Fool Me TWICE

LADIES *of* WORTH

PHILIPPA JANE KEYWORTH

ISBN (eBook): 978-1-9998652-4-5

ISBN (Print): 978-1-9998652-6-9

For Bennetts

Thank you for showing me the value of historical research, the beauty of words, and the importance of an author's sense of humour.

"It is a far, far better thing that I do, than I have ever done; it is a far, far better rest I go to than I have ever known."

CHAPTER ONE

London, England 1774

"Are you always so demanding?" asked Lord Avers, smiling saucily and flashing his white teeth as he gave up a card to the player beside him.

"Always," replied Angelica Worth, turning from the retreating waiter she had ordered to do her bidding and plucking a card from the table with her small, sprite-like fingers. Her blue eyes glinted as they ran over the cards in her hand. "I like to have my own way," she said simply, preparing for her last lay, "even if it is detrimental to my circumstances." She extracted some cards from her hand and placed them on the table. "In this case, it is not."

As she leant, far from innocently, across the table and draped her elegant hands across her winnings, she was greeted by a cacophony of groans. Players threw down their cards, the game over, but not one failed to notice the pale white bosom of the female gamester. Angelica knew what she was doing. Of course she did. This was not the first time she had gamed in a hell, and it was not the first time she had won from these men. Let them stare, let them imagine, let them fantasize about the woman they thought a harlot. If it distracted them enough to forget they had lost to her, to play her again, and to lose again, then all the better.

"Alas, in this case it is to *my* detriment," said Lord Avers, still put out by his loss.

Angelica returned the saucy smile he had given her earlier. A delicate crease appeared at the corner of her mouth, causing the patch near her red lips to lift teasingly. Her light blue eyes gave him a coquettish look, and she parted her lips to reveal a hint of her white teeth.

At this display of her charms, Lord Avers' face softened. It always worked—the hint of suggestion and those feminine wiles with which she could even the odds in a male-dominated arena.

A waiter appeared, offering Angelica a glass full of amber-coloured liquid on a mock-silver tray. She took a sip, the sweet orange-flower Ratafia leaving honey-like trails down her throat. She rarely drank, especially whilst gaming, but this evening was at an end and she deserved it. By the sheer exercise of her wits, she had dragged her household out of the financial gutter it had dug itself into over the last month. She would drink now and enjoy these short hours of respite before more money needed to be won.

In the brief quiet while she sipped her drink, she forgot about the staring Lord Avers and glanced over her glass rim at John Williams, the servant she always brought with her. He stood at the far wall, blending into the mahogany with his brown woolen frock coat. If he had been a more noticeable person, he might have looked out of place, but he was the kind of man who was invisible. That was why Angelica brought him, as her protection, as a sort of bodyguard-come-chaperone, if a bastard female gamester could have one of those. All she asked of him was that he stand by while she gamed for hours. He would say nothing, do nothing, but his presence would inevitably calm her, and she always received his company gratefully on the dark, early-morning journeys home. John acknowledged her look with a brief glance and then resumed his study of the middle distance.

"You know," mused Lord Avers, watching the card dealer clear the table which was now empty of players, "I think you some kind of witch. You fly in, you take my money, and I am all the happier for it." His brown eyes were the sort a woman could get lost in, his smile the kind that would melt a heart of ice. But Angelica Worth was not interested in getting lost, and her past had more than hardened her heart. She had come to Town for one reason, a reason that would not be served by an illicit liaison.

She laughed suddenly, the action lighting up her often-serious countenance. "You flatter me, my lord." And it was real flattery. She was quite aware of the sway Lord Avers held over the marriage mart with his dashing good looks. She had watched him, in another time, at another place, as another person, captivate many a woman who afterwards set their cap at him.

Unfortunately for her, Lord Avers was the third son of the Duke of Mountefield, destined to play his life out as an officer in the army with no larger financial prospects. And for Angelica's alter-ego, the full daughter of her father, her real self whom she played during the day, such a match would be impossible. Miss Caro Worth—a respectable woman who would have no more to do with gaming than she would a low-cut dress—would not spend the rest of her life trailing after his Majesty's army, no matter how beautiful the eyes of the man.

"I had rather catch you than flatter you, O Beauteous

Wood-Nymph." Lord Avers' fingers brushed across Angelica's, halting them from tracing a pattern over her empty glass.

Angelica's body stiffened then. She was not Miss Caro Worth this evening, and Lord Avers was not a potential husband here. It left a bitter taste in her mouth, the knowledge of whom she played on these dark nights and of the values she let slip so easily through her fingers. She was merely a bastard gamester of no virtue in these haunts. She was not scared by his touch, but she was no fool either. She trod a dangerous line in this precarious world. That was why she had rules. That was why she was always aloof, always superficially charming, but always a foot away from everyone.

She noted the movement John made at the side of the room, treading closer in reaction to Lord Avers' touch. She shot him a quick look to make him stay where he was and then slipped her hand out from beneath Lord Avers' caress.

Her coy smile resurfaced. "If you were to catch me, my lord, I am afraid my magic would be lost. Is that not the way of phantoms or magic beings? We are not for catching but for admiring." Her full lips curved up on one side, her stomach tight as she waited for his response.

Lord Avers eyed the heart-shaped patch so coquettishly placed. He sighed, resigning himself to the fate of all Angelica's would-be lovers. He threw up a hand, the gold embroidery of his cuff catching the candlelight. "Very well, I will content myself with looking."

She breathed easier then, her spirit greatly relieved but also a little deflated. That roguish smile appealed to Angelica in spite of her rules. If she did not have a plan, one that required strict adherence, she would have said she liked Lord Avers. She had played with him several times, and he was not tinged with the same competitive desperation as many others.

He turned away from Angelica, looking for his next game

as she would be doing tomorrow night. For now, she must deposit her winnings.

Angelica rose and gathered her takings. Then, swinging her full skirt round, she traversed the gaming tables. The hell was full tonight, the air lying thick between the gentlemen as they played. The dark panelling of the establishment only added to the feeling of vice as the darkness shunned in other places bred excitement in the hell.

As she looked about her, she saw the usual gamers scattered across the card room. Sir Denby, Mr. Ashby, and Lord Maltravers were at piquet a short distance away. Mr. Went was playing whist with Sir Percy and two other gentlemen. Lord Fitzhubert and the Earl of Bevenshire had just now arrived. Those were the notables; they were interlaced with other persons and personages less important to Angelica—gamers without the deep pockets she wished to plunder.

The candlelight half-shadowed the faces of the players, the dimness masking their concentration, despair, or triumph. Other faces, those watching the play, were animated by conversation and liquor, and still others keenly scanned the room for the few ladies present.

Angelica herself attracted attention at each table she passed. She had only been in Town a year, and the presence of a bastard female gamester, one who had gained admission to the hells through her aristocratic father's soiled connections, had intrigued gentlemen young and old.

She had known it would, and she had helped in that regard by refusing to powder her dark hair and thus making herself stand out from any other woman of fashion. She was not averse to attention, as long as she could control it. Society enjoyed a scandal—she had firsthand experience of this—and if she could give it a scandal of her own devising, then she cared naught for what was said.

For now, she ignored the scattered glances and stares she

evoked by her passage, confirming her position as the untouchable gamester Angelica Worth, too haughty, too aloof, too distant to approach. She passed a group of revelers just arrived through the two bolted doors guarding the hell's entrance, and made her way to where Mr. Russell, the proprietor of the establishment, stood. He nodded to her.

"Good evening, Mr. Russell." She inclined her head to the short, stout man.

"Good evening Miss Worth." Mr. Russell's neat little wig bobbed just below her nose. "I see you had luck on your side at tonight's play?"

"You are correct, Mr. Russell. May I use your private rooms for a few moments?"

"But of course." Mr. Russell reached into his waistcoat and fished out a long golden chain—the line appeared neverending until the soft, light tinkle of a key could be heard as it popped over the edge of his pocket.

He escorted her through the double doors opposite, into a room set out for hazard and other games of chance that Angelica had never played, until he came upon a hidden door, paneled just as the wall was, barely noticeable in the dim light. She could hear the slide of the lock drawing back, and then Mr. Russell's short legs trotted to the side so that she might enter. She dropped several coins in his hand as she passed. He gave no acknowledgement that he had received them other than closing the door behind her.

A small library opened up before her, the candles lit in the sconces casting a warm glow over the whole room. Books lined two of the walls, or—as Angelica knew from previous visits to this room—what might better be described as a façade of books. Mr. Russell was aware of the environment in which his clients enjoyed relaxing, but he would not spend his hard-earned money lining shelves with expensive volumes.

Angelica moved forward, the wide hips of her *robe à la*

française twisting and turning between the small table and the two wingback chairs while avoiding the fire that burned merrily in the hearth. For the first time since she had entered the hell this evening, she breathed deeply. This was the moment she longed for each night that she entered Mr. Russell's establishment—the moment when she felt the relief of financial pressures, the moment when she received respite from the role circumstances demanded she play, the moment when she could prepare for her homeward journey and the sleep stolen from her by her nocturnal profession.

She had never been robbed, but as a woman travelling in this world of men, she could not risk losing the precious money she won. Her first lot of winnings had gone to Mr. Russell to ensure he spread the rumour that she kept her winnings in his private rooms and sent for them at a later date. The rumour worked well. Only he knew that she took them with her each night, and he would not tell anyone, not after the money she had paid him and continued to pay him.

She ran an unthinking hand over the spines of the false books and sighed. She was tired tonight, ready for the evening to end. When she came to the final column of books, near the far corner of the room, she stopped. She fingered the line of her silk dress and cast one last cursory glance around the room before raising her foot onto one of the lower bookshelves. Her heel clicked against the faux volumes below as she quickly pulled up the layers of her dress and petticoats. Silk ran against silk until all that was left was a pale white leg showing in the warm candlelight through the sheerness of her shift.

She would have to be quick. John would already be calling her a carriage after seeing her leave the room with Mr. Russell. Angelica's dressmaker, Madame Depardieu, had not only lowered the neckline of this gown, but she had also added a secret pocket. Stitched into the underside of her petticoat, it was the perfect place to hide her newly-acquired blunt. Unlike her pockets which could be reached normally, this compartment was only accessible from the underside of the gown.

Now came the tricky part—the buttons. Thankfully, the Lord had blessed Angelica with a particularly long set of fingers and, despite the tiniest of buttons and the difficult positioning on the inside of her petticoat, she soon had the compartment undone. She folded the notes and laid them flat in the pocket so that they would lie unseen against her body for the journey home.

She was just fastening the last button when she heard the door open. Her raven-haired head shot up, and her large eyes darted in the direction of the intruder. No one had ever entered when she had been in here alone before. What was Mr. Russell thinking? He always left her in peace until she left of her own accord.

So shocked was she, she failed to remove her foot from its perch on the bookshelf and cover herself before a gentleman entered—a gentleman that was *not* Mr. Russell. At least, that is if you could call the man who entered a gentleman at all. The man in question practically fell into the room, sloshing the tankard of ale in his hand and taking more than a few seconds to find his footing.

Angelica watched with horrified fascination as the tousled hair escaping the pathetic ribbon at the back of his neck flicked up and down while he gained his balance. For a moment she wondered if he would merely stumble back out again, quite unaware of her presence. But fortune would not smile upon Angelica a second time tonight.

In spite of his graceless entrance and obvious inebriation, the man's eyes were exceedingly quick. As he righted himself, they made contact with a heeled shoe, a pleasingly long leg beneath the flimsiest of materials, and a gathering of skirts. His eyes continued their journey upwards, over her bodice, her neck, and then they stilled at those indefinable blue eyes.

In the odd pause that followed, a cat-like smile slowly unfurled across the young man's face. Angelica threw down her skirts and stepped back.

"I say…" was all the gentleman offered. He half-raised the tankard as if in salute, and Angelica could only be thankful that he had knocked the door shut during his imbalance. Or was she thankful? She took another step back, hitting the panelling of the wall.

She did not recognise the man, but he was undeniably handsome. Aware that she was looking him over, his boyish face gained a mischievousness. His green eyes twinkled merrily at her, lingering—to her utter infuriation—on her lips. He stumbled towards a book-lined wall and rested an unsteady elbow upon one of the shelves, leaning jauntily on one leg and most clearly making himself at home.

"I say…" he repeated himself, but he did not move towards her as Angelica had feared.

Her wits finally returning, she put some ice into her stare. "You say what, sir?"

She was buying time. She was not yet sure how to work the situation to her advantage. Should she play upon his intoxication and hope a little flirtation would gain her access to the door? Or should she give him a set-down and storm out, risking that he might attempt to stop her? If it had been someone she knew, she might have been able to guess which would be the best course of action.

As it was, she could not rely on John's appearance—he always waited downstairs for her with the carriage.

"I say," the man responded affably, as if they were acquaintances encountering each other during a promenade through Town, "that is a rather clever trick you have there." He gestured to the compartment recently concealed in her skirts.

"I don't know what you mean," she replied too quickly, her heart still fluttering.

The gentleman merely smiled and shrugged his shoulders. As though he had not just learnt a valuable secret. As though he did not intend to rob her. As though...well, as though he cared not a whit for the precarious position in which he had found her. Apparently he was not going to take advantage of it —but neither was he planning to ignore it.

Angelica was momentarily stumped. But then, choosing the course of action that had worked most successfully in the past, she took two small steps forward. She raised her head so that her neck was shown to the best advantage, relaxed her full lips so that they pouted attractively, and brought a hand up to play with the cravat encircling the man's neck. Teasing at the folds, she noted that although she had first guessed his age to be just above twenty, a closer inspection showed him to be nearer thirty.

"And just whom do I have the pleasure of addressing?" Her tone dripped with honey, though her eyes still searched his face shrewdly for any sign as to his intentions.

"Pleasure?"

For a moment he looked dashing. She found herself looking no longer at his eyes but at his lips as they curved in a pleasing smile. Her stomach fluttered.

"Is that what you feel?" He was leaning closer now, sending the smell of cloves and ale wafting toward her.

The spellbound moment ended rather abruptly. The gentleman's elbow, which up until now had been wedged between two rows of false books, slipped. The jolt of movement turned his enticing lean into a headlong plunge towards Angelica's bosom.

Angelica immediately assumed he was attempting to steal her winnings—or worse.

"Oh...oh, I am sorry!" he managed, pulling himself out of her décolletage and into balance.

But even his boyish green eyes could not save him.

Angelica delivered a resounding slap across his face. Gathering up her skirts, she marched from the room without a backwards glance. If she had looked behind her, she would have seen a gentleman utterly bemused, his mouth hanging open like a catfish while he stared after the angel who had departed so suddenly.

CHAPTER TWO

A ngelica arrived home near four in the morning. The hackney she had taken with her footman John had dropped them off three streets distant as it always did, and when she descended the carriage steps, she was in the same old, patched cloak with which she always covered herself after leaving the gaming hells. It belonged to Libby—wife to John and maid to herself. In this disguise she could come and go from her London home after dark without anyone noticing. To passers-by she was just a maid returning to her place of work.

The streets were quiet but by no means asleep. Dark figures moved up and down their lengths, and Angelica and John were careful to avoid them. They arrived at the Town house façade soon enough, and John opened the gate in the railings which allowed them to descend damp steps to the servants' entrance below street-level.

As her first silk-shoe clad foot stepped over the threshold of the kitchen, she stepped from the fictional Angelica, bastard of the late Lord Worth, into the flesh-and-blood Caro, legitimate and respectable daughter of the same dead Lord. It always happened like that—a simple movement across a threshold to exchange one identity for another. The relief she felt when closing the library door behind her at Mr. Russell's hell was nothing compared to the feeling of stepping over the threshold of her home.

Once they had exited the kitchen and stillroom, they ascended the servants' stair and came out into a well-furnished hall and a waft of warmth from the recently banked fire. Libby always kept the fire burning in preparation for their return. Caro, too concerned for the household expenses, had never asked for it, but every time she returned home in the unholy hours of the morning it was a welcome sight. Economy was the rule of this house, and after several years of such economies, Caro's eyes were used to seeing by firelight rather than by the light of the carefully hoarded candle ends.

"Brandy, Miss Worth?" John always asked her that, the solemn lines about his mouth remaining straight, not betraying the tiredness he must feel as she did. She knew that her answer would be read by Libby. The maid taking the borrowed cloak from her hands must be wondering how the gaming had gone that night. Had her mistress made money? Had she lost? Were they to avoid life on the streets another week, another month, or were they done for?

"A small one, thank you, John."

He handed her the glass. Libby's face softened a little as she folded the cloak and took it away to be hidden downstairs until it was needed again. Unlike Libby, John's face showed nothing; Caro doubted it ever would. She had known John Williams since she was a child, and she had never seen emotion register on his countenance.

The two servants disappeared down the stairs leaving Caro to herself for a few moments. She wandered towards the heat and glow of the fire, her eyes transfixed by the dancing flames. The warmth permeated her clothing. Mesmerised, she felt the heavy weight of the blanket of weariness that fell upon her so often now. Playing two people's lives took its toll, and now, in these dark, lonely hours, it seemed too hard a task to maintain.

Libby's bustling reappearance dispelled her growing worry. The middle-aged maid came immediately to her mistress, chattering about the coldness of the night, the cost of fuel for the fires, and the fresh linens with which she had made up Miss Worth's bed.

"Oh, Libby, you needn't have bothered with fresh linens just yet. I could have had those ones another week."

"Nonsense!" barked the maid, taking her mistress' gloves. "We may be forever circling the pauper's drain, but we have enough to afford the soap for your sheets. Besides, I shall be adding those covers to the ones I've already put on your bed, for I know you must be too cold now at night, though you tell me nothing. Skin and bones! Skin and bones you are!"

Caro allowed Libby's scolding but rebelled as the fussing servant tried to push her towards the stairs. "Just a few moments more, Libby," she begged, turning her face again towards the fire, the heat having already rosied her pale cheeks.

"I have banked one in your room tonight."

"You haven't!" exclaimed Caro, astounded by the extravagance.

"I have, and I shall not have you rebuke me. It is November now, and two mornings ago I found ice on the inside of your windows."

"But, we cannot—"

"Hush with you, child!" said the maid, the scold coming out more like an endearment. "Up to bed with you. We shall have you undressed before the fire, and you shall be warmed right down to your cockles."

The maid pushed and fussed Caro all the way upstairs until she was seated before the fire with John's glass of brandy at her elbow. The only pieces of furniture in the room were the chair, the table, the bed, and a small commode. Everything else was bare, but Caro did not notice the lack anymore.

In the beginning, when the stark upper rooms of the house had first been furnished with what little she could afford, she had been affronted by the vulgarity. But her spirit had grown since then. A little was better than nothing. The lower rooms of her Town house were another matter. They were furnished in the manner to which the gentility of Town were accustomed—that she might accept their visits as though she were the moderately wealthy woman she claimed to be. The upper echelons of the house were solely her domain, and no pretence was needed.

With no family left to her, she was an independent woman in the eyes of Society, without even a maternal relation to be her companion. Society forgave her a little for it, pitying the lonely existence that had been thrust upon her. Whenever she was Caro, she would go out with Libby for respectability. Whenever she was Angelica, she would go out with John for protection.

Here she could sit in a bare room, sip at the warm brandy, and forget about acting—forget about all the little nuances she must remember, forget that her life was played out precariously and that one day the house of cards might fall.

If she had not been tired, if she had been more herself, she would not be thinking such things. But whenever she came home to the two servants who had remained faithful through all, the two servants who relied wholly on her for their livelihoods, it was then that the magnitude of her responsibilities weighed so heavily on her that not even brandy could lift her spirits.

She had managed, in the past two years, to drag herself up from destitution to become the lady of quality she had once been by right. The creation of a bastard sister had been a stroke of genius allowing her the chance of a successful future without destroying her virtue. The fictional Angelica allowed her to earn her living the only way she could, and the factual Caro allowed her to search for the security she desired above all else. She knew, from two years alone, without the protection of a man, exactly how dangerous a woman's position could be in this world. Soon it would be the beginning of the Season, the time to find a husband to secure her future.

She peeled off the heart-shaped patch at the corner of her mouth and placed it in a patch box. Then she pushed the raven-black wig from her head, revealing the golden hair beneath. Angelica had been banished for the moment, and she was now Caro once more.

She thought of her mother. If she could see her through this glass, what would her mother think of her now? She had been a respectable woman. She had not lived to see the self-destruction of their family. Caro had avoided that destruction for a time, but was it still waiting to consume her? In the darkness of the night, her life, her thoughts, her worries, all became too much.

She would feel differently tomorrow. Her bright blue eyes stared to the side of her glass, watching the flickering of the flames behind. Her golden hair lay loose upon her neck and bosom, a far prettier covering than the moth-eaten blanket that kept the chill from her back.

The fire was on the turn. Soon it would burn low and cold would creep into the room slowly but surely. She wished to be abed before then. Drawing back the covers, she smiled at the sight of the warm brick Libby had put there.

The maid had taken her winnings to hide in a trunk in the attic. When she examined the accounts tomorrow, she would know how long that money would last—not long, she suspected, fearing the return to the hell that awaited her.

Who was that man? She recalled his irrepressible grin as he stumbled upon her in Mr. Russell's private room—and his exclamation of dismay as he had plummeted toward her bosom. She had slapped him hard. Her hand had hurt all the way home in the hackney—it still hurt a little as she ran it across the bedclothes. It had not taken long to realise that his plunge towards her had been merely a loss of balance, but it was too late by that point. And besides, the slap had afforded her the opportunity to escape.

Had the situation been different, she might have apologised, given him an indulgent smile, and perhaps even blown him a kiss whilst walking away. But the situation was not different. She had spent a year building up her identity, her credibility, her desirability in that establishment, all in the pursuit of a higher goal—wealth and security. No risk could be allowed no matter how mischievous and irrepressible that grin had been.

She rolled over in the bed, her golden hair spraying out behind her like rays of sunshine. As the cotton bedclothes brushed against her leg, she thought of the man's eyes running over that very same limb earlier this evening. She hoped she would never see him again. She doubted she would.

Admiral Viscount Felton was growing exasperated. His second son's propensity for funning, his fondness for drink, and his inexcusably unconventional hours were becoming unsupportable. The Honourable Tobias Felton never rose before midday, never tired before four in the morning, and was always abominably late to every engagement. Yes, the Admiral, quite frankly, had grown weary of the boy, and his wife, the sweet-natured Lady Felton, had urged her husband to leave Tobias to his own devices. Such a strategy would, hopefully, encourage the onset of manly maturity.

Submitting to his wife's sage counsel, Viscount Felton had

relieved his son of all responsibility. He had ceased his frequent lecturing. He had curtailed his regular reprimands. Unfortunately, thus far, the cunning plan had failed to nurture in Tobias Felton a sense of familial responsibility and societal duty.

This morning, the Viscount had arrived along with his eldest son, the Honourable Frederick Felton, as agreed, at a quarter to eleven to breakfast with young Tobias. But instead of greeting them at the breakfast table, Tobias was hard at work in his bedchamber, doubled-over his chamber pot casting up his accounts. Frederick turned his nose up at the acrid smell and walked over to the window, thrusting the sash up and causing a gust of cold winter air to enter the room.

"Thank you, Frederick," said Viscount Felton. His florid countenance was looking at his younger son's backside with such fury that if his son had seen it, he might have been mildly flustered. "This is not the manner in which I am wont to see my son."

"That's rather unfair on poor Frederick, Father." Tobias' voice echoed from the depths of the chamber pot. "It is hardly his fault he is wont to look like a dull dog."

Viscount Felton made a sound betwixt a cough and a growl.

Tobias' head came up a little, and he wiped the back of his hand across his mouth before his valet could offer the customary towel. "Oh, you mean myself?" The amusement in his voice was easily detectable. "It's not the manner I like to see myself in either."

His father tapped a buckled shoe on the thick carpet.

Frederick sighed in a condescending way and turned to look out of the window as if it might provide a more satisfying view. "This is what comes of giving a mere boy freedom he knows not what to do with."

A flicker of annoyance passed over Tobias' face, but it was

gone in a moment, and an easy smile replaced it as he pushed a hand through his disheveled hair. "Alas!" he exclaimed, assuming the theatrics of an actor from Drury Lane. "The things I do for pleasure! My pleasure leads to displeasure— rather a paradox, don't you think?" He finally took the towel from his waiting valet, a small, mean-looking man, who bobbed away to fetch his master's clothes.

The tall Viscount clasped a pair of lean hands beneath his round belly. "Ridiculous and wearing thin, I assure you, my boy. Your charming and youthful qualities are rapidly becoming dissolute and debauched!" In spite of his red face, the Viscount did not drink, the pattern of purple veins on his cheeks due to having spent the best part of his life aboard ship in His Majesty George III's navy. "I am only glad I consented to giving you your own lodgings in Town. If your mother were to see you in such a state, she would be devastated."

Tobias refrained from explaining his mother had seen him exactly so a number of times before. His father always did have a desire to protect his mother, a desire which Tobias admired but hardly understood, considering his mother was as strong a woman as any he knew. It took a certain kind of woman to live aboard ship with her husband, sailing to the far corners of the map with naught but men for company.

"Then praise be that she is safe and sound in Mount Street! Now come, Father, less of your anger. Let us have breakfast together. Frederick may even join us if he can lower his nose a little."

"Breakfast!" exclaimed his lordship, his face taking on an even more crimson hue. "Frederick and I have already eaten— at least your butler had the common courtesy to feed guests under your roof. He offered us food and we are both well satisfied. You cannot tell me that you were unaware we were waiting downstairs for over an hour?"

"You've eaten? How ungenerous of you." Tobias skirted

the issue of them waiting for him. He did know, but until the expulsion of last night's dinner, he had barely been able to maintain a vertical position. "Now I shall have to eat alone."

He sighed in a way that he knew would irritate his father. Truth be told, the Viscount's thundering was exacerbating his headache no end, and he was rather looking forward to the prospect of eating alone—especially if it meant the weight of Frederick's ugly condescension would be lifted from the room. His brother had not waited for him to be back a week before he had begun parroting Father's lectures.

Lord Avers had invited Tobias to that hell last night. It had been a welcome back into Society, and after Tobias had lost a deal of money to his friend at faro, he had resorted to wasting the rest of his allowance on drink to alleviate his sorrows. The image of a long, slender leg, appearing through the finest of muslin shifts, arose in his mind. Most gratifying. An indolent smile unfolded across his face.

"And what about our inconvenience is so amusing to you?" demanded Frederick. "I am kept from urgent business to wait on you, for Father asked as much of me—not that I would willingly spend a moment, much less a morning, in this debauched den of yours. But I see my influence is like to have no effect. It never has."

"Oh, don't say that," said Tobias, the same flicker of annoyance reigniting. "I find you influence me immensely. Just now, for instance, I realised that I should never like to rise before noon if it should do that to my face." He pointed at his brother's solemn, lined countenance.

Frederick's eyes took offence at this, but they kept up their stare nonetheless—at least until he turned to his father, pretending not to hear what Tobias had said. "Father, I must go if you wish me to meet our solicitor. I wash my hands of this unkempt vagabond."

"Oh, do," said Tobias, making washing motions with his own hands.

Frederick exited the room without grace and left his father and younger brother alone together.

"I don't know how you stand the dull dog, Father."

"Urgh!" The Viscount threw his hands up in the air, almost disturbing his powered wig. He strode about for several minutes trying to regain his composure, leaving Tobias to his thoughts and his headache once again.

Last night had burnt a bit of a hole in Tobias' pockets. He would have to go to his mother before long—only she was able to loosen his father's purse strings in a time of need. Devil take that scoundrel, Lord Avers! He was a lark, but he was also one of the luckiest men Tobias knew—a younger son who was allowed his own head and who had never been placed beside his siblings in a race.

As he recalled the thrashing he had taken from Lord Avers, he also recalled that leg again. Had it been attached to a lady of significance? Or a lady at all? Or was alcohol becoming more intimate a friend than ever to Tobias? He really would not be surprised.

"I have tried," his father burst out. "The Lord Almighty knows, I have tried, but I will not, I cannot, be in your presence again until some sense has found you. Look at Frederick —even he, a man so near your age, cannot stand to be around your childish antics."

"You have already lectured me many a time on how poorly I measure up to Frederick." Tobias' cutting tone hinted at the rawness of the nerve on which his father was pressing.

"You think life one grand joke, and I remember thinking in such ways once upon a time, but things change. *You* must change. Frederick has always known his responsibilities, and he has fulfilled them. Now he is a man finding himself a suitable bride and settling down to the business of the estate. But you..." He was unable to finish his unsatisfactory sentence describing his unsatisfactory son.

Tobias knew how this lecture went. He knew how it ended. "...are not Frederick," he said, finishing the sentence for his father.

Viscount Felton's silence was confirmation enough. He finished pacing and stared hard at his younger son, but then— as if unable to find the puzzle piece he was searching for—he sighed and turned away.

"I shall quit your presence as you have quit on all your prospects. If you are to continue down this dissolute road, I shall have no part in funding it, be sure of that, my boy." He nodded, agreeing with his own decision. "When you have gained enough common sense to hold a reasonable conversation with your brother and me, I will return."

The older man took no leave of his son—he merely left. Tobias was alone again, apart from his valet who had been standing in the corner all through this exchange.

"Quite a show for you, Coker," said Tobias in a sour tone, picking up a comb from the table and drawing it through his tatty locks. He wondered, for a moment, whether his father had indeed just cut him off? He wondered if he would have to change? If he would have to submit and become like that dull dog of a brother, Frederick?

But even a few moments among such solemn thoughts were enough for him. Quickly, his mind moved forward, away from the present and toward the brighter future. He had an engagement with that devil Lord Avers, and at least *he* would be in good humour. His father's words could wait. Being sensible—being Frederick—could always be tried another day.

"And must we keep the rooms in Little Hart Street?" asked Libby as she bustled around the trunks in the spare attic room, dusting the few pieces of furniture. "It drains the coffers no end."

"I'm afraid we must if the pretence is to be upheld, Libby." Caro sat on an old blanket on the floor. Libby had insisted on it though Caro would have been perfectly happy on the scrubbed floor-boards. The skirts of her open-fronted gown lay in high piles of ruffled silk, letters from landlords and household bills slotted between the folds of material as though her skirts were a letter stand.

"Does John still go and light the candle?"

"Aye, in the window, every evening for an hour." Libby wrinkled her nose.

"I know you think it a drain on resources, Libby. But it is necessary. No one has questioned the deception so far, or pried much into my past, but they may—and we have to be ready to cover our tracks. Trust me?"

She asked that last question gently, knowing full well the answer. Libby and John Williams had trusted her implicitly since she had been born to Lord and Lady Worth, they had trusted her long after her parents were dead, and they would continue to do so no matter the aspersions cast upon her name.

"Of course, miss, now don't be silly asking me such foolish questions." Libby dusted a wall hanging embroidered with the image of Mary Magdalene wiping the Christ's perfumed feet with her hair. They had brought it from Sussex when they had moved to Town a year ago.

"I know we cannot yet place this downstairs, for you want to keep it safe in case we fall into trouble with creditors and it be sent to—" Libby broke off, realizing what she was saying. "I am certain that shall not come to pass—our good Lord will see to that. I am only wanting to say that it looks better hanging up in the attic of this house than those other filthy rooms."

Caro agreed. It had been far out of place in the sordid rooms of Little Hart Street near Covent Garden in the midst of an area of pleasure and vice.

But then the strong irony of that thought hit her like a lash —who was Mary Magdalene but a redeemed harlot? Her place would have been in an area like Covent Garden before she met the Christ. Perhaps she would have lived in Little Hart Street if she had lived in London.

As it was, Caro had removed the embroidered hanging along with herself and her retainers to this respectable Town house about six months ago under the pretence of having lately arrived in London. Caro had brought what family treasures she had managed to save from their Sussex home before they had left in ignominy. In this house they could be stored in a more stately manner than had been afforded previously whilst the Little Hart Street rooms were maintained as Angelica Worth's dwelling.

Caro, ignoring the letters scattered across her lap, gestured toward the wall. Libby opened the trunk sitting there and removed a bag full of blunt, the treasure won at such a cost last night. Caro shuffled through the bills and began to count the coins. She laid them in piles on the sturdy oak chest beside her.

"Are we to avoid the streets and pay for the fire I made you last night?"

"I believe we are, Libby, at least for another month or so."

"What a trick you have to make money in that way. If only your f—" Again Libby broke off.

Caro's heart felt a slight twinge at the unspoken words, and she was thankful that the usually frank Libby had refrained from bringing up a painful subject. "You can go shopping now, Libby, without writing any notes of promise—

how exciting for you!" Caro's eyes twinkled briefly at her maid.

That was how it was between them since coming away from Sussex. The past would be alluded to by mistake, and that allusion would be ignored, and the change of conversation, like a new deck of cards, would remove any remembrance of what had gone before.

"It *is* exciting, though I know you poke fun at me, miss. There is nothing I like better than a well stocked larder. I may even buy beef and make my stew."

The thought set Caro's mouth to watering. She became acutely aware that she had not yet breakfasted this morning.

"And I shall purchase fresh eggs to make that hair of your mother's shine again." Libby nodded towards her mistress' fair head.

Caro touched a hand to the curls, much softer than the dark wig that had concealed them last night. "What's wrong with my hair?"

"Naught that a good wash cannot fix. I already have a portion of rum and some rose water I made last month."

"Extravagance."

"And one well worth having if we are to get you wed!"

Caro replied with a sigh, piling the papers and letters together in her lap and placing them beside her on the floor so that she could rise to unlock the great oak chest. She placed the money within and relocked the chest. Holding the key dangling on its long chain, she passed it to Libby.

"Before you go downstairs, I will redress your hair. It is not sitting as it should today!" The old maid dropped the chain over her head and the key between her ample bosoms where naught but a madman would attempt to pilfer it. "You must look quite as à la mode as Lady Fairing if you are to keep up with her in Society. I have my eye on a new hair style which will look lovely on you, my child."

"Yes, but I mustn't be late. Lady Fairing has much to tell me, or so her letter said, and I do not wish to miss any news."

Caro retrieved the papers she had left on the floor. The letter from Lady Rebecca Fairing was the one piece of correspondence with a friendly tone to it. As for the rest, there were no missives from friends or relations, no sweet letters with foolish nothings for her to pore over. They had all ceased over a year ago, and now her only correspondents were shopkeepers, landlords, and dressmakers.

"Will you put these in my bureau downstairs, Libby? Then I shall sit as still as school child at lessons for you to do what you will with my hair. You always know best."

"No school children I ever knew sat well for lessons," said Libby dubiously. But nevertheless, she took the papers from Caro's hands and followed her down the attic stairs, eager to trade her task for obedience from her mistress.

CHAPTER THREE

Caro sat with her friend Lady Rebecca Fairing in the window of the Pot and Pineapple, a small confection-er's shop owned by Mr. Negri and housed snuggly in Berkley Square. The view afforded by the November sunshine showed the square in the best light. A few persons of quality milled around the edges while others ventured onto the brittle grass in the centre of the handsome classical buildings.

Caro's spoon twisted mindlessly in her rapidly melting pistachio ice as she gazed out the window. A moment ago her friend had been describing the dress worn by Lady Curshaw's daughter at Lady Ophelia Carey's ball. But with her wandering thoughts, Caro was quite unaware that Lady Rebecca had finished both her parmesan cream and her conversation.

"I swear," Lady Rebecca declared suddenly, "I shall dash the remnants of my ice over your head if you ignore me for another minute! First you are adamant you wish to hear all the latest *on-dits,* and then you are more interested in the hackneys passing outside. I love to talk, it's true, but I draw the line at talking to myself!"

Caro jolted to wakefulness, her blue eyes refocusing on her friend's brown ones, searching Lady Rebecca's face for an explanation of what was wrong.

Lady Rebecca's gloved hands fell in exasperation on the table causing her teacup, saucer, and spoon to jump and jingle.

"I am sorry," Caro replied automatically. When she had come back into Society, she had been avoided by most of the debutantes swelling the drawing and music rooms of London's finest homes. Not many wished to associate with Lord Worth's daughter.

The ripples in Society's pool that her alter-ego, Angelica, was creating had only worsened matters. It was easy to separate herself mentally from her false identity, but far harder for Society to separate the two persons, no matter what effort Caro put into it. The financial benefit of living two lives must always be weighed against the damage Angelica's reputation caused. Caro could only hope that the money earned at the gambling table would allow her to make an advantageous match to a man who cared little whether she had a bastard sister or not. This negative perception under which she suffered made her friendship with Lady Rebecca all the more remarkable, all the more precious.

"It is most unkind of you!" said Lady Rebecca, refusing to curtail her remonstrances. "And to think, I even went as far as to describe the different breeds of flower on the Honourable Miss Curshaw's dress! I do not even like botany. In fact I dislike it excessively. You make me describe everything of Society to you, and then you ignore it."

Lady Rebecca's friendship was invaluable to Caro. She granted her access to far higher circles of the Ton than she could ever achieve on her own. It had been Caro's initial reason for seeking the friendship of a woman with whom she had no previous connection. No doubt Lady Rebecca had her own reasons for befriending Caro—a delicious pool of salacious scandal in which she could dangle her toes while sitting quite safely on the edge—but she had never flaunted those reasons openly.

At first, Caro had not expected to like Lady Rebecca. Caro had not *liked* anyone she had met for a long time, but Lady Rebecca was not like most people. She seemed to see past the fickleness of Society, and her predilection for truthfulness, bordering on shocking, appealed to Caro from the midst of her life of lies.

"I have been a poor friend," she admitted honestly. "In truth, I feel a little worn—"

"And you look it," Lady Rebecca cut in with her customarily unorthodox style. "You are looking quite drawn. This is not the first time, my dear...."

Rather than acknowledge the reprimand and answer the implied question, Caro continued hurriedly. "But I beg of you, for the sake of my maid's sanity, that you refrain from dashing anything over my head. You have no idea how possessive she is over the dressing of my hair."

"Well," said Lady Rebecca, her chocolate brown eyes softening a little, "I can well understand why. The gold of South America is threaded through your locks—I am exceedingly jealous of the fact. It always causes a stir when you arrive at a party, and the rest of us have our hair powdered as the fashion says." She sniffed, readjusting the placement of the spoon on her upset saucer and patting her fingers along the line of her highly piled, powdered hair. "I suppose you may repay me by telling me the dressmaker responsible for that fabulous caraco."

Caro looked down at the aquamarine material swathed tightly around her upper body, the tiny flowers of the embroidery so fine they looked half real. She wished to oblige her friend, she really did, but she could not risk Lady Rebecca being associated with anything from her other life. Madam Depardieu was one of those associations.

"I cannot rightly remember her name." The honeyed lie was sweet to the ears, but poisonous to the friendship. She hated herself for doing it. "I can look up her details when I return home. Tell me,"—again she moved quickly on, trying to escape the feelings of guilt—"are you to attend the theatre on Friday? I hear the play is a good one."

"Yes, and so is the Marquis. And the play will be far more interesting than those hackneys you were watching from the window." A mischievous grin took over Lady Rebecca's face.

"Indeed?" Caro played coy. She knew exactly why Lady Rebecca mentioned him. He had been at a small card party they had attended together two weeks since and was quite the eligible bachelor. A fortune, a title, an estate—just the sort of gentleman that could secure Caro's future. At the moment she was merely a cloud flitting across the surface of his moon; she would need to become a brightly shining star if she wished to capture his attentions.

"Indeed," replied her friend, her tone playful but her lips refusing to give anything further away. "Do you know," she said, toying with the silver spoon on her saucer once more, "if we were not such bosom friends I should be quite offended that the mere mention of a gentleman's name elicits more of a response from you than does anything else I have uttered all morning."

Caro felt herself colouring a little. She had to be careful. She did not want to be labeled as a woman dangling after a rich husband. Gentlemen would avoid her for it. But she did need to secure her future, and the Marquis answered those practical requirements. Love was too expensive for her to afford if she wished to gain the security she yearned for. She had tried to hide her excitement upon meeting him from Lady

Rebecca, but Caro's friend had a habit of reading her mind—a habit which worried her.

Rather than pressing for a response, Lady Rebecca continued. "The Marquis of Ravensbough was at Lady Carey's ball, you know, and though he did not ask after you immediately, once I happened to carelessly drop your name into the conversation, he did acknowledge that he had seen a fair-haired woman in my company of late."

"Carelessly?" Caro could not decide whether to be joyful or angered by Lady Rebecca's actions.

Lady Rebecca only laughed in response, that same wicked laughter she always emitted when she was proud of some hijinks she had played. It was infectious and Caro could not help smiling.

"After he settles his father's estate, he plans to spend the whole Season here, so we shall see much more of him—at least we will if he does not succumb to that extravagant itch that every gentleman of consequence is determined to scratch."

Caro grew very still at Lady Rebecca's allusion to gambling.

"Oh!" said her friend, all the hard confidence in her face melting into compassion. "I am sorry. I know you do not wish to talk of such things."

"It does not matter," replied Caro. This subject had come up a few times, and each time it was more difficult to handle, the lies harder to tell, the truths harder to keep hidden.

"I know you have said before you do not wish to speak of it, I just...." Lady Rebecca broke off, and Caro, in spite of her self-imposed rule that she would not bring up one of her roles when playing the other, desired to hear more. There was always the possibility it was something she could benefit from knowing.

"What is it?"

"Only, well, I do not wish to be a bearer of bad news but,

well, you must know Society talks of her. She has been gaming again. I hear she has been losing at the tables recently, people may...they may talk when you are out at the theatre on Friday. I just...."

The frequent pauses were unlike her friend—Caro knew that she must be wording things carefully in order to spare her feelings.

"...I wondered if perhaps her actions upset you? That might be why you feel so worn."

"Why should they?" Caro's voice was suddenly clipped. It was imperative to exude repulsion at such things whenever she was playing the respectable Miss Caro Worth. It was the only way she could be accepted and maintain her place in Society. "It is nothing I have not heard of her before."

Inside, she smiled a little at the rumour of Angelica's losses. It was a delightful false trail that led away from her door. If Society thought Miss Angelica Worth was losing at the tables, then Caro's recent rise in income would never be questioned.

"She is becoming quite famous, my dear." The excitement in Rebecca's voice showed none of the repulsion that Caro must pretend. After all, how many female gamesters were there in London? How many women were permitted to attend the hells that respectable women only mentioned in hushed whispers?

Rebecca reached a gloved hand out across the table toward her friend and cast down her eyes to moderate her enthusiasm. "However much you endeavour to hide it from me, I can see the concern in your eyes whenever she is mentioned. Only last week I heard of one of Sir Camberley's sons gambling away half his inheritance. His father quite cut him off, and he had creditors after him before long. Apparently, he only just escaped to Paris in time, and they say the creditors will follow him across the Channel."

"How very foolish." Caro's words were cool as images of the past filtered through her mind. She tried to blot out the picture of herself being cast out onto the streets.

"Very. I knew you would not like it." Lady Rebecca glanced cautiously up from her study of the table to look at Caro. "But I should like to see Miss Angelica Worth. She is a reputed raven-haired beauty, did you know that? And she wears her hair quite as unpowdered as you."

"I have never met her," replied Caro, for once an ounce of truth in what she said. How could she meet a bastard sister that had never existed? She lightened her voice. "But I suppose that is why you befriended me, for access to my notorious half-sister because you delight in all oddities and adventures."

Although the smile in no way reached Caro's eyes, the lightness of her tone did alleviate the conversation a great deal, and soon they were back to talking of Lady Carey's ball, oblivious to the frequent tinkling of the confectioner's bell as persons of quality came in and out of the little shop in Berkley Square. At least they were oblivious until a pair of particularly loud visitors came through the door.

"I say," said a male voice, "I didn't realise you could obtain such excellent sweetmeats outside of Italy itself."

The exclamation did not immediately capture Caro's attention, but as the owner of the voice carried on, Lady Rebecca's words began to fade a little from her hearing.

"I say," the owner of the voice exclaimed again, "I am not at all sure about the Bergamot Ice. I mean, I like the smell of the stuff, but surely that is a better use of it than infusing an ice with it? Oranges are grown in orchards in Spain—they aren't created to be tasted cold but in the heat of the Iberian Peninsula!"

"Ah!" said Lady Rebecca with a sharp intake of breath.

Caro jerked to attention, certain that her friend's exclamation was the prelude to another scold. Lady Rebecca must have noticed her concentration drifting towards the voice that sounded worryingly familiar.

However, as Caro looked to her friend, she was surprised to see Lady Rebecca's gaze was not directed towards her. Instead, the dark beauty with her white-powdered hair was looking over Caro's shoulder, her face breaking into a radiant smile intended for someone else.

The recipient of the smile hailed Lady Rebecca. Caro placed that voice, and as she did, her worries grew.

"Lord Avers!" Lady Rebecca responded with the same warmth she greeted every friend. "And who is this gentleman with you?"

Caro was immediately and acutely aware that it was not the voice of Lord Avers that had made her stomach turn. It was not his voice that had spoken of sweetmeats and Bergamot ices, and it was not his voice that sounded again, this time far closer to Caro's ear.

"Oh!" continued Lady Rebecca. "It is Mr. Felton!"

"Lady Rebecca,"—the other gentleman bowed, his hat creeping into the corner of Caro's vision—"I have been dragged here most unwillingly to order some kind of pastry for Avers' mother's ball, but now I see you here I am quite pleased I relented in my protestations."

Caro turned then, using all her strength to break out of her statue-like trance. A closer inspection of the gentleman confirmed her worst fears.

"How delightful it is to see you again!" said Lady Rebecca, oblivious to her friend's discomfiture. "I had no idea you were back from your Tour."

"Ah, yes, the weather of Europe is nothing in comparison to that of England. I quite missed the rain, you know?" The man's voice was full of amusement, so like it had been last night when he had accosted Caro while she played the role of another.

"Are you still a scoundrel?" One of Lady Rebecca's fine dark brows rose, her characteristic truthfulness challenging the man playfully.

"My long-suffering parents will confirm as much."

Caro breathed rapidly, dreading the moment that Mr. Felton would turn towards her. She reminded herself that she was not Angelica Worth today, but the fair-haired Caro. He would not recognise her—others did not. She must not panic. All would be well.

"Lord Avers, Mr. Felton, may I present Miss Worth to you both." Rebecca stretched a hand out, gracefully indicating Caro, and both gentlemen turned their attention to the golden-haired woman dressed in dazzling aquamarine.

"Miss Worth," Lord Avers bowed and smiled affably, "An additional pleasure to find you in the company of Lady Rebecca once again."

"Miss Worth." Mr. Felton, being the nearer of the two gentlemen took her hand and bent over it in a perfunctory bow.

That same boyish face Caro had seen by candlelight was before her now. By the light of day, Mr. Felton's face still held the handsome, careless, amused expression that had captivated her for a brief moment last night. But the same face in the morning's light was more worrying than captivating. Her legs began to tremble beneath the full skirts of her gown.

When Mr. Felton's head lifted, he caught Caro's eye, and the look that appeared on his face sent ice running through her veins. It was recognition.

"I say," he said, repeating his customary exclamation, "how intriguing."

His green eyes ran quickly over Caro's face. They paused on her hair for a moment, his brow furrowing and then clearing, and then they returned to her brilliant blue eyes once more.

"Am I remiss? Have I not made your acquaintance before?" His brow was furrowing again. He was trying his hardest to place her face. She was praying her hardest he would fail.

"I do not believe so, sir." Caro removed her eyes from his, desperate to keep away from his intent stare, desperate to steer his mind away from remembering. "I am sure of it, I would not forget those eyes anywhere, or...." Mr. Felton stepped back a little, looking down at her skirts as though expecting to see through them. To anyone else he looked as if he were only trying to gain a better view of the woman he thought he recognised, but Caro knew exactly the memory that was being conjured up in his mind. "You look very much like a woman I have already met."

She coloured.

"I dislike excessively to say it, Miss Worth," said Mr. Felton, a boyish grin resuming mastery over his shapely lips, "however, I believe if we have met before as I suspect, it was in quite different surroundings."

Clearly, he thought he was being subtle, but Caro knew the irreparable damage he could do to her. Tongues were already wagging where Caro was concerned, and his attempts at the finer arts of concealment were poor. Caro was overcome with a desire to strike him again, wishing to destroy that amused smile on his face that so carelessly put her future at risk.

"I don't know what you mean." Caro's body stiffened, her voice containing the same rigidness reflected in her frame. She suppressed her urge to react and instead resurrected the feeling of satisfaction she had gained from slapping him last night.

"That exact turn of phrase," he murmured again, still staring at her.

His words were far from proper, even to those whose minds could not fully understand what their ears were hearing. Caro was aware that other guests in the confectioner's shop were leaning in to hear the unusual conversation from the loud young gentleman.

Both Lady Rebecca and Lord Avers had been staring at the interchange, confused—however, the latter was rapidly catching up to his friend on the gentleman's path of assumptions.

"But that hair...." Felton murmured to himself.

He was looking at her gold curls, trying to reconcile them with the raven hair he had seen, with the wig that sat on her dressing table at home. He recognised her face, her eyes—but the hair remained her one defence.

"Yes, I do not powder my hair. My mother always told me not to because of its fine colour." At least there could be a little truth in her life of falsehoods. "I dislike the way you stare, sir," Caro used her severest tones, trying to break through the mesmerised state the gentleman seemed to be in.

"Felton." Lord Avers stepped forward, attempting to stop his friend before more damage was done. But his friend carried on like a runaway horse pulling away from its pursuer.

"I have never been so sure and so unsure. Are you not the lady I met last night at Mr. Russell's?"

Again she blushed, and taking her blush to be confirmation, Mr. Felton gave her a saucy wink.

Caro shot up from her chair in a surge of red hot fury. "Sir! I must ask you to desist!"

"Mr. Felton," he corrected, not in the least perturbed, the curl of his grin still evident on his mouth.

She was trying her best to ignore those lips, the ones that had uttered the word "pleasure" in such a fascinating way last night. She hated how his careless attitude at once riled her and intrigued her. Her anxiety was laced with a desire to meet this gentleman on the word-sparring field...but she knew better. She shook off any vestiges of her ridiculous humour. Now was the time to draw the line between her identities in indelible ink before he had a chance of furthering this course of inquiry.

"You are mistaken, sir. I can guess which surroundings you refer to, and they are the haunt of my father's illegitimate daughter." If the house of cards was to fall, she would be in control of its destruction, not some impertinent cad.

She watched with satisfaction as Mr. Felton's face faltered. She must carry on if she wished to dash the water of explanation over the flames of scandal. "Her name is Angelica Worth, and I am not she. I should thank you to refrain from associating me with such an improper hoyden and instead to respect my position as Miss Caro Worth."

She managed the speech with dignity and had the satisfaction of winning the audience to her side.

"Hear! Hear!" cried Lady Rebecca, positively thriving off the drama.

"I tried to warn you, old boy," said Lord Avers, shaking his head, one hand upon Felton's arm and another upon his own brow. He tried to pull his friend away from the embarrassing encounter.

Yet in spite of his faux pas, there was still a half-cocked grin upon Felton's face. He leant back on one leg, surveying Caro as a duellist might an opponent. Caro returned the stare measure for measure. She could see his hair remained unpowdered, a style they frustratingly shared, his hair tied imperfectly at his neck with a plain ribbon, a few pieces of it falling about his shoulders. His red silk suit was well-cut, but the buttons were only half done up, the lace at his collar less than dazzling.

The brazen green eyes danced over her face again and again. Did he not believe her? Did he not believe the friends she had vouching for her, no matter their status? *He* could not be quality. He might be handsome in an infuriating way, but he was shabby, improper, and still he stared! He was as shocking now as he had been last night, except this time she was sure he was not foxed. At least, surely not at eleven o'clock in the morning?

"Sir!" she reprimanded, continuing to stiffen her shoulders.

"Mr. Felton, as I said, you intriguing woman—the Honourable Tobias Felton. Has anyone ever told you that you are quite beautiful?"

"*Mr. Felton.*" She spoke the name without reverence and ignored the shocking compliment as best she could. "I find it hard to believe that you hold the word 'honourable' in your name. I was half inclined not even to call you 'sir,' so ungentle-manly is your behaviour."

The words were a barb, but they only served to tickle the gentleman further. Apparently, even her best thrusts were easily parried. A little chuckle gurgled up in Mr. Felton's chest, and Caro saw his eyes brighten with something she did not trust.

"Well, she has you there, Felton." Lord Avers was looking particularly uncomfortable by this point but trying his best to promote amicable relations.

Lady Rebecca, on the other hand, could not have been happier. After so many Seasons out in the Ton, she adored ripples in the usually stagnant waters of Society. "She has you indeed," said Lady Rebecca. "Honestly, Mr. Felton, I thought European circles would have sharpened your wit, not blunted it."

"My apologies," murmured Mr. Felton, the look of taunting disbelief wiped from his face.

Caro felt the tightness of her chest relaxing a little. Did he believe her now? Would he grant that she was not Angelica Worth?

"I have clearly been mistaken in my assumptions. May I reintroduce myself and hope that in time I may enter your good graces once again?" Mr. Felton attempted to take her hand again, but Caro was slow in offering it.

That light in his eyes had dulled, but it was still there. She wished to withhold both her hand and her good graces, but she knew she would have to concede. He had apologised, and if she did not accept it, at least publicly, rumours would spread. She would follow the dictates of Society, but in the future she would have to keep this man at arm's length. He had come closer to the truth than anyone in the past year, and he had an odd ability to trip her up. Such a man could be nothing but dangerous.

"Very well," said Caro with grudging politeness.

"I have been abroad this past year, gaining maturity my father tells me, and I had not been back in London more than two days when I met your...Miss Angelica Worth at...ah...."

"You needn't say it," Caro replied coldly. All affability had disappeared from her face. "And if you would be so good as to never mention my name alongside hers again, I should be most obliged to you, Mr. Felton. She is a disgrace my family must bear, and one which I will not allow to drag me down. I no more wish to be associated with her than I wish to be accosted by you." At least that was truth, and she could utter those words without the guilt she was accustomed to.

"I do not blame you," said Mr. Felton in a cavalier tone.

His relaxed attitude only aggravated Caro's tense mood further. She felt like a Boulle clock whose mechanism was being wound too tight—before long the cogs would start flying. She exhaled. She must remain calm and controlled, no matter her feelings—it was the only way she would avoid slipping up in the mire of her own lies.

"Now I have caused such a stir, shall we sit and enjoy a calming cup of tea?" asked Mr. Felton, still apparently untroubled by the upset he had caused her.

Caro could not tell if he was serious. He seemed to be in

earnest, but the tone of his voice and the gleam in his eyes suggested something different. She could read a hundred faces at a ball or in the hot confines of a hell, but not this gentleman's face.

Lady Rebecca, seeing the harassed look upon her friend's face finally allowed compassion for Caro to overcome her enjoyment of the unusual situation. "I am afraid we are expected at my aunt's, gentlemen." Lady Rebecca stood with great imperiousness, her curvaceous figure rising from behind the table. Her chocolate-coloured eyes swept over to Lord Avers. "You will excuse us."

"But of course," Lord Avers replied, making a bow, no doubt relieved there was to be an end to the unpleasantness.

"I shall bid you good day then, Miss Worth," said Mr. Felton, once again unfazed by the coldness from Caro. Without waiting for permission, he whisked her hand from her side and placed a soft kiss upon the back of her glove.

Caro was too shocked to resist; however, when Mr. Felton raised his eyes and bestowed another wink upon her, she snatched her hand from his fingertips.

"I shall look forward to seeing you again," he said and then turned his attentions to her companion. Caro's mouth dropped in surprise as Rebecca smacked Felton's hands off hers with her fan.

"That's enough of that!" Without so much as an apology, Rebecca swept outside of the confectioner's. Caro followed, the tinkle of the bell on the door an oddly joyful sound since it meant escape. The cold November air hit Caro's hot face like a welcome relief.

"Well," said Lady Rebecca, taking her footman's hand and stepping up into the waiting carriage, "that was all rather thrilling."

CHAPTER FOUR

"Tobias Felton? The dear boy is back in Town? How delightful!"

Caro could not agree with Lady Etheridge's statement. She could not, by any stretch of the imagination, consider Tobias Felton's presence a delight. She still had the vision of his green, winking eyes in her mind. He was quite honestly the most shockingly saucy gentleman she had ever met.

"You met him at The Pot and Pineapple?" Lady Etheridge queried. "How curious! The haunts of young men have changed quite considerably since my day." Lady Etheridge, known by most of London Society as an eccentric, spoke her mind without the least reserve. It endeared her to some and made her formidable to others who knew better than to shun a lady of her stature.

"He was there with Lord Avers ordering desserts for the upcoming ball," explained Rebecca, "but, he was most unpleasant to poor Caro." She widened her dark eyes in a telling way.

"Was he indeed?" Lady Etheridge's keen blue eyes switched to Caro.

Caro averted her face, staring a little too intently at the scene depicted on the far wall's tapestry. She would much rather stare at scenes from a battle than think upon the fiasco of this morning. At least she had held her own admirably—not that anyone knew enough to admire her for it.

"Europe has done that young scoundrel no good I take it?"

"Aunt, language!"

Caro looked between the two and thought with wry amusement that Lady Etheridge was merely an older, less restrained, version of her niece. Lady Rebecca, who was all for adventures and intriguing situations, often felt obligated to upbraid her unorthodox aunt for things she would have said herself. When Lady Rebecca aged, she would no doubt endure upbraiding from her own niece—such was the nature of the world.

A childless widow, Lady Etheridge doted upon her sister's daughter. While Rebecca's parents were abroad, seeking warmer climates for Lady Fairing's frail health, Rebecca had been left in her aunt's charge. Caro reflected that Lady Etheridge must enjoy the excitement Rebecca brought to the old Townhouse. The dwelling had not been updated since Lord Etheridge's death almost a decade earlier, and the furniture was covered with rococo fascinations that were beginning to look out of place compared with the new classical aesthetic.

"And what say you, Miss Worth? You refuse to look at me or speak of this morning's events. I am quite intrigued."

The old woman was seated in an old-fashioned, open-fronted mantua gown in a pale blue which picked up those twinkling eyes of hers. She had a cap upon her powdered hair. Caro always found the high cheekbones of her countenance quite striking, and the apple cheeks which would appear below whenever she smiled. At this moment those twinkling eyes were mining into Caro's own for gems of information.

"What did you think of young Mr. Felton, Miss Worth?" Her ladyship refused to be ignored.

"He...I...he was rather...abrasive. A scoundrel as you say."

Lady Etheridge laughed, the well-used lines about her mouth creasing as she smiled. "Abrasive indeed. No doubt you would find his older brother Frederick more agreeable, though I understand he has recently become engaged to Lady Cynthia Reynolds. I, for one, could never turn down a scoundrel."

Caro remembered how Lady Etheridge had described her husband. A stealer of hearts, a breaker of most, the keeper of hers. It had sounded so romantic, but if Lady Etheridge really meant that her husband was similar to Mr. Felton, the story instantly lost its appeal. Mr. Felton was risky. Besides, Caro did not have time for romance, only for marriage to a man who secured her future.

"What did he say that upset you so? I declare I have never seen you looking so sullen, Miss Worth, and it is all the more surprising for you are serious most days, are you not?"

"Aunt! That is abominably rude."

"I hardly mean she does not look attractive, Rebecca. You and I both know her to be a unique beauty. I speak only the truth about her character. I wondered what attracted you to the woman for she is a great deal more serious than you, Rebecca."

"We have been friends these past six months, and now you say such things. You may think what you wish, Aunt, but you mayn't say it!"

Lady Rebecca was sighing in exasperation and beginning to tut, but Caro felt a giggle bubble up from her chest.

"Ah," Lady Etheridge's eyes twinkled. "Do you find my opinions humorous? Now I can see the attraction." She shot a provocative look at her niece and then turned back to Caro. "Come, tell me what he said to you."

"He..." There was nothing to lose, everyone would know

by now anyway, and besides, Lady Etheridge had already accepted her into her circle knowing her scandals. "He thought me my father's illegitimate daughter, Miss Angelica Worth."

"Did he, by goodness!" exclaimed Lady Etheridge, her eyes alight with the same excitement her niece often showed. "What a scoundrel, but I thought Miss Angelica Worth had dark hair?"

"She does." Caro paused, realizing that her statement could insinuate an intimacy between the two half-sisters. "I have heard about her like the rest of Society has."

"A bold statement to acknowledge. You must be very like her for Mr. Felton to confuse you with her." Lady Etheridge's remark sent a shot of anxiety through Caro. "The fact that you both leave your hair unpowdered is most curious."

"I am sure Caro does not like such a similarity drawn," Rebecca said. "It was most distressing and he made quite the scene. I wish he were not so droll, for I found it quite hard to be cross with him."

Caro had found it just as hard. Towards the end, when the reality of the damage he could do had dawned on her, she had been angry, but not at him, at his carelessness.

"Mr. Felton is a tear-away and a scapegrace, but no real harm ever comes of his youthful excitement. In fact, before he went away, I remember him as one of the most amusing young men about Town, forever funning and quite charming when he wished to be, though his father was exhausted with him by the end of it. Still, he has a soft spot in my heart. Do you know he once wrote me a poem? He said I was the most beautiful older woman he'd ever had the pleasure of laying eyes on—the young scamp!" Lady Etheridge chuckled at the memory, but drawing herself back to the present, she turned to the subject of the morning. "I can see it is poor Lord Avers who deserves our pity—that gentleman despises a scene. He is quite the most affable man in London."

Lady Etheridge knew almost everybody in Town. Now that the loss of her husband had abated to a dull ache, she busied herself with knowing everything about everyone. She was well known as the Lady of Society who could spot a match a mile off. She knew enough of the many scandals simmering beneath Society's surface to curl a more proper madam's toes.

"Well, I am obliged to you for divulging the story so promptly, my dear," she said to Lady Rebecca. "I would have hated to have heard it secondhand from that vulgar gossip, the Countess of Goring. She is bound to have had her nose pressed up against the window if she was not inside Mr. Negri's shop at the time. Tell me, do many people mistake you for your half-sister?"

Caro saw Lady Etheridge turn towards her. Apparently, she was not going to be left alone so easily.

"Oh, here she goes again." Lady Rebecca threw her hands up in the air before leaning back upon the brocade sofa in an unladylike fashion. "Aunt shall be pumping you for all the information you have. She is quite the Societal bloodhound."

"I confess I have never been fond of that breed of dog." Caro forced a smile onto her face. The longevity of the conversation was most distressing.

"Oh, Rebecca, you are ungenerous to me." Lady Etheridge leant forward and swatted her niece's hand with her handkerchief. "If it were not for me, you should have bestowed your favor on that cad, Lord Melchant, had I not told you of his...er...less salubrious dealings."

For the first time since Caro had known Rebecca, she saw the lady blush, the red stealing up her cheeks and her eyes darting nervously.

"Aunt! I was quite the green school-girl at that time. I was swept away by ridiculous fancies." Rebecca seemed determined to alleviate her embarrassment by pushing the attention back onto Caro. "You had best tell Aunt or she shall not be satisfied."

"No," Caro obeyed. "I have never been mistaken for her before." So why had she this time? What was the trick of this Mr. Felton?

"Ah." Lady Etheridge's intent face softened a little. "I do feel for you—no parents, your brother away in the West Indies, and you coming to London alone without any friends from Sussex. It is all most distressing."

The mention of James sent a lancing pain through Caro's chest. She pushed it away immediately. She would not think of him.

"What made you come to London all by yourself?" asked Lady Etheridge, insensible of Caro's distress and led only by her own curiosity.

"I came to Town in search of a husband." There was no point in pretence. Where deception was necessary Caro used it unwillingly, but here, where she felt the company almost safe, she could be truthful in some respects. She liked Lady Etheridge—what she thought was the same as what she said.

Even though she was accustomed to plain speaking, such an abrupt reply from Caro took Lady Etheridge aback. She sat in stunned silence for a few moments, putting down her teacup and staring hard at Caro. Then the light of approval began to shine in her eyes, and she resumed drinking her tea.

"Honesty. I can admire that."

Rebecca giggled. "Oh, Caro, you are too awful! You have said as much to me, but we are bosom friends. I hope you do not go around all your acquaintances declaring such shocking truths."

"None of my acquaintances have asked such direct questions," Caro replied candidly.

"Ah, yes, my flaw, I am afraid," said Lady Etheridge, her light eyes twinkling, "and my niece's too. Let us cease this interrogation, shall we?"

Caro smiled. "Yes, my lady."

At least here, among these two women she called friends, she had not yet lost all that she had worked for. It showed her that the rest of Society was still under the spell of her lies as she had hoped. Her secret was safe, at least for the time being.

"Ah, *ma chérie*, we meet again, what a delight." Felton whispered the words into Angelica's ear, his breath tickling her neck and making her jump a little.

She refrained from turning her head. She was at play, but she knew exactly who was addressing her.

"Good evening," she replied, cursing the inconvenience of his appearance. "I trust you are not intoxicated yet?" It was only twelve and Angelica knew he was not, but there was no harm in insulting him. As Angelica, she could say the things she wished without worrying over the repercussions as Caro must. Pushing him off his game, whatever it was, was for the best.

"Alas, no, I have yet to succumb to the dizzying heights of inebriation this evening. I trust you have not undressed in the library yet?"

Angelica felt the sudden and surprising pull of a rebellious smile tugging at her red lips, tweaking the angle of her heart-shaped patch. This man was utterly shocking! At least in this guise she might enjoy his improper humour. She saw how it was now. Mistaking Caro for Angelica had shown him that her respectable self was forbidden fruit—now he was trying the alternative he thought available.

She turned her head very slowly until her eyes were

looking directly into his. "If we were not in company, Mr. Felton, I would slap you."

Mr. Felton flinched, drawing his head back slightly, but it was only to show her his wide grin. It seemed this man was perpetually amused.

"I know exactly how your fine hand feels against my cheek. No, I thank you, I am glad we are in company. Though," he leaned even closer, "I hope to catch you out of company at some point this evening."

"Many hope that," she teased, but despite the urge to get lost in those humorous green eyes, she knew she must resist. "They are always disappointed."

She had never spoken with such familiarity to a player before, and here it must end. She needed to be on her guard, just as John was where he stood against the wall, ever-watchful. She must cease bantering and start ignoring the attractive lips which were proving more than a little distracting.

She had wondered if she would see Felton again. Last time his appearance had been a disaster, and this time she knew her self-control was lacking. She regretted her choice to enter the hell tonight. It had taken weeks to be admitted to this gaming establishment. Mr. Russell knew her and she knew the players. If Felton's distraction ruined this, she would have to frequent a new establishment and start again, research the players again, earn the trust of the proprietor again. Being a woman in this game made earning trust difficult, not to mention the tediousness of keeping a half-decent gaming reputation. She should have paid the heavy Joey to bar Felton's entrance tonight. If only she had thought of it before.

"I see you are at loo." Felton stood up, cheerfully resigned to her coldness, and looked over the table where several other gentlemen sat. Each had a varying degree of concentration marking their faces. Lord Avers was lounging back in a chair, a position that juxtaposed awkwardly with the etched concentration between his brows. Mr. Went and Lord Bivens were also seated at the table, each joking with one another about their latest bits of muslin, but neither taking their eyes from their cards. And then there was a quiet gentleman, a gentleman of particular interest to Caro Worth, who was seated across from her.

Angelica did not respond to Mr. Felton's obvious statement, but he was not so easily deterred. He beckoned for one of Mr. Russell's men to bring a chair and was soon seated to her right, the skirts of his carelessly donned jacket admirably displayed in the relaxed position he took.

"You are still here," she said, laying a card.

She took the hand that she had just freed of its cargo and laid it on the richly coloured silk of her stomacher, all the while smiling coquettishly at Lord Bivens across the table. She could always distract him from his play with a little flirtation. It was easy. After a day of difficulty and tension it felt good to be playing this relaxed, dangerous version of herself, if only for a few hours. If only she could get rid of Felton....

"I wish to watch you play," he said, leaning closer. "I hear you are quite the gamester. You fleeced my friend Mr. Leeden of two thousand pounds just three weeks ago."

"Did I? How clever of me." She laughed softly and played another card.

"You know I met your sister."

This cavalier statement brought her up short. She tried not to react, but Felton saw her hand stop toying with her stomacher to grip her cards more tightly. Distracting the players was no longer a priority—distracting herself was the new objective.

"Did you?" This was how she could maintain control. Asking questions, remaining calm and disconnected.

"You are very different from your sister, you know." A

little smile tugged at his lips. "Such exquisite raven hair—like an Italian beauty."

"Half-sister."

"I say! Come on, Miss Worth, you are hardly in this game." Lord Avers reproached her while laying the winning card upon the table.

Roused from paralysis, Angelica saw that she had just lost five hundred pounds. Exhaling sharply, she discarded the rest of her cards onto the table in a series of flutters.

She could feel Felton watching her. She hoped that he had missed that initial expression of fear. Five hundred pounds! Still, all could be well if she could regain her garments of self-possession.

"Unfortunate." Mr. Felton clicked his tongue against his teeth. What was wrong with this man? If she believed in bad luck, she would say that he was it, lingering like the smell of the Thames on an unpromising morning. She held back a huff of irritation.

"I am not a bird in a cage—stop staring," she commanded. There were times she was thankful not to be the proper Caro Worth, and this was one of them. Let her emotions be seen if he was so intent on looking.

"So another commanded me." A lilting grin appeared on his lips. "And I would call it a gilded cage," he added provokingly.

"What?" Her eyes darted towards him in anger. "I am no kept woman." Her words snapped like twigs cracking under foot.

"That was not what I meant, but thank you for clarifying."

She looked away, ignoring the embarrassment. This man was infuriating. He led her into one ill-spoken, impassioned speech after another, whichever of her two roles she was playing.

"No matter," she said, pretending the last part of the conversation had not occurred. She had a role to play, she had an identity to conceal, and seriousness and anger had no part in the saucy and playful character of Angelica Worth. "I am sure my luck shall change; it never does leave me behind for long. But I think my ill-fortune was caused by you, you know. You are an unlucky charm." Mr. Felton's eyes were unnerving, but she willed herself to maintain her saucy façade. "Not to mention an irritation."

"A dagger to the heart, dear lady. I love to be an irritation to many people, but you are not one of them." He finished with mock sincerity, but he still watched her with more intensity than she liked, as though he could see into her soul and read its secrets without permission.

She said nothing in reply, but apparently Felton needed no encouragement to continue the conversation.

"Yes, indeed, I cannot rightly say why." He leant back, his coat flaring out on either side of him displaying lavish but tarnished embroidery that glinted in the candlelight. His hair remained unpowdered and tied only loosely at the nape of his neck. He still looked shabby and unkempt. Apparently he cared little for other people's opinion of him. For a moment, Angelica was jealous of his carefree spirit—but it was different for him. His future was secure.

Resting his chin on his hand, he repeated himself. "You and Miss Caro Worth are quite different."

"Is that not obvious?"

"Not to me." He was staring at her, his green eyes taking everything in, seeing beneath her skin, beneath her lies. Did he know?

There were many who had seen her game and then danced with her at a ball the next evening none the wiser. But then again, she never usually let anyone so close, and it was proving almost impossible to keep this man away. He was like a puppy too enamored with his favourite stick to bring it back to his master—and she was the stick he had decided to play with.

"Your mind fails to work quite as well as most then."

"An insult." The side of Felton's mouth curled. A flash of white teeth showed, and a gleam appeared in his eyes. "This is only the second time we have met—I hardly think you have the ability to judge."

Angelica bit her tongue.

"Then again, as such an accomplished gamester, you are clearly a good reader of people. Can you tell me why you misread this table?"

The majority of the players were still at the table, talking, drinking. A few took notice of Angelica's conversation with Felton. One in particular, the man across from her, watched with some interest.

"I was distracted." That distraction had cost money— money needed to order more candles and more dresses. Caro had to have a new gown for the theatre on Friday. She had worn her current gowns too often, and she couldn't risk people thinking her less independent than she had let them assume. A respectable reputation was built up over months; a bad reputation could be caused in one careless moment, and a bad reputation scared off suitors.

At the thought of potential suitors, she looked up. She had been worried when the Marquis of Ravensbough sat across from her. She did not want anything reminding a potential suitor of the scandals connected to the Worth name. But he had not spoken two words to her over the course of the game, and aside from catching his eye several times, she had barely thought of him since he'd sat down. Now, however, she was horrified to see him rise and come towards her.

Felton carried on talking as the darkly clad presence descended upon them. Flustered, Angelica heard nothing of what was said until the Marquis stopped beside Felton's chair.

"The lady does not wish for your company, boy." The Marquis' dark eyes looked at Angelica as he spoke.

"Boy?"

For the first time since meeting him, and no thanks to her own best efforts this evening, Angelica thought she heard something akin to irritation in Felton's voice. Apparently a simple slight from this Marquis had found the joint in Felton's armour that her barbs had missed.

Felton didn't move, his right elbow still on the table and his back towards the interloper. His eyes were fastened on some distant scenery over Angelica's shoulder. After being the sole captivator of his attention this evening, she now found herself beaten by the mahogany walls behind her.

"Yes, boy," the Marquis confirmed, his tone condescending.

Angelica looked up at Ravensbough whose dark features were considered handsome by many and whose fortune was the envy of the other eligible bachelors among the Ton. She had only spoken to him a handful of times and had hoped for more conversation from him as Caro Worth, but he was here now and all she could do was listen.

"Are you not Frederick Felton's younger brother? I've heard about you and your supposed exploits. Those of a reckless boy, don't you think? We've not been introduced, but you must know who I am—the Marquis of Ravensbough." The older man did not bow, and the younger man did not acknowledge the introduction. The Marquis was in control of this conversation.

"Being Frederick Felton's younger brother would make you less than thirty and less than independent, would it not? I think the woman would prefer a real player. Perhaps you should run along to bed now and let the lady play me at piquet. Are you game, madam?"

Angelica was not game. She no more wished to play

Ravensbough at cards than she wished to sit with the inquisitive Felton. The insults the Marquis was raining on Felton dismayed her, and though Ravensbough was a marriage candidate by day for Caro Worth, Angelica wanted nothing to do with this side of him.

What was happening to the perfectly controlled world she had created? She caught eyes with John, willing him to come and whisk her away with some small whispered message in her ear.

"I shall partner the lady. Miss Worth?" Felton's tone was more clipped than usual, his joviality strained as he rose and held out his hand to Angelica. All she could do was admire his rising to the Marquis' challenge. "I am one of her favourites after all." Felton laid down his own gauntlet.

"Are you indeed? I have not seen you in her company before though I have seen her gaming a number of times."

Had he? Angelica felt a shiver of unrest at the thought of being spied on.

"Miss Worth?" Felton's eyes searched her own. She looked between the two and, not sure how to extricate herself, consented.

"An interesting choice of partner." The Marquis cast an indifferent eye over Felton as the gentleman took Angelica's arm. "It is unfortunate, Miss Worth, that we finally make the acquaintance I've long desired under losing circumstances, especially as this next game may prove much the same for you." There was another look at Felton and then a lingering gaze on the hand she had placed on Felton's arm.

The party was moving towards a table ready for piquet. John followed them on his well-beaten track along the length of the wall like a yearling pacing a fence. They could have sat down silently, but that last comment made Angelica look up warily. The Marquis had been wanting to make her acquaintance for some time? This was not good. More than that, his arrogance niggled Angelica's competitive nature.

"You assume my defeat, my lord?" A light came into her eye. "But you lost the last game, as did I, and assuming never did anyone any good, did it?" She would sever this unhelpful acquaintance with caustic words and by winning his money. If she was to be acquainted with the Marquis, it would be as Caro Worth.

As she laid this challenge, Felton straightened at her side, a smile creeping onto his face.

The Marquis' response was far more menacing. "Indeed," he said, a flash of anger suffusing his face. But rather than reneging on the game, the Marquis sat down at the table, his eyes relentless as they preyed on her face.

Felton, having regained his humour, leant forward to the now-seated Angelica. "Now, no more distracting me, Miss Worth. I must be at my best, for last time I was partnered at piquet I lost some ten thousand pounds."

The jovial words hit Angelica's chest like a stone from a sling. She felt the air flee from her lungs, and the beat of her heart sped up in panic. Ten thousand pounds. Ten thousand! That was more than Angelica had access to by any means. She could not run that deep in this game—she had already lost five hundred pounds, and her plan to pocket a thousand pounds this evening was not looking promising.

She tried to think of an escape, but if she wished to save face she could not leave. Were she to abandon the game, people would talk, perhaps assuming she had no blunt. She could not afford that.

She would play with Felton and the Marquis but, while they were playing with the cream scraped from the top of their fortunes, Angelica was playing with her livelihood, her future. The odds were too high to accept and too high to refuse. More than that, she needed to dissuade the Marquis' attentions.

Angelica was so distracted by her dilemma that she hardly noticed Felton observing her. Even the Marquis was busy ordering a drink and pulling at the cuffs of his well-ordered jacket. It was left to Felton to observe that look of fear on her face, to note the hand which held her fan shake a little, to see the way her brow puckered.

When the final player, apparently a friend of the Marquis, was seated, and the cards were dealt, Angelica tried to make sense of the numbers and suits before her. But her mind would not be quiet—it would not cease running through the possibilities, the evils that would transpire if she failed to play well. She stood on the edge of a precipice overlooking the dark chasm of loss.

As she turned to her partner Felton, she noticed his face had changed. There was no teasing on his lips, and instead, a hint of concentration. His eyes darted upwards and caught with hers. He grinned. After that there were no more smiles and the play was high.

CHAPTER FIVE

"Do you know I find myself quite jealous of how you feel about the Marquis."

"Do you?" Caro smiled but kept her eyes on the objects in the glass case before her. "And how do I feel about the Marquis?"

They had come to Montagu House on Great Russell Street to peruse Sir Hans Sloane's collection. Lady Etheridge had wandered off to conduct her own tour, and so far the selection of manuscripts and tables displaying prints and drawings had done less than interest Lady Rebecca. She was following Caro, rarely looking down at the treasures available to them. Caro on the other hand was bending over each case in turn, reading the minute text or following the lines of fine prints with avid interest. She was trying to ignore the finely pointed shoe which peeped from beneath Rebecca's blue gown, tapping on the floor with excess energy.

"You know! The way you are setting your cap at him." Rebecca turned and placed two gloved hands on top of one of the display cases. The frame rattled and a small man with a puff of gray hair, lined skin, and wiry legs, came dashing across the room to shoot a reproving look at Rebecca. He glowered like a parent at a disobedient child.

"You needn't look at me like that, you silly little man. I hardly touched it." Rebecca looked formidable as she retracted her hands from the case. "You would be better off investing in more substantial cases for these...what are these, Caro?"

"Manuscripts, Rebecca."

"Manuscripts!" Rebecca nodded briskly and walked on without a backward glance.

The little man darted forwards after they had moved on, his pale eyes scouring the case for damage and his small wrinkled hands checking that the treasure-holder was stable.

"As I was saying," Rebecca carried on, following Caro to the next case and paying no heed to the custodian, "I am quite jealous because, well...." The fearless woman hesitated.

"What is it?" asked Caro, ceasing her examination of the artefacts and turning to face her friend. Her expression was soft and her face open.

It was amusing how Rebecca could at one moment be the bluntest and most truthful woman in London—perhaps excepting her aunt—and in the next be shy and vulnerable. "Oh, I know I can be honest with you, but it is a little embarrassing."

Caro was enjoying this visit. She had never been to the British Museum before, and the knowledge that lay behind glass cases and on well-lined bookshelves excited her.

More than that, for the first time in many weeks, she felt like she could enjoy herself. Felton, in spite of his irritating manner, had helped her win a great deal two nights ago, and with that influx of monetary funds, Caro was free to enjoy this time with her friend without distraction.

Even if Felton had caused her trouble, the service he had done her alter-ego Angelica could never be repaid. She felt a little softness towards the mischievous gentleman. She was not hoping to meet him again, but at least she could now think of him without so much aggravation. More than that, the good mood he had managed to awaken in Caro made her wish to be a better friend to Rebecca whom she had neglected of late.

The ladies moved out of the elegant room and into the next which was currently devoid of visitors. "What is it? You may tell me." Caro drew Rebecca towards some chairs placed before one of the large windows overlooking the formal gardens that were laid out behind the property.

"I have never felt particularly attracted to any one man. I think it's why I have yet to marry after two Seasons. I simply have not met anyone at whom I've wanted to set my cap. What I mean to say is, yes, I find them physically attractive, but I have never desired to speak to a gentleman above any other. I enjoy their flattery, their conversation, but there has yet to be a man whom I desire to spend time with over and above the rest."

Sunshine was drifting in through the window, and with the pane of glass keeping the chilled November air outside, the beams were warming and pleasant.

"This is how you must feel about the Marquis, isn't it?"

Caro frowned a little, not quite knowing how to answer. Did she wish to spend more time with the Marquis? As Caro, not Angelica, she certainly did, but not because she enjoyed his company. She barely knew the gentleman as of yet. Rather, it was his ability to provide her with security that made her wish in turn to secure him. Did that make her callous?

"I'm not sure." Rethinking, she spoke again, "That is to say, I find him attractive."

"Half of London does!" Rebecca replied. "My aunt has said to me before that if you can, marry for love, if not, marry for like. It is not at all what my father says, but I do not think them much alike."

Caro laughed. She had not met Rebecca's parents, but she could not imagine anyone being like Lady Etheridge.

"I know, I know!" Rebecca giggled. "But I do value my aunt's words. I remember a little of my uncle, and I know what people say of them both. Do you know when they married their story was all across London? A love affair which everyone spoke of, especially when they married without his father's consent. He eventually forgave them, but it was quite the scandal at the time. I think that's why Father wasn't quite so happy for me to stay with my aunt whilst they are abroad."

Caro wondered at the love affair between Lord and Lady Etheridge. How could they have jeopardised their future in such a manner? All in the name of love they had risked everything. It was fortunate for them that it had turned out happily —not all lives worked out so easily.

Being such a romantic was out of the question for Caro. She had never thought of feelings when she had planned her trip to London a year ago. It was not feelings that would feed her and Libby and John. Perhaps that was why she found it hard to answer Rebecca's questions about the Marquis.

"From what I know of your aunt, I am not surprised—she does not care for others' opinions." But Caro had no choice in that quarter. People's good opinions were vital to her plan.

"No," Rebecca's eyes lit with amusement as they so often did. "I don't suppose you can be much surprised when you have known my aunt for some time. My sister Rachel is just as bad, but my parents were quick to marry her off before she became a nuisance. Compared to her I am as meek as a church mouse!" She sighed. "I know I am outspoken, as do you,"— she giggled sheepishly—"as does most of Society, and I have not yet met a man who can match me. It is not that I think myself above the gentlemen of my acquaintance, but I can hardly say that I have respect for any of them, and I wish to be able to respect the man who would look after me as his wife."

The serious tone of the conversation was unusual for Rebecca and, as if realizing this herself, she turned the subject. "Do you know that the field of the forty steps is in that direction?" She nodded towards the window.

"The field of what?" Caro was fast realizing that she would have to relinquish her hope of further study of the museum's treasures. She had been looking forward to examining some of the literature bequeathed by George II, hoping to satiate her desire for reading here when she could not do so in the sparsity of her own home.

"Forty steps." Rebecca's eyes sparkled with the same excitement she always exuded when speaking of some salacious story. She took one of Caro's hands in her own and guided her out of her chair and to the window, coming so close to it that it looked as if her nose would soon be pressed up against the pane of glass.

"Over there, beyond the formal gardens and the fountain, where you see the land changing to fields."

"Rebecca, I find it utterly ridiculous that we have come to the British Museum to view its treasures, and you are more intent on showing me things outside of it!"

"Oh, yes, I know you are bookish—I accompanied you with my aunt when you asked, did I not? But give me this one moment, and then I shall look at prints and trinkets to your heart's content. Do we have a deal?"

Caro nodded, and Rebecca's gloved finger pointed against the mottled glass pane. "Those are Montagu Fields, and in them is the field of the forty steps." Her tone became theatrical as though she were imparting a great secret to her audience. "It is said that two brothers fell madly in love with the same woman. Not satisfied to yield ground to each other they met in the field below."

Caro was beginning to realise that she had heard this story, or a different version of it, before.

"The woman they loved sat on a bank as they measured out their paces and then fought each other."

Rebecca's voice rose to a dramatic crescendo causing several visitors who had entered the room to glance their way. Caro could see the curator they had upset in the previous room hovering in the doorway, watching them with his pale little eyes.

Rebecca was oblivious—or impervious—to her growing audience. "In the end, neither won. They killed each other with the woman they loved looking on. And ever since, their forty steps have been marked in the ground. No grass will grow there to cover the tragedy of the place."

"Well," said Caro, seeing Rebecca relishing the story even after it had been completed, "that is a highly unsatisfactory tale, is it not? Surely even your dramatic palate is a little ruined by such a sad story of pointless endeavour?"

"Not at all!" cried Rebecca, moving away from the window and placing her arm in Caro's as they walked through to the next room. "I find it highly romantic—imagine having the sort of love for someone that you might sacrifice yourself to have them? Really Caro, I know you are a practical sort of woman, as am I, but wouldn't it mean something to you if the Marquis were to make such a gesture?"

Caro highly doubted she was far enough in the Marquis' affections to warrant a duel being fought in her name. She thought back to the anger he had shown at the hell when he had lost to herself and Felton.

"I wouldn't want anyone to sacrifice for me in such a way. It was a waste of life, and in the version I have heard, it was not over a woman but over political loyalties during a rebellion." Caro's brow raised as she challenged the authenticity of her friend's story.

"Oh! You are not romantic at all! Honestly, Caro, how you not wish to be loved like that? I, for one, am waiting for such a love. A man willing to fight for me is a man I can respect—and a man worth giving up my independence for, no matter what my father may wish for me. I would rather have a love like my aunt had or none at all."

That was just it. Rebecca *was* independent, Caro was not. Besides, if anyone were to know the truth, they could hardly love her. She was the hollow shell of a woman of quality with a scandal hidden just beneath the surface. If her outside self were ever to crack, people might see her, and she had no intention of letting that happen. Felton might have been able to crawl beneath her skin for a time, but she would be resolute. As she had thought before, love was expensive, and she was in no position to pay the price.

"Well, perhaps we should make another deal then?" Caro said.

"Yes?"

"You will be the romantic, and I shall be the practical one."

"You *are* silly—there are times, I am sure, when one can be both. I love that story, but if you will not love it as I do, then I will have to be the romantic for both of us. The only problem, as I have said, is that I have not yet found the man to die at the end of a duelling sword for me."

"Life is not always fair."

"No, indeed. Oh," she said, patting Caro's arm affectionately, "I do so love that we may be honest with each other. I swear, before you came to London I was wont to drive away any respectable woman's acquaintance with my candid words. Father calls them as blunt as a butter knife."

Caro giggled.

"Ignore your father!" Lady Etheridge was moving between dried plant specimens in the room they had just entered. "Charles can be quite foolish sometimes. I do not know how my sister abides him and his antiquated ways."

"Oh, Aunt, Father is not that bad."

The older woman fell in step beside the two ladies.

"Yes, my child, you know I love him as a brother, but that does not mean I always like what he says, and he says a great many foolish things in my opinion."

"How do you even know of what we are speaking?"

"I have the ears of a bat, my child. And I do not happen to be decrepit just yet, I might add."

"Of course not, Aunt."

"And it is better to be a butter knife than a fool in my opinion—at least a butter knife serves a useful purpose. A person who cannot speak truthfully of her feelings is of no use to anyone!"

"Aunt,"—Rebecca changed the conversation—"have you heard the story of the field of the forty steps?"

Caro rolled her eyes dramatically. "Say yes, Lady Etheridge."

The older woman's eyes twinkled at Caro and then looked to her niece. "Of course I have, my dear. One of the most sensational stories to have happened in Bloomsbury, I dare say."

"You see Caro," said Rebecca, "I am not the only one who enjoys the romance of the story."

"Romance? It was on account of the Duke of Monmouth's rebellion, was it not?"

Caro looked at Rebecca and promptly set off into peals of laughter at the disappointed look on her friend's face.

CHAPTER SIX

"I have heard...that you won a great deal at the tables Friday last."

"Town talks," Felton replied in less than jovial accents.

He had been standing with Lord Avers at the Mires' ball, but when that gentleman sloped off to procure drinks, Miss Caro Worth had detached herself from her party and actively sought him out. If he had not been in so foul a mood, he would have found that action very interesting.

"Five thousand pounds," the fair-haired woman said tentatively, her large eyes watchful.

"You have knowledge of the amount?" He turned his green eyes upon her for a few moments, her persistence too much to ignore.

She coloured, looking like a startled deer, but Felton failed to chase her. He felt no inclination tonight and instead turned his attention back to the array of ladies present. Most were wearing the fashionably wide mantua gowns, and he supposed that should the height of hair continue to increase, houses would soon require substantially higher ceilings.

His silence was solace. Words seemed as pointless as past

victories in the face of his father's latest rebuke. He might have won against the Marquis and shown himself to be more than a mere boy, but his father had not appreciated his son's activities as heartily as the rest of London.

"It is a great deal," said the fair-haired deer, nibbling persistently once again at his attention.

"You are surprised I could do it?"

His barely-controlled temper threatened to erupt. She thought him incapable just as his father did. Just as everyone did.

He gritted his teeth. It was clear that he ought not to have gone out in Society so soon after receiving a verbal thrashing from his father. Apparently hells were not how he should be spending his time—despite his winning more money than Frederick would make on the estate in half a year. *Those* establishments were not respectable haunts for a Viscount's younger son. Town did indeed talk.

"Are you well this evening, Mr. Felton?" The fair-haired woman had changed her tack and was now watching Felton with something akin to wariness.

He saw it and turned his unflinching stare upon her. "Do I look well to you, Miss Worth?" If she was so impolite as to force conversation upon him, he would be impolite as well and forbear from disguising his true feelings.

He could hardly be blamed for his low spirits—he would be cut off at this month's end if he did not find a suitable bride and settle down. Settle down! A curse on the man who had invented such a thing. He was to find some respectable woman who would temper him—those were his father's words, though he heard his mother's wish in them—and he must settle to a profession that should provide for the children he was destined to have.

He might well want to spread his blood someday, he might even enjoy having a brood, but until that day came, the only way he could think of pleasantly spreading his blood without responsibility was at the tip of a duelling sword.

"No."

He found the blunt reply eminently pleasing, a damp cloth to his hot, angry brow. It made him feel far more inclined to converse with this woman. Memories of their first adversarial conversation surfaced, and an amused smile formed on his mouth.

"What do you mean, dear lady?"

"I...I would not venture to say." She stammered a little, apparently regretting her candid response. "It would be—"

"Improper. I think you have already crossed that line."

"True." She looked away from him and towards the dancers. "You seem frustrated, or maybe angry."

"You think me angry? Dear me, what a front I am showing you. I should do better to conceal my ill-humour. I should not allow a lady to see me so discomposed." Felton's mouth pulled up into a sardonic smile, his green eyes glowing with ire. "How do I look to you now? In full possession of my faculties and in devilish good spirits no doubt."

He watched as Caro's delicate nose wrinkled and her red lips pursed.

"Perhaps I should go."

"Oh no, it is a task to gain the truth from you, and now I have your more candid side revealed I will not let you escape." He raised an eyebrow. "Please tell me what thoughts are passing through that mind of yours and why your face has taken on such a disapproving look?"

"Oh no, I—"

"Go on."

"I do not mean to appear disapproving, but I dislike the lie your face shows." Her eyes flicked down to the line of his jacket and the flourish of his laced cravat. "It is better to be oneself if one can be."

"Novel," replied Felton, watching the woman with even more interest, pleased that her mind ran along the same lines as his. Perhaps he could be enticed out of this foul mood. "And quite the same as my own thoughts on the subject. We are kindred spirits."

He saw the slightest flicker of concern pass over her face at the comment, and it set his anger to burning once more. She disliked the idea of them being kindred spirits. He did not temper his next words. "And, my dear redoubtable Miss Worth, so very sincere and truthful, do you think that of your half-sister?" Let her feel the full extent of her own unsuitableness as he had been forced to feel his this evening.

"I..." Again she faltered. Apparently Miss Caro Worth was not the conversationalist her illegitimate half-sister was. "That is not a proper line of conversation."

"And my mood is?" he countered. "You are telling me that a respectable woman such as yourself learnt of my gaming wins from the tittle-tattle of Society? Would it not have been easier to speak to your half-sister?"

She inhaled sharply, raising her fan to her mouth and concealing herself with shadow. "How can you say such a thing?"

"Why, because my person holds no expectations of being proper." He came in close to her. "For instance, I can say to you that you are looking beautiful tonight, Miss Worth—quite ravishing—and that I desire to kiss you."

He could smell the scent of roses on her skin before he stepped away, smiling at the blush he had caused.

"I can say what others will not because I am the wastrel younger son of Viscount Felton." He couldn't hold back the bitterness in his voice, nor did he wish to. "My reputation is tainted."

He looked pointedly at her. "Besides, you told me yourself, you dislike lying. Therefore, if only for your benefit, I am being myself. It is not my fault you dislike my character. Most do. And what of your own hypocrisy? You complain about my own impropriety, but a moment ago, you were delving into my deepest feelings—most *improper*. Perhaps you and your half-sister have more in common than I at first thought."

He pushed the conversation onto her, feeling exposed after laying bare such inner thoughts, and he had the satisfaction of seeing her eyes grow wide and dart around the crowd a little frantically.

"You wish to escape? Do you fear your own tongue? Why should you? When we say something improper, it is like a brief streak of lightning. It ignites the field below in a brief blaze. And yet sometimes the ground must be razed by fire, Miss Worth, for the good of the next crop."

"Much good it does you," she said, swinging back around at him, a sudden fire in her eyes.

"And there it is," he said with satisfaction. Something was driving him, whether it was the frustration he felt after the meeting with his father or the words of Miss Worth he did not know, but he could not stop himself. The delight he gained from prodding her was like the gratification one received from lancing an infected boil.

"Perhaps you should not fear speaking your mind as much as you do, for is that not lying by omission? You disliked the lie my face showed—what about the lie you show perpetually by letting Society bridle your tongue? Is it not better to be yourself?" He looked at that face, so similar, and so different to her half-sister's. The desire to kiss her came stronger than ever. "Have you ever thought of wearing a heart-shaped patch just here?" He tapped a finger to the corner of his mouth.

"That is not what I meant." She ignored his second question, her eyes darting away from the part of the face his finger pointed to.

"Was it not?"

"I merely meant I detest lying! I loathe falseness. It weighs heavily, and if one can avoid it then why would one willingly put it on?"

Her frustration was plain, but it seemed to be rooted in something larger than him. Her words lay on the surface of much deeper thoughts, and Felton was intrigued anew by this mysterious side of Miss Worth—indeed, of the two Miss Worths.

As her agitation grew, he began to be sorry for the teasing that had occasioned it. Even he, the wastrel son of a Viscount, had a heart. His face broke out into a genuine grin, and he declared with his usual forthrightness, "I like this uninhibited side of you, Miss Worth. But though I have enjoyed being candid with you, I fear I have put your nose out of joint. Shall we call a truce?"

The lady coloured a little, rich scarlet creeping up her neck. Rather than agreeing to his proposal, she looked more tormented than ever.

"I must leave, Mr. Felton." She would not look him in the eye again.

He felt a stab of remorse and quickly reached for her hand. Holding it warmly in his, he spoke earnestly, finally ridding himself of his sardonic tone.

"Very well, Miss Worth, but believe me that, though I do not deny what I have said this evening, I did not wish to cause you pain. Pay no heed to me. I am only, as my father puts it, a hot-headed boy. May we part as friends despite my ill humour? I beg it." He bowed low and did not rise again until he felt her hand move a little in his.

When he caught eyes with her, he could see her conflicted emotions but failed to decipher them. He did not know what turmoil went on in her mind. He had been so obsessed with his own worries this evening that he had not attended to her reactions as he ought—he was ashamed at the realisation. She looked unhappy.

"Please," he asked again, another stab of regret in his chest. For all his fun and games, he never wished to hurt her.

"Yes, Mr. Felton," she said in a hollow voice.

"D'you know, I think I prefer it when you call me, sir." He winked at her, squeezed her hand, and then reluctantly let it go. What was it about those two sisters that captivated him so and drove him, at least this evening, to the edge of madness?

After Caro left Felton, she was asked quite swiftly onto the arm of an effeminate young gentleman. He was one of the many that Lady Rebecca had trailing after her, and he had seen Miss Worth's need of an escort as the best way to gain admittance to Lady Rebecca's circle this evening. The man talked of the ball to Caro, of the attendees, the turtle soup, and of course, Lady Rebecca, in a sycophantic manner—a manner which would have irritated Caro had she been listening. As it was, she cared not for his thoughts or for the use he was making of her to gain the attention of Lady Rebecca. In this moment her mind was racing over other things.

What had just happened? She had not known Felton to act like this before. She had thought he would be in good spirits—he seemed the kind of man that always was, his humour irrepressible. In fact, she had been certain of it after their stupendous win at Mr. Russell's on Friday. She had expected joking, frequent winks, a little sauciness, which is what had made his reaction all the more surprising. Was she upset that he had not been flirtatious? After all, the kind of sauciness that Felton displayed was most improper. And yet, the bitter cup of conversation they had just drunk together was also hardly proper for an unmarried young lady to have with an unmarried gentleman.

No young man had ever spoken to her with such truthfulness before. She thought of his compliment to her again, of his admission that he wished to kiss her, and she found him baffling. He had clearly been in an ill humour, he had said it himself, but she had never expected the candour of his words or that cutting wit.

It was not his words that upset her, however. It was her own. She had risen to whatever madness was holding Felton in thrall and in the process had demolished the wall of respectability that had taken so long to build. He truly brought out the worst in her. When she was Angelica he drew her into conversation when she needed her head clear of distraction to game. When she was Caro he drew out a spirit residing within her which only risked her respectability.

Worse, what had they argued of? Lies. She had pronounced her hatred for lying. She swallowed back a bitter laugh at the irony. How had she dared to speak thus to him? Lying was her forté. The unstable cornerstone of falsehood held up her house of artifice, and the very presence of Felton seemed to make the collapse of her house more inevitable.

Why had she struck up conversation with Felton alone instead of waiting for Lord Avers to make a third to the exchange? It had been her most decided mistake, but she had felt gratitude towards the man for her win. He had helped her finances immeasurably, but he had also increased her risk. When they had first begun speaking this evening, she had resolved that Felton was a thoroughgoing cad—and then, at the end of what could only be described as their argument, he had taken her hand and begged her friendship.

At least Caro knew the two roles she was playing—that man seemed confused as to exactly who he was. Was he a scoundrel or a gentleman? Was he careless and shocking, or was he honest and charming? But who was she to judge him? Was she respectable Caro Worth or infamous Angelica the gamester? After that tête-à-tête she wasn't sure herself.

"Oh, Caro!" called Lady Rebecca, piercing Caro's thoughts with her joyful voice.

Caro's eyes drew back into focus. She saw the radiant smile on her friend's face as she ignored all the gentlemen thronging about her to look solely at her friend. The crowd of admirers parted like the Red Sea as Caro walked through to her place at Rebecca's side.

"I saw Mr. Felton conversing with you. After his awfulness at The Pot and Pineapple, how remarkable that he should seek out your company again!" There was a sparkle in Rebecca's dark eyes.

"He did not. It was quite by chance that I spoke to him. It was only while I waited for you to return from speaking to your aunt."

"Oh, that was too bad of me. After having my cloak taken and seeing my aunt, I simply could not get back through the crush I am afraid. Oh, Mr. Daniels, how amiable of you to bring Miss Worth back to me. Might you fetch some drinks for our parched throats? It is as hot as the great Sahara in here!"

The young man bowed overly low, his young cheeks dimpling with pleasure at being spoken to by his goddess. "Most certainly, Lady Rebecca." He turned upon his heeled shoe and disappeared into the crowds.

Many of Lady Rebecca's other admirers slowly filtered away too. The second dance was assembling, and they could see their Aphrodite was to be ensconced with her bosom friend for this particular musical set.

"Caro?" Lady Rebecca stared at the pale face of her friend. "My dear, what's the matter?" She laid an arm around her smaller friend's shoulders and drew her closer.

"Oh, nothing, nothing at all—it is merely quite hot in here."

Caro could not repeat the conversation she had just had. It had been too confusing and too raw. It must have been by happenstance, but she could swear he had almost spoken to her as if he knew the roles she played, as if he knew the thoughts she had. Impossible!

And besides, he had been speaking as much to himself as to her. She had seen it in the way his eyes had avoided her at points when his feeling had overcome him. He had been arguing with himself, battling his own thoughts, and she had merely been there to witness it.

At least, she hoped that was the true explanation—for how could a man who had known her so little time see through her charade? He could not, she told herself.

"Well," said Rebecca, "Mr. Felton can be a cad when he wishes, but Aunt says he can be quite the gentleman when he wishes too. Was he funning at your expense?"

"No, he..."—he had been angry, he had been honest—"he told me he wished to kiss me."

"What!" Rebecca gasped. Her hands seized Caro's. "He did not!"

Caro nodded, a little smile playing on her lips in spite of herself. "It is a shame that he managed to be as rude as he was forthright."

"He insulted you again? I supposed that he had a liking for you, but I thought it might have been related to.... Ordinarily I would not go on, for I know you do not like to speak of her, but the gossip I have is so connected to you both that I cannot fail to mention it."

"Go on." Caro was interested now. She needed to keep up with the tittle-tattle surrounding herself so that any malevolent spark which might damage her carefully constructed deception could be stamped out before it lit a fire in Society.

Lady Rebecca dragged her over to a chaise lounge and tapped rapidly on her arm. "Do you like my gown?" she asked, something akin to childlike mischief lighting her eyes. Rebecca's arms spread wide showing off the fabric of the dress.

"Yes," said Caro, a sinking feeling in the pit of her stomach. She had noticed nothing remarkable until Rebecca had drawn attention to it, but in this instant she recognised the material. "It is very becoming." It took all of Caro's control to school a look of mild interest on her face.

Those miniature gold flowers. That deep crimson silk. The neckline. The whole design—it was the same dress as one which resided in Caro's home. One which she only wore at night. One which came to the hells with her. One which belonged to Angelica Worth.

"Well, you know I was asking for your dressmaker's details? I no longer need them. I stumbled across this delightful little French modiste, come over from Paris, Madame Depardie."

Caro resisted the instant urge to correct the name. As Caro Worth she didn't know Madam Depardieu. She had never ordered a dress from her. She had never been to her shop.

"You see the fabric, these beautiful little star flowers? They are the very same as those worn by your half-sister Miss Angelica Worth!" Lady Rebecca's triumph lit up her face. "I could not believe it, and I know, it is quite naughty of me to have a dress made up like Miss Angelica Worth's, but that lady has taste." She touched a hand lovingly to her waist.

"Rebecca!" said Caro, in an admonishing tone. "That's scandalous!"

She wanted to fix the matter by dissuading her friend from going there again, but it was already too late. A bridge had been built between Caro's two lives.

"Scandalous? I hardly see how. I've already had half a

dozen compliments from the gentlemen of my acquaintance who are here this evening. Anyway,"—she brushed off Caro's words while smiling dazzlingly at a lingering admirer—"that is not even the most scandalous part."

Caro could tell that Rebecca had read her rebuke as the very essence of encouragement. "Isn't it?"

"Are you not interested to know how I found out Miss Angelica Worth patronises this Madame Depardie?"

Again Caro resisted the urge to correct the mispronunciation of the modiste's name. How *had* Lady Rebecca found out? And even more concerning, had Madame Depardieu spoken of her identity? Was she a leaky water cask that would need stopping with a roll of soft? Caro had been sure she could trust the woman.

"I saw her there!" Lady Rebecca whispered with great delight. "I saw her walk out of the shop when I was on the other side of the street with my aunt. I looked towards her because she was most striking in this fabric in the middle of the day. When I saw the dress and her raven hair, I guessed. I went in to demand it from the modiste, and when I gave the exact name, the poor honest woman could not lie to me. Miss Angelica did not see me, of course. I was most discreet until I was wresting the truth from the modiste."

Indeed, Angelica had not seen her. Caro would have taken serious note if she had glimpsed Rebecca anywhere near her dressmaker's. Her last visit had been just before the game of piquet with Felton. She had arranged for Madame Depardieu to replace the tiny buttons in the secret compartment of her dress with ribbons. The time it had taken her to undo the buttons in Mr. Russell's library had started all her troubles with Felton. She had gone to Madame Depardieu to eliminate such instances in the future.

"I must say, I can see why your half-sister has set the Town, and especially every gaming gentleman, talking. She is quite ravishing I must own. I was struck by her likeness to you in features."

"In appearance perhaps," replied Caro, a little too coldly, "but in nothing else."

There she was, lying again. How could she do it so freely after the conversation she had had with Felton? That argument had made it clear that her true identity was part-Angelica and part-Caro. The sardonic words which so characterised her gaming self and the temper she tried to keep from both had invaded her respectable self this evening.

"I have to disagree," cut in a male voice.

Before she could stop herself Caro retorted, "You have a habit of cutting in most impolitely."

There it was again, that side of her she tried to keep hidden. And there *he* was again, able to bring out her temper with four little words.

"I do, don't I?" said Felton, grinning.

Why was he here? She was not prepared for more confusing conversations in which she might give too much away.

"Then again, it is the best way to hear what others are thinking but will not tell you." His voice was back to its usual amused tone. Perhaps he had come in peace and his mood had lifted.

"You are monstrous," said Lady Rebecca with humour. "Have you not taken up enough of my friend's time?"

"No," he said, looking at his fingernails and flicking a bit of dust from his sleeve. "I don't believe so. Besides, I feel I owe her a debt for a more amiable conversation."

"Apparently you struggle to be amiable to my friend, Mr. Felton." Lady Rebecca's cutting words were only softened by her brilliant smile.

"That's not entirely true—did she forget to relay to you that I told her she was beautiful? I say it again now. Her hair is the colour of the sun itself, and I am much obliged to her for leaving it unpowdered as her mother bade her."

"She said you told her something else too." Rebecca refused to let the smile at the corner of her mouth take over. "Something far more...intimate. You must stop it. I told you last time we met it was enough. If you are not careful, you will receive the wrath of my fan once again, Mr. Felton!" She brandished the implement.

Caro could see that her friend was enjoying this, but Rebecca's enjoyment was not performing the necessary office of making Felton disappear.

"I thank you for the thought, Mr. Felton, but our conversation was amiable enough, and now I am conversing with another." Caro gestured to Rebecca, praying that Felton would take the not-so-gentle hint.

"Alas, I can see that, but I have already cut in, and I do dance rather well. Will you accompany me as recompense for upsetting you?"

"You upset her?" Lady Rebecca looked interested. By now, she was apparently used to hearing that others were upset by Felton, but to hear him admit it himself was something entirely different.

Caro's mouth fell open in disbelief, but in the next moment she resurrected her self-control. "Do not be foolish, Mr. Felton, I was not upset." She managed to speak with some authority, but she ignored the look of criticism in Felton's eyes. She was being the hypocrite he had accused her of, and he could call her out if he wished. She prayed he would not. "I am afraid I am too engaged to dance."

"I see," replied Felton stiffly, clearly considering his next move. "You are too frightened I will cause you to fall into trouble."

She hated him in that moment—hated that he could read

her thoughts so readily. "I am not frightened of a lively discussion with a gentleman," she said with some fierceness.

"Yes, but he is an incorrigible gentleman, one who says things he oughtn't," said Rebecca. She looked back and forth between the two, not fully understanding, but undoubtedly drawing her own conclusions.

"It is a shame." Felton seemed to change tack. "You were conversing quite happily with me a short time ago, as you yourself attest, and now you refuse to dance with me, though I have seen you dance with no one yet this evening."

"I have been asked," replied Caro, her cutting words drawing a look of surprise from her friend.

"I say, you two will be at dagger-drawing soon," Rebecca cut in. "Just as well the drinks have arrived."

As she spoke the gentleman they had dispatched some time since returned with glasses of Ratafia.

"Ah, I see," said Felton, leaning back on one leg. He watched as the gentleman gave each woman a glass and then settled into conversation with Lady Rebecca. "I am quite unneeded with all of this male attention at your fingertips." He spoke to Caro alone, and his eyes flashed a challenge to which she rose without flinching.

"Quite," she agreed. "Unneeded."

"I know you do not understand me."

Again he read her thoughts! Was he intending to explain himself further?

"I came in a form of truce. I *did* feel incorrigible after the way I spoke to you, and though my humour is not fully restored, I have enough of it back to feel guilt over my treatment of you. Can I not persuade you instead to take a turn about the room with me? Is my character so much on the precipice of undesirable?"

Caro took in a breath. He had just admitted his wrongdoing, he was attempting reconciliation in more than a spoken apology—but she needed him to leave. She could not trust herself to the temptation of honest words again this evening. It was too hazardous.

"It is, and as I do not have a parent or a duenna to accompany me, I must be my own protector. Please, leave me."

Felton's eyes lit with the same anger they had contained earlier in the evening, but this time she was the cause. A twinge of remorse rippled through her mind. She had upset him.

"Very well, I see no one is happy with me this evening. Neither fathers, nor prospective brides, nor the intriguing Miss Worth. I will bid you good evening once again." He bowed stiffly and left.

Caro watched his fine form dissolve into the crowd. She opened her fan and hid the confused expression she wore behind it. This evening had become even more bewildering. First he was angry, then provoking, and now he had come back with a form of apology. Yet he seemed almost vexed at the men who danced attendance upon them with drinks and words of flattery.

She had thought after their first meeting that she would not see the strange man again. After their second she had hoped it, but on their third she had gone away with gratitude toward him. Now she was just confused. It was essential that she understand those around her so she could predict how they might affect the fragile structure of her life. But that man was unpredictable, incomprehensible, and now, he would not leave her thoughts.

CHAPTER SEVEN

Later that same night Angelica, robed in her newly-altered red dress, entered a hackney bound for Mr. Russell's hell, accompanied by her redoubtable manservant, John. Mottled shadows covered his old, lined face as they travelled through London's streets.

"It will not be a late night tonight, John. I am in no mood for more than what we need, and we need only a little after last week's win."

"Very good, miss. It is a happy time we are in, being deep in the pocket as we are."

"A happy time," she echoed, her thoughts elsewhere.

It was a happy time where finances were concerned, and she was happy that at least Libby and John could sleep in peace, but every other part of her life seemed to be unravelling faster than she could knit it back together. Her hands rested lightly on the skirts of her gown, and she could gauge through the thick material where the secret compartment lay. The quick-fastening ribbons would save her from predicaments like her first fracas with Felton....

Just thinking of the man made her stomach contract with

guilt. He had won her two and a half thousand, half of the total winnings, but he was no doubt off in some dark haunt licking his wounds—both those he had gained elsewhere and those she had inflicted on him at the Mires' ball. She had cut him and, as much as it was essential to her plans to catch a more eligible husband, she had not enjoyed doing it.

Even now, as she travelled to the hell through the narrow streets, she wished that Felton was her partner for tonight's play. Previously, she had taken advantage of gamers who were foolish enough to play. But wounding a man who was foolish enough to show her kindness was unforgivable. She did not wish to think of it. She switched her attention to the man whose kindness she desired.

The most eligible bachelor of her acquaintance had attended the ball, but she had not been able to speak to him. The Marquis of Ravensbough had continually been surrounded by half the women in Society. It had been frustrating. After her caustic words and winning against him last Friday, Caro had wished to reacquaint her better self with him —to interest him in the identity of hers which could eventually secure him in marriage. As it was, the flock of other interested parties had edged her out.

But in some kind of painful irony, when she glided into the hell on small buckled shoes, the first person she locked eyes with was the Marquis. She did not want him watching her, not as Angelica. She did not want him to notice her in this life —it did no good for her position as the eligible Caro Worth.

He was now sans that frustrating flock of women from earlier. His dark eyes flashed up from his game of piquet, and they watched her, following her movements through the hell as a cat would the flitting of a bird upon the ground. She saw him whisper something to a man at his side, no doubt some friend of his, and then go back to looking at her. She had failed to gain his attention at the Mires' ball, even for one conversation, and now here he was rapt at her very presence.

She traversed several tables, John finding his customary place near the wall, until she came beside a waiter. She raised her forefinger, and the man nodded and scurried away, fully aware of what her regular order was. She turned back upon the room, using those few moments to assess the players present, to estimate the amount of drink in each one, and to decide which table was the best target.

As she came across the piquet table, she ventured another glance at the Marquis. To her dismay he was still watching her. The last time he had seen her at the hell, he had been interested. This time he seemed determined, his eyes roving over her entire form. As she moved under that gaze, for the first time since Felton's appearance, she felt a stab of that old isolation she had become hardened to over the past two years.

She knew that look in the Marquis' eyes, that licentious interest—she had seen it in many a man's eye before, and she had sent all of them away from her, believing her still the flirt, that she might maintain their distracted interest, and keep her unrecognised virtue intact. That action had always been accompanied by an acute loneliness—loneliness from sending away companionship, though she loathed its form, and loneliness knowing that she must be her own protector because there was no one else. She was not sorry she had cut Felton, but in this moment she realised the value of the companionship the young gentleman had given her—however irritating it might have been.

She pushed Felton from her thoughts and turned her mind to the gentleman present. Let the Marquis admire from a distance, as most did, and she would keep him safely there. She would pursue him as Caro Worth, and as Angelica she would ignore him. This evening, as with every evening, she needed to win.

"Miss Worth, you are well this evening?"

It was Lord Avers, hailing her from a table to the side that was determined on whist. The friendly voice and address in such a moment brought an odd kind of relief.

"My lord." She curtseyed and approached, taking the offered chair and agreeing to be dealt in. She barely noticed John shadowing her movements and coming to a rest against the part of the wall nearest the table.

"I shall partner you."

Good. She liked Lord Avers, and Lord Avers enjoyed talking. She would allow him to do so, and that would enable her to concentrate fully on the game. He rarely needed responses in order to carry on his conversation. There needed to be no distractions tonight. There had been too many recently.

"So, how do you fare, fair-lady?" asked Avers, his dark eyes smiling at her.

"All the better for winning a week since," she replied matter-of-factly.

"Now it is customary for you to ask me how I fare."

The dealer was from the other pair. He had finished shuffling and was now dealing cards in neat piles. Lord Avers watched the progress as he spoke.

"But I know you shall not, for you never do, so I will endeavour to fill in the gaps nonetheless. I fare well. I thank you for your imagined interest, though I must admit to feeling stung by your admission of joy when I am on a losing streak."

"Losing streak?" She affected indifference, but he was her partner and she was not indifferent.

"Indeed, ever since you came to the tables, Miss Worth, I have had undeservedly bad luck."

"A rare compliment," replied Angelica, a wave of relief passing through her body and that coquettish smile taking over her red lips once again. Her eyes, as they withdrew from his face, caught those of the Marquis yet again over Lord

Avers' shoulder, and she retracted them quickly. She must ignore him. She did not wish to engage him anymore as Angelica. Lady Rebecca had been speaking just this evening of the vast inheritance he had received upon his father's death, and as a Marquis he was second only to a Duke. He could secure her future.

"Your lay, Miss Worth. Ladies, as always, first." Lord Avers let loose his charming smile and awaited her play, his broad, athletic frame leaning back casually in his chair, dwarfing the furniture.

He was a decent player and a good match for her. They both won, and each of their purses were seven hundred and fifty pounds heavier by the time they were done. Angelica rose from the table, exchanged a few flirtatious words with Lord Avers, and then folded the notes and tucked them into her normal pockets.

"I shall bid you adieu then, Lord Avers."

"So soon? The night is young and full of promise."

"And full of danger too. I hold no desire to upset the happy result we have come upon this evening. I thank you for your partnership." She curtseyed and moved away before he could try to persuade her to stay. This was why she had not been ruined by that extravagant itch, because unlike other gamesters, she was controlled. She knew exactly when to stop and exactly when to go all in.

She moved away from the table to the admiring looks of a few gamers—though not so many turned now. They were getting used to her presence.

"Time to retire, John."

Her retainer nodded and followed her like a faithful hound. His presence calmed her, and she knew in the next few minutes he would be calling a carriage to carry them to the safety of their home—the most favourite part of her evening.

Mr. Russell was standing beside a small desk examining a

ledger that recorded bets made by his patrons. Behind him in the adjoining room, a few gamesters' faces brightened at the thought of Angelica joining their tables. But their hopes were dashed just as quickly when she hailed the proprietor and stopped in front of his desk.

"A full house this evening," he said with a smirk.

"Indeed." She never knew why he bothered with small talk. She paid him a small fee to use the private room, and that was that. His attention fell on ungenerous ears.

"Although you played with another partner tonight, was luck still sitting upon your shoulder, Miss Worth?"

"Myself and luck are boon companions, Mr. Russell." She exuded the confidence that characterised Angelica, once again enjoying the license of her gaming identity.

If she were to make such sweeping comments as Caro, she would appear arrogant or missish. Here it was allowed, even expected.

She glanced back at the gaming room behind her to see that Lord Avers had struck up another game with a new partner. The Marquis, however, had disappeared from his table, no doubt the game finished and his tastes better sated elsewhere.

"I am in need of your library again."

"Of course, Miss Worth. It is empty and at your disposal." Mr. Russell's tongue passed over his teeth and then wetted his lip, and a brief shadow passed over his face. Angelica should have done more than notice it. She should have taken heed of the tell and wondered what the hell proprietor might be thinking. As it was, she was longing for her bed, happy with her winnings, satisfied at the feeling of control she had regained, and failing to take note of anything else.

"Thank you," she said, following Mr. Russell to the library door. As she turned towards the room, John peeled away from them, going to call a carriage home as he always did when his mistress was safely installed in the room.

Angelica heard the click of the door and felt the customary peace as the jostling and noise of the hell dulled and the evening's gaming subsided into past memory.

"I was wondering when you would come in."

She jolted, her eyes flying open. The peace that had descended upon her flew up like birds disturbed from their roost.

Seated in a chair behind the large leather-topped desk was the Marquis of Ravensbough. At Angelica's arrival, he rose from his chair and stalked towards her. "I have been watching you for some time, and I noticed a hiatus between your playing and your departing. Mr. Russell obligingly related that you use this room regularly after your rounds of gaming."

The snake! Russell had known. He had allowed it. His face had told of his deception—she should have noticed!

"I found it intriguing that you come in here...*alone*. I know not for what purpose, but I decided to join you."

She could see that. And she could see why. Angelica wondered if Mr. Russell had accepted a good greasing of the hand to allow this. She was a loyal and lucrative customer, but evidently, a titled man was more important than a whore gamestress. Once again life had dealt another an easier hand than her.

She had not moved from the door. Her right hand was still twisted behind her back, resting upon the handle. What the Marquis wanted with her she could guess. After all, he wasn't the first man to proposition her in such a way. The only question in her mind was how to deal with the situation. How could she extricate herself without damaging her respectable self's chances?

"You are quite a fascinating woman, Miss Angelica Worth. I see you play expertly, though not as well as the best." He examined his nails briefly before turning his attention back to her body. "And I hear something quite remarkable—that you are kept by no man...*yet*. I have a proposition for you, Angelica, you raven-haired minx."

He was still advancing towards her. The way he used her Christian name felt invasive, and suddenly she felt less concerned about extricating herself carefully. She just needed to extricate herself at all.

Where was John? He would be getting the carriage. He trusted, as she had, that Russell would let no one else in the library. That is what she paid for—the exclusive use of this room. There was no reason for John to return—he would be waiting for her at the door like he usually did. She was alone here.

"I do not feel inclined to hear your proposition at present, my lord. Perhaps later after a little wine?"

"My lord," mocked the Marquis. "All the manners of a lady from the lips and body of a bastard whore."

Angelica's eyes hardened at his words. Fiery anger shot through the coldness of her fear but not of sufficient heat to melt the fear altogether.

"A whore with no keeper." The Marquis launched himself forward and reached out a hand. Angelica stepped backwards, but there was nowhere to go. His hand ran over her dress and paused, grasping at the pocket through her skirt.

"Do you know how much you won from me at piquet, Angelica?" His face was a mixture of lust and fury.

"Friday last?" she asked, attempting to maintain an air of indifference. Ignoring the danger.

"Five thousand. Five thousand pounds of my money." He was so close to her now she could not bear it. "Lost to a woman!" He lurched forward, breathing in a lusty breath of Angelica's scent.

She recoiled instinctively, the back of her bodice hitting

the handle of the door, crushing her hand, and making the door rattle. She winced.

"I do not lose to women."

Angelica emitted a surprised laugh. "You want your money back, my lord?"

"Do not laugh!" hissed the Marquis. He raised his voice only loud enough to scare her, not enough to penetrate the din next door.

Angelica released the door handle surreptitiously and slid to the side of the frame, making ready to open it and make her escape.

"No," said the Marquis, moving in front of the door and forcing her to circle round. "I don't think so." He was in between her and her exit now, his demeanour altogether menacing.

Angelica thought fleetingly of her ambitions, of her desire to capture this man's attention, of her assumption that he would give her security. Then she looked into those dark eyes —those eyes that seemed to have no end to their lustful depths —and the unrelenting anger that was displayed there, and she felt shaken to her very core. What kind of a man was this? How could she have been so foolish?

"You can't have it," she said, side-stepping him, her voice wavering in spite of her desire to appear uncowed. All of the wind which had been in her sails was knocked out. She was stranded in the middle of a mill-pond, desperate to get to shore with no hope of doing so.

"I won it." She spoke again, this time her voice stronger. At least she could pretend her courage, even if she did not feel it. That was what she was good at, pretending.

"I am well aware of that," replied he. "But as I have felt,"— he looked toward the pocket which held her winnings—"you are in no need of winnings. You are, however, in need of a schooling."

"A schooling?" Her mind went blank. What did he intend?

"Give me what you have."

Though she wished to protest, she knew it would be dangerous to do so while she was alone. If she gave him her winnings, then perhaps when he got outside the door she could call on Mr. Russell's heavies to assist.

If only John were here...but even as she thought it, she changed her mind. She would not want the older John facing this young, virile Marquis. The malevolence in his eyes guaranteed that he would not hesitate to beat any servant that stood in his way. The only thing that protected her, even a little, at this moment, was her sex. It was also the thing that trapped her.

She drew her winnings from her pockets and handed over the paper notes. They rustled as the Marquis' long fingers closed around them.

"Seven hundred and fifty," he said, after counting them. "You shall reimburse me for the rest when next we meet. In the meantime, you will become my kept woman. I shall be the first to master you." The feeling obviously excited him. He reached for her. "My mistress."

She stumbled back, turning to flee, but before she could do so, the Marquis delivered her a hard push that sent her reeling into the wall. Her face struck against something hard, a wall sconce, causing her head to jerk back painfully. The lit candle wobbled, sending scalding wax in a long spatter down her cheek, burning her soft skin and half-covering her patch.

Shocked by the sudden violence she turned only in time to be thrust back once again. One of his hands snaked its way around her waist. The other, which had shoved the bank notes into a pocket, was clutching at her hair. She moved with his pull, frightened her raven wig would fall. His mouth descended hard and fast. If lips could be cold, his were. She felt numb to his touch at first. Everything was happening too fast.

Then she came alive, her body tried to wrench away from him but was obstructed by the wall. As her hands reached upwards to push viciously back at his chest, his head lifted for air and to dispose on her a lecherous smile.

She used that moment to scream.

The high-pitched cry for help was cut off halfway as his mouth descended again and his hands found their way all over her body, following her curves, pulling at the fastenings of her dress. A tear slipped down her cheek running into the hand that was now clamped over her mouth, cracking the wax that had cooled on her cheek. She tried to sob but was denied even that.

Then, with as much suddenness as the Marquis' assault had begun, the man was removed from her. His hands released her in surprise and failed to regain their purchase. He toppled backwards, arms flailing, before he was flung to the other side of the room. Through her tears, Angelica saw a figure before her, standing between herself and her assailant. Her knees failed her and she crumpled, shaking, to the floor.

Seconds passed, and her hands rubbed at her eyes, begging them to clear, begging them to see if she was still in danger. What she saw was a blow delivered to the Marquis. The aristocrat was on the floor, another figure leaning over him. She could see him now. She could see Felton.

"Get out!" Felton barked, his voice unlike anything Angelica had heard. He delivered a kick to the Marquis' side.

The man on the floor spluttered, his fingers scratching at the rug, trying to pull himself up from the ground. Bank notes littered the floor. The Marquis' dark eyes saw them and, in between coughing fits, his long fingers snatched them up. Then, rising to his full height, he stuffed the bank notes in his silk pockets and began to curse.

"You cursed interferer! What right do you have?"

"The woman does not desire your attentions." Felton's lips were pulled back, his teeth bared like a dog's.

"I'm a Marquis, you cur! You have no idea who you're dealing with."

"The Marquis of Ravensbough, a peer of the realm—and yet, I am sure you do not wish to have it made known to your friends next door that you were just floored by a mere untitled second son." Felton's brow rose challengingly. "I know exactly what kind of dark devil you are."

The Marquis growled, casting a fury-filled look at Angelica and then suddenly smiled that same lecherous smile he had disposed on her earlier in the evening.

"I shall find another time to speak to Miss Worth…alone. I must discuss the repayment of her debt to me as well as the…interest."

He stood there a few moments longer, staring at Angelica in a way which made her feel as though she stood before him half-dressed.

Felton did not back down, not even by an inch, and Angelica stood behind him. He was taller than she had thought, and broader. He might be the younger son of a Viscount and he might be forever upsetting her world, but in this moment she was only glad he was here.

"Until another night, Miss Worth." Ravensbough nodded to Angelica, but it was Felton who answered on her behalf.

"I think not."

The Marquis ignored him and finally flung round on his heel, leaving through the door which Felton had been careful to close when he had entered. Felton closed it again now and then turned back to Angelica who had sunk to her knees shaking uncontrollably. He came to her side and, placing an arm around her waist, lifted her gently. He walked her to a chair placed beside the hearth and cast his eyes about until they alighted on a decanter. Pulling the stopper, he found port rather than brandy but poured it out regardless. He carried the glass to Angelica and, placing another arm around her, gently pressed the glass to her lips.

"I can drink it myself," she spoke suddenly, the words disjointed, her tone unsteady. She needed to keep his hands from her, to keep his touch away. She took the glass in her own two hands, carefully avoiding his fingers, and tipped some of the substance between her lips. After the first few drops, she drained the glass in one go. It was sweet, and the warmth of the liquid curled up at the base of her throat.

"Another?"

She nodded. He poured another glass. She drained it just as quickly.

"Again?"

She shook her head, passing the glass back to him and touching a hand to her jaw. She flinched, the area tender to the touch. The sconce the Marquis had shoved her into had been unforgiving. Her fingers could feel that the jaw was already swollen, and the pain which she had not felt at first was rapidly becoming a sharp ache.

She stared, replaying the events in her head, unsure in all the tumult what had really happened. Her glance floated upwards and caught Felton's eyes for the first time.

"You were at the Mires' ball."

"I was." He replied calmly to the statement, nothing showing on his face.

"How did you...?" She did not know how to phrase the question.

"I came to play and Mr. Russell, upon my greasing his palm, told me where you were." He leant on his fingers, the tips pressing into the leather top of the desk. "He told me not to disturb you, but I thought better of it—so I disobeyed him." The amused lilt in his voice came back then, just at the end of his speech.

"I'm glad you did." She emitted a sharp laugh. It stopped suddenly, and she continued to stare directly ahead.

"So am I," he said with feeling. "I hazarded a guess that the rendezvous was not your idea." His voice rose towards the end of his statement, implying it was a question.

"No," she gasped. "No, it wasn't." He must believe her. He must. She would never arrange such a meeting, nor attend one.

"I know. You do not strike me as the sort who would.... That needs a cold compress," he said, changing the topic of conversation fluidly. "Port should not hurt," he said, pouring some onto a white handkerchief he had drawn from his pocket.

"Don't," Angelica protested.

He looked from handkerchief to the woman. "I really don't care about it." He shrugged and pressed the stained fabric against her jaw. She took over the pressure from him.

"You need to go home," he said firmly.

"Thank you," she replied. She had an overwhelming desire to cry, but she stamped it down. "Thank you," she whispered again.

Felton did not reply—he merely bowed. The whole interview had been one of seriousness; the gentleman had not made one joke. Even now he stood there with a look of intense concern on his face. She couldn't bear it. She swallowed. She needed to go home.

"I will ask Mr. Russell to call a carriage," he said, apparently reading her thoughts once again. He always did that.

"John has already done so."

"I will see if it has arrived," he said without hesitation, leaving before she could protest. He was gone some time, and Angelica found herself needing another glass of port. She was halfway through it, this time sipping slowly, when he let himself back in. He shut the door with some deliberation.

"Miss Worth, I am afraid that the hell's patrons are aware something has happened in this room. Though they are still guessing what, I am afraid you have been plunged headlong into the waters of scandal."

The calmly spoken words sent spikes of anxiety pricking into Angelica's stomach. What were they saying? What did they assume? The lump in her throat returned, and she fought off the urge to cry.

"Has the carriage arrived?"

"Yes. I advise you not to talk to anyone. I have informed your man of what has occurred." He watched for her response.

"Thank you." She bowed her dark-haired head. He had done the right thing. She could not bear the thought of explaining it to John or Libby herself. Shame was already seeping through the cracks of her shattered identity, settling like tar in her depths.

She rose and went to the door, waiting for Felton to open it. It was not until that moment that she realised the din from the hell had quieted into nothing. The door opened upon a sea of faces which, although their owners were at play, were directed subtly towards the door. She walked through a forest of whispers, vaguely sensing that the leaves of every tree were blowing with the breeze of scandal.

She made her way past the two now-unbolted doors and down the stairs onto the street outside. She turned to Felton. He had followed her out.

"Miss Worth." John greeted her much as he would normally, but she could see the concern marking his usually placid countenance. His hand was already on her arm, hiding behind the guise of helping her to the carriage but in reality steadying her.

"I shall be fine now, thank you."

"I will escort you home," replied Felton.

"No." She put up a hand. "You saved me from...from I daren't think what, but I wish to go home alone." She had remembered her role. Remembered that he did not know who she was and she could not let him. Now John was here she was safe. She felt safe.

"Very well," Felton said reluctantly. He bowed stiffly, and Angelica wished in that moment that he would lighten the mood and act as if all of this were nothing.

"No wink for me?" asked Angelica, her injured face peeping out the window of the hackney.

Felton's eyes widened at the questioned. He frowned at first, confused. Why was she making light of the situation? Then something in him understood—she needed to make light of it or the heaviness would crush her entirely.

He winked. As he watched the hackney pull away, he smiled. His suspicions were solidifying, and soon they would be hard, irrefutable fact.

He raised a hand for a hackney and upon entering, told the driver to follow the carriage in front. He could still escort her home even if she had no knowledge that he was doing so.

CHAPTER EIGHT

Caro was unaware that Felton had been admitted to the morning room of her Town house. First, John had tried to keep him out but had been forced to admit him to avoid a scene on the street. Then, Libby had tried to fob him off with excuses that her mistress was keeping to her bed today. After leaving him in the morning room, the two retainers exchanged worried whispers in the hall.

"How does he know where she lives, John? And why is he here?"

"I don't know, love, but he's the one who saved our mistress last night. I don't want to believe he has come with any mischief in mind."

"No mischief, indeed! Have you seen the look in his eyes? As mad as a March hare he looks, and pacing like a man awaiting the birth of his firstborn!"

"Well, he won't go, my love, so what's to be done?"

"What's to be done?" echoed his wife, her voice less authoritative than usual. She had put her mistress to bed last night with a great dark swelling on her jaw and a look in her eyes so desolate she might have been attending a funeral.

"Keep him there as long as you can," said John. "Mayhap he will go away afore long if we make him wait."

Felton knew that the old manservant and his wife were putting him off, but nevertheless, he waited, and waited, and waited. Intent on his goal, he ignored the maid's frequent appearances to tell him that her mistress was still indisposed. Upon the seventh such announcement, Felton could see the late night and early morning were taking their toll on Caro's trusted watchdog.

"I'm afraid, Mr. Felton, that you cannot see her this morning. Miss Worth is still abed as I told you before, and it is best if you come back in a few days' time when she is fully recovered."

"Fully recovered?" Felton eyed the stout servant, noticing that another set of eyes, ones belonging to Angelica's servant John, were watching him through the doorjamb. "Do you expect me to be turned away so easily? I must speak with Miss Worth, and I shall sleep on this dashed chaise lounge if I must!"

"Mr. Felton, my mistress is not well."

"I can very well believe it."

"She does not wish to receive visitors. I ask you to go, Mr. Felton, please, for my mistress' sake, please go." The maid raised her hands as if she were shooing birds from her path.

"You *will* let me see her." The strength of Felton's words and his sudden step forward forced the maid back and forced the manservant from his hiding place behind the door.

"Ah, and here is my helper from last night. What a coincidence that I find you here in Miss Caro Worth's home." The frustration at waiting had only increased the sarcasm in Felton's voice.

"Now, Mr. Felton, we ask you to leave our mistress in peace."

"And just which mistress are you referring to?"

That left both servants speechless for some time. They stared at him without offering any response.

"Tell her I am here, and let me see her now." He did not raise his voice, but the tone brooked no denial.

After he had followed Miss Angelica Worth home last night, his suspicions had put down roots, and now he wanted to replace those speculations with facts. All the lack of perseverance his father bemoaned in his character was being turned on its head in this moment. He was in no mood to be denied, and he would not be deterred.

"We will not!" The servants stood together in a wall, blocking his way.

Felton was about to launch into another tirade when a soft voice entered the fray and a small figure appeared behind the domestics.

"What's all the noise?" asked Caro Worth.

Felton vacillated between stepping forward to confront this woman and stepping back to allow her entrance into the room. The tired, frayed tone of her voice decided it for him, and he retreated to let the scene unfold.

This morning, unlike all his previous encounters with her, her face was not bright with animation. There were dark shadows beneath her eyes, and her usual air of wariness had lifted a little. She looked thin, and despite her best attempts at applying powder, the swelling of her jaw could be seen on a face framed by her fair locks. That was why he had come today. That was why he had not waited. Her face could not lie to him as her mouth had done so often.

"I knew it," was all he offered in a husky whisper. "I knew it." The look in his green eyes was akin to wonder and not far from admiration. But mingled with that was concern. What was this woman about? Why was she taking such a risk?

"Libby!" Caro Worth paused on the threshold of the room. "You did not tell me there was someone here." Evidently she had expected a tradesman or a servant, not the younger son of Viscount Felton. She stood in hesitation.

He watched her perfect small mouth try its hardest to form words directed at him. Would she curse in surprise? He would not blame her.

Her brilliant blue eyes regained their lustre, but they were also shocked and unsure. The control she usually displayed over her feelings, the control he had been endeavouring to understand, had disintegrated, and before him stood the true woman. The half-identities, that appearance of pain and sorrow, the defiance which still glowed like small embers in the back of her eyes—it was all laid bare before him.

"Mr. Felton," she said, "we were not expecting you." Her fingers traced the lines of the old open gown she wore, a threadbare garment unlike the intricate dresses and refined gowns Felton was used to seeing her in. She had not been expecting *him*, but she had clearly heard someone's entrance, otherwise she wouldn't have bothered to cover her face in powder.

"I am feeling unwell this morning. Perhaps if you could come back another day."

Felton wondered if that tense frame had gotten any rest last night. There was a sharp look in her blue eyes, and he could hear the panic rising in her voice.

In this moment he wished to calm it all—to replace her prison of fear with a cloak of peace, to exchange her weariness for hope and her worries for rest. He wished to touch her arm, to pull her towards him, to soothe away the rigidness of her frame and feel her relax against him.

"Miss Worth, or should I say both Miss Worths." He bowed.

Why had he come? How could he word himself?

She had started off as some kind of puzzle to figure out, a challenge to rise to, a truth to uncover. But now it was something else. Last night had turned everything on its head. He had never felt the fury that had so consumed him in the moment he had come upon Ravensbough assaulting Angelica, or Caro—yes, he meant Caro. She had always been Caro Worth. He had never known such an overpowering desire to protect someone. He had never cared that much before—and the feeling was strange and disconcerting for him.

"Miss Worths? I don't know what you mean." Something flickered across her face as she spoke the lie. "As much as I enjoy your funning—another time, when I am feeling more myself perhaps." She extended a graceful arm towards the door behind her, inviting him politely to leave.

He had left politely at the Mires' ball last night when she had asked. He would not be leaving her this time, and he would not be lied to either.

"You know what I mean." He sighed, his shoulders slumping slightly, his whole aspect losing any appearance of threat. She was frightened, no doubt, especially after last night. "I mean you no harm, Miss Worth, I mean to...to offer you my assistance."

"Your assistance, with what?"

"With the Marquis."

"The Marquis?"

"Curse it, Caro! I shall not call you Angelica. We know she no more exists than does justice for that wretched nobleman."

He moved towards her but halted when he saw her stumble backwards, fear flashing across her face.

"Caro,"—he used her Christian name again—"I know the truth. You asked me to wink at you last night when you entered the carriage. And yet I have only ever winked at Caro Worth, never at Angelica. And if you do not believe me on that count, though I listen far more than people give me credit for, then I can wipe the powder off your face and reveal that bruise you have so poorly concealed—that bruise which the Marquis gave you."

His face took on a look of deep sympathy, his green eyes soft and open. "You told me you have no protector, but...but I wish...." He didn't finish. He couldn't when she looked like that, so hurt, so vulnerable, so incomplete.

Caro's shock dissolved into a cough which turned into a choke and then into a whimper until eventually she began to cry. The maid came to her side, and the manservant went to the sideboard to pour out a nearly empty decanter. The maid administered the medicinal alcohol to her mistress, and Felton resumed his pacing.

"It's about time someone guessed," said the male retainer gruffly from the position he had retreated to by the door.

"We were always a-feared of this happening," agreed Caro's maid, looking up at Felton with more than a little kindness in her eyes. "John told me what you did for Mistress Worth last night."

"You should not be here," said Caro hoarsely.

"And yet I am."

"He means well, miss," urged the elderly maid, her arm still around her mistress.

"Oh, he may," Caro huffed angrily and then glared at him through her bright tears, "but I do wish he would go away!"

That was far more like the Caro, and the Angelica, that Felton had come to know, and the harsh statement brought a smile to his lips. He had been thrown quite violently into a front row viewing of her vulnerability, but there in the midst of that frailness was a spark of her courage, and of her rather idiotic indignation.

"Well, I can hardly do that," said Felton. He relaxed slightly and brushed a hand over the skirts of his frock coat in an effort to do something with himself. Though she might have a good reason for her lies, it did not change the fact that she had lied so easily to him—to everyone.

"Why not?" A frown puckered the delicate skin between Caro's brows, and her incomprehensibly large eyes were doing much to thaw Felton's frustration at her deception.

"Because, Miss Worth, I know your secret."

She did not respond. Instead she took the offered handkerchief from her maid, wiping the tears which were rebelliously pouring down her face. Once she regained some of her composure, she rose to face her intruder. Felton watched her try to gain some height—and authority—by straightening her shoulders and raising her chin in challenge.

"It looks painful." Felton gestured to the bruise that her tears had revealed. He took a tentative step forward and touched a gentle thumb to the swelling. She allowed it, much as a frightened horse might allow a caress from a human while blowing and shivering in fear. After only a brief moment, she pulled her face away from him.

"It's nothing."

"Oh yes," he replied, dropping his hand. "It looks like nothing." His frustration at her deception rose again.

"Something I did by accident—I tripped and hit my chin."

Felton's temper rose. "Do not try to deceive me. Your deception is over, at least where I am concerned, and I shall have no more of your lies."

Fear showed in her eyes. She must be considering the awful truth that he could out her secret if he wished.

"I have had my suspicions for some time," Felton continued, his tone more moderate. "They have merely been confirmed this morning. If I had any intention of outing your secret," he added, "I should have done so already."

The woman remained silent as did the servants.

"What? No thank you?" he said, a sudden mischievousness coming back into the voice which really had been sounding far too serious today. "You really are impolite in the mornings."

The humour managed to lighten the mood a little. "I wished to come this morning to see if you were quite well after last night." He took a seat on one of the winged chairs and leant forward. "Not just to confirm my suspicions. How are you feeling apart from bruised?"

Felton watched confusion crawl across Caro's face and rest there. He looked again at the dark circles beneath her eyes. She almost certainly had not slept, no doubt haunted by yesterday's events, and now she had no answer to his simple question.

"I am well."

At least no truthful answer, but Felton let this lie go. He could not imagine the fear she must have felt last night. Coming home to a house filled with only these two servants and no family or friends to comfort her must have made it all the worse. "Perhaps your maid can bring us up some tea?"

The elderly maid looked to the man in the doorway for direction and upon an infinitesimal nod from him left her mistress to do as Felton suggested.

Caro, after withdrawing to change into a more acceptable floral *robe* à l'*anglaise* for a morning visit, came back into the morning room to see Felton pouring tea. She would have laughed had the situation been different. She never would have thought that Felton *could* pour tea, let alone *would* if called upon. He looked up as she entered, his eyes flicking over her as she walked to the sofa.

She sat down as he finished pouring. Libby took up her position in the corner of the room as a chaperone. The young gentleman lay back in his seat, his legs stretched out and his back thrown against the cushions as if he were in his own home. He looked at her again, and she could feel his eyes on the area of fresh powder and rouge she had applied to re-cover the swelling.

Caro had loosely dressed her own hair, leaving large curls either side of her face, and thanks to the rouge and a bit of bread and butter John had brought up to her, she was looking far more like herself, far more equipped to deal with whatever was to come.

"How long have you been posing as your illegitimate sister?"

The question was blunt but expected. Caro had been taken off-guard before, but now she'd had time to adjust to the new situation she felt calmer. She knew Felton would have questions, and at this present moment she had nothing to lose in telling the truth. All was already lost once he revealed her secret anyway. "A year."

"And no one knows of this deception?"

Caro shook her head tentatively. Felton held her life in his hands. "Only Libby Williams, my maid, and her husband John Williams who accompanies me to the hells for an escort and protection."

She noted that Felton refrained from chastising John for his failure last night. It was not his fault, and in the end Caro had been glad that John had not found himself between her and Ravensbough. Much worse could have happened.

"And this,"—he gestured at their surroundings—"this is all for show?"

"This is my home."

"These are your lodgings," he corrected. "Where did you live before your arrival in Town?"

"Does it matter?"

Felton regarded her silently. "No, I suppose not. You must forgive my curiosity. I knew of your father—I believe I even met him once—but I don't recall his home county." He shifted on the sofa. "Here." He passed her a cup of tea and then took up his own, stifling a yawn before he sipped at the hot liquid. Caro realised for the first time how tired he looked.

"Thank you." She turned the cup on the saucer, threading her fine fingers around the handle and raising the cup to her lips. She took a sip. "I hail from Sussex, though I claim no house there anymore." She took a breath. "Would it be fair if I were allowed to ask questions too? You are intent on interrogating me as if I were some exotic creature, and I find you quite as intriguing." Some of her courage had come back when she had gone to change. She discovered that she was just as fascinated by Felton's interest in her as he was by her double life.

His brows rose at her request, and then his face broke into that charming grin. "Why not? Though I confess, compared to your double life, my single life is far from interesting."

"That's not what I wish to ask about. I wish to ask *why* you care to know about me?"

He looked as if he was going to respond immediately and then thought better of it. Caro waited.

"You're quite captivating," he answered at length. "I don't know anyone else who is so skilled at deception that they can pretend to be two separate characters in public."

She believed he was trying to compliment her, but she felt the familiar guilt at her deception. Skilled at deception? How could he compliment something so sinful?

"That bruise that Ravensbough gave you," said Felton, his voice deep and gentle, "does it hurt?"

She almost said no. The lie was instinctual, but this conversation had given her a distaste for falsehoods. "Yes."

"Forget basilicum ointment. Put a steak on it, cold from the larder...or if you have none, I shall send one round."

"Send a steak to a lady's house? How novel."

"A sister with the same bruise as her illegitimate counterpart is equally novel." The grin on his face accentuated the innocent humour of his words.

"Did the fact that I asked for a wink from you last night really give me away?" The ludicrousness of that slip made Caro cringe inwardly.

"It confirmed what I had been assuming, but I would have followed you home last night all the same if you had not asked."

"You followed me home?" Caro's brow lifted.

"Yes. I could hardly risk you being accosted again by Ravensbough on the journey home. That man is a dog. I almost lost you and your manservant when you walked the last part, but I kept up." The corner of his mouth curled up. "Besides," he said, raising himself a little and readjusting his position on the sofa, "I had my suspicions for a long time before last night. There was something in your face when I met you at The Pot and Pineapple and mistook you for Angelica. It was—how shall I put it?—guilt at being found out, rather than the shocked innocence you tried too hard to project."

His words felt like an attack, and Caro shot back instantly. "I do not feel guilt over my life. I hardly chose to be put in a position which necessitated my gaming. My father drank himself to death when his gambling debts grew too shameful. We were left destitute after the house paid the debts. I had no other income." Her back was straighter than ever, and she raised her swollen chin defiantly. "I support myself at the expense of men too intoxicated and too rich for their own good, and in doing so I support Libby and John as well."

Her sharp words were as much a justification to herself as they were to Felton. They were meant to push Felton and his questioning away, but they did the opposite.

"So you make your living at the tables? It is not an addiction?"

Again his words riled her. "My father played cards." Her words contained no fondness. "He called me his golden angel, Angelica. It seemed fitting." She swallowed back the lump in her throat, the knowledge that this name was the only gift her father had given her. "It did not seem a stretch for my father to have an illegitimate daughter—he probably does somewhere— and he left me with nothing to live on. I found I had skill with the cards, and so I made an opportunity to use it."

"You do indeed," he concurred. "But I recall Lord Worth having a son? What of your brother?"

Caro's hands began to shake, and she fought to steady her teacup. "He believed me less than I am.... He is not here—I do not wish to speak of that."

She breathed more surely once Felton allowed her to close that door.

"I presume you have been careful not to let *this*"—he gestured between himself and her—"happen before? No one has guessed?"

"No one has been so..."—she tried to find a word, but none of the ones which came to mind were flattering—"... persistent." He was being persistent now, poking her, prodding her, testing her for weaknesses.

"It must be an incredibly lonely life."

The truth of what he said pierced her armour like a lance. It knocked the breath from her, and she felt the pricking of unbidden tears behind her eyes. Why was he here? Why was he doing this to her? What did he really want? Surely he could not mean to help her? All she wished was to be alone as he so poignantly put it.

Felton's gaze which had wandered off to the other side of the room drew back to her, for what reason she knew not. His eyes were intense but also kind in their stare. He was reading her face behind the mask which she had let slip. His eyes dropped from her face and took in her hands clasped tightly around her teacup. He seemed poised to say something but also undecided as to what.

"I...I should probably leave you."

As Felton uttered those words, Caro felt a sudden sharp desire that he stay. He was humorous and sure of himself. He made her feel more secure in spite of the precarious situation. And yet, just a moment ago, she had wanted to be alone? Indeed, he *must* leave. He was risking too much by being here, and he was asking questions she had no desire to answer. She felt wounded and tired.

"What do you plan to do with the information you have discovered?"

Felton's green eyes fixed themselves on her face. Apparently he liked staring at her in that manner.

"I don't see that I will do anything with it."

She sighed with relief inwardly but outwardly kept her face blank. She had shown her vulnerability to him once—she would not do so again.

"However," he began.

Her back straightened.

"What happened last night will cause ripples, and from what I have heard about Ravensbough, I do not believe this is the last harassment you will receive. I don't wish to frighten you, but I do wish to be practical."

"I shall not go to Mr. Russell's from now on."

"I'm not convinced that will answer. It would be best if

you left the tables altogether for the time being. Your only safety is in your real identity of Caro Worth."

Perhaps he was right, but that did not change the bills Caro needed to pay, nor the lack of money she had to settle them.

"He stole my winnings last night."

Felton did not respond with words, but his lip curled back and his eyes hardened. After whatever emotion had muted his voice had passed over him, he spoke again. "I can lend you money if you are in need of some."

"Why?" The situation was becoming too much for Caro, and now she felt exasperated. "Why do you wish to help me?"

"You're amusing," replied Felton without pause, "and I am so rarely amused."

"This is not a game—it's my life."

"But a most amusing life."

"You are intolerable!"

"Alas, so my father tells me." He smiled, apparently happy that he had managed to drag some sort of feeling other than hopelessness from her.

"What else does your father tell you?" said Caro, pushing the focus off herself.

"That I am a reprobate with no redeeming qualities and a lack of desire to shoulder any familial responsibility. Call me pleasure-driven."

She chuckled, her body unused to the sensation of genuine laughter. But at the same time, her confusion about Felton's motives was unallayed. What possible reason could he have to help her?

"I cannot accept your money or your help, though I will thank you a thousand times for your services last night."

"My services?" scoffed Felton. "Well, you may not want my help, but that will in no way impede my giving it. Rest today, do not game tonight, and I shall visit on the morrow."

"Here I thought you were a pleasure-lover, and instead you command me like an officer."

"And why should you object to that?" replied Felton, always ready to fire with his quick wit. "I don't recall saying you were a pleasure-lover as well, and perhaps some direction would do you good. But I should warn you that the army was not my forté—though Father had me try it. Something about disobedience not being a good quality in an officer —*disgraceful* was the term that was applied if I remember correctly."

"A deceptive woman leading two lives, lying to her acquaintances and making her living at the tables—what do you call that then?"

"Desperate."

Again, the quick word and its sharp truth pricked Caro's shell. She *had* been desperate. She had no money and had lost the one last protection afforded to her—her brother.

Felton rose to leave and bowed low to say his farewells. "The bruise does nothing to diminish your ever-present beauty," he said with the same confident amusement that so characterised him—as though he had simply stopped in, as a friend, for a morning call. He straightened. "Good day, Miss Worth."

Caro inclined her head a little, finding the formal gesture at odds with the situation. And then, just as suddenly as he had appeared, he was gone.

Libby came to clear the tea things, and Caro sat there for a little while longer running over all that had happened this morning and last night. She felt like a woman in a lifeboat, lost at sea.

CHAPTER NINE

L ater that night Caro was happily ignoring the advice of her new self-appointed protector. She had thought on it, long and hard, and she had come to the same conclusion each time. He did not understand of what he had spoken. He had no idea of the repercussions if she did not game. Staying away from the tables not only meant avoiding risk, it meant avoiding reward, and she knew that her household could only survive a short time without any further funds coming in.

How was the pampered younger son of a Viscount going to understand that situation? Understand her predicament? The answer was simple. He might have good intentions, but he could not comprehend who she was or what was demanded of her. She was thankful beyond words for his assistance, but she could not sit idly by and watch the world she had built crumble.

With that in mind, Miss Angelica Worth was entering the gaming hell of a certain Monsieur de Sauveterre, a French gentleman who had set up his establishment a year ago. She was hoping that the newness of the hell would protect it from the *beau monde* and, in particular, from the Marquis of

Ravensbough. Even the thought of him sent a shiver down her spine. She pushed the thought away as quickly as she could. John was here and was carrying a small club in the pocket of his frock coat. He would at least be on hand if anything untoward were to happen.

She entered the hell through a doorway on street level and was escorted upstairs. She noted, as she entered the upper rooms, that the gamers present were those most devoted to the sport. It was not like the amusing atmosphere of Mr. Russell's which attracted both hard gamers and the young pups who only wanted to dip their toes in the waters. Monsieur de Sauveterre's appeared to attract a far more serious clientele, one which failed to laugh, one which spoke but little, and one which would win or lose a great deal in the small hours.

She would not have come if necessity had not bidden her. She had wanted to stay away, at least until the scandal she had caused last night had died down and until the threat of Ravensbough had dissipated, but it was impossible. Felton might have a choice, she thought bitterly, but she did not. More than that, she knew that she must pay Ravensbough the money he had asked for last night. If she did not, she had no idea how long this drama would go on or how long he would hold it over her head.

She was dressed in a slightly more demure gown than usual, one of blue silk with a higher neckline than her daring red ensemble. Her face was powdered heavily, and she wore a new patch lower than usual to cover the bruise on her jaw. The new sun-shaped patch had been sent round by Felton to replace the one now covered in candle wax, and though he had meant it to be used by Caro, she had appropriated it for Angelica's use.

The swelling had gone down considerably thanks to the steak Felton had sent to accompany the patch box. She had wanted to refuse it initially, but Felton's slight and mean-looking manservant had disappeared before she could send it back. Libby had insisted that her mistress use it, and John had agreed it was the best medicine, having often used the same remedy after boxing in his youth.

Monsieur de Sauveterre's establishment was thick with the smoke of cheroots and the smell of liquor. There were four tables placed equidistant from each other in the first room she entered. These were the games of chance—hazard and faro— neither of which she wished to play. She won because of skill, not because the goddess of chance smiled kindly upon her. The goddess never had, so why would she now?

Decorated in rich colours, the room was dark with an aura of hopelessness. She saw a few familiar faces among the players, but the majority she did not know. It would not take her long to gain the measure of her opponents, however. She felt confident that she would win—she had to.

She noted the varying attitudes of the gentlemen at play— the winners leaning forward ready to take their game, the losers twitching their hands and shifting their legs in their chairs. Just inside the entrance of the room, there were two men standing near her. They were the guards for the entrance to the hell, both large, broad-shouldered men with faces that brooked no argument. They wore plain woolen frockcoats in sombre colours, and their shoes were made of black leather with only the most modest buckles.

The man on Angelica's right bore a scar in a jagged line down one side of his face, the result of a broken bottle being raked through the flesh. She knew this heavy—she recognised him as one who moonlighted at Mr. Russell's hell. She glanced to her other side. There were no defining scars on the second man, but the ear facing Angelica was like a cauliflower, the top full of extra flesh bubbling up under the skin—an ex-prize fighter, no doubt, lending his much-needed skills as a gaming hell guard.

The man with the scar noticed Angelica's look and gave her a smile which sent the jagged line puckering up as his cheek rounded. Despite his huge size and the way he towered over her, she found herself smiling back. Joey had always been kind to her.

"Evening, Miss Worth." He nodded his head to her manservant. "Mr. John."

"Good evening, Joey," said John, the shadow of a smile on his lined face.

"We was not expecting you 'ere tonight." The heavy spoke to John, but the insinuation immediately made Angelica's frame tense.

"Well, we are in attendance and hope for no trouble." John patted the object in his frock coat pocket to which Joe nodded.

"What tables are good tonight, Joey?" asked Angelica, bestowing a smile upon the guard.

"Well," said he, drawing breath. "I knows you like piquet, Miss Worth, and the second table to the left through those doors 'as a...good gentleman to play with. I believe 'e's just finishing up his game."

She understood his implication with little trouble. She had spoken to Joey before and asked him about players. He knew the type of men she liked to game with and so this good gentleman he spoke of was most certainly drunk.

"I think you are my favourite doorman, Joey." Angelica felt a surge of the old control in her veins. She was the cool and collected Angelica again, and not the vulnerable girl she had been made to feel last night. She would not be defeated. She had a role to play, and play it she would.

"And you my favourite player, Miss Worth." Joey said her name again with the odd lisp he harboured thanks to losing one too many teeth and tugged his forelock before straightening into his guard's stance once again.

Angelica nodded to John, and they both set off through the room. Several faces turned their way, and they were already trading whispers. Her brief sojourn in the doorway had afforded any familiar faces the time to relay Angelica's latest gaming fracas to the rest of the room.

Usually, as Angelica, she could withstand this kind of brazen staring. She could wear the scandalous identity she had formed with only traces of embarrassment. This evening, however, she felt what they saw—she felt the dirtiness of her identity, the use of her lips for another's pleasure. In the midst of this, she felt the burning of injustice coupled with the shame of allowing herself to be tricked. Each pair of eyes that turned her way were like a shot from a crossbow, the bolt piercing her armour and lancing deep into her flesh. The only thing which kept her from turning around, from running away, from leaving this place, was John's presence. He reminded her of why she was here, of who relied on her.

With her chin held high and a challenging light in her eyes, she made her way between the players of chance and into the card room. She glided towards the tables on her left. Upon arriving at the second one, she produced a dazzling smile, ignoring the pain in her injured jaw, and said in her sultriest voice, "Good evening, gentlemen. I see you are nearly finished." She glanced down at the player who looked the most inebriated. The gleam of initial intoxication was long gone in those listless eyes, and his chin sunk heavily upon his chest. She did not recognise him, but his intoxicated state was all that mattered.

"You wish to play me?" asked the other player, a youth whose eyes were bright with interest.

She shot down his attempt swiftly. She had no time for children. "Alas, no, though I am sure you are as fine a player as any. I was speaking to this gentleman." She gestured to the other and allowed a smile to play around her lips for his benefit.

"Were you now?" replied the older man, slurring his words. "The famous Miss Worth requests to be paired with me? How amusing." His hand clasped his wine glass like a claw, drawing it to his stained lips and dropping bad Bordeaux after good.

Angelica felt a tremor inside of her. She was not used to be left waiting. She was always accepted at once. Half of the gaming men thought her an easy target due to her sex—the other half wished to lust after her during play. The drunken gentleman did finally acquiesce, however, stretching a hand to order another chair to be placed at the table.

"Excellent." She descended gracefully into a chair, fanning herself gently.

"I am Mr. Rivers and I won the last game," he said, "so I think I shall reserve the right of being the Elder Hand."

Angelica did not care about his name, but her ears should have pricked at the admission of his win. She should have perhaps questioned Joe's proposal of a gaming partner. She should have perhaps cried off from the game.

But Angelica was not herself. Her senses had been so overcome in the last twenty-four hours that they were stunned. All she knew was what she felt she must do, and that was win, so she trusted in the man's intoxication.

"Very well, I will allow it," she said, maintaining the appearance of control and allowing him to forgo the usual method of choosing a dealer by cutting the pack. Men enjoyed women being forceful, unlike the women who were their wives, mothers, or daughters.

Mr. Rivers smiled in response. "I have never played a woman before, but I have heard from those who have played you that it is immensely pleasurable."

She did not respond but instead dealt the cards. Let him

be the Elder Hand, it would set her at a disadvantage initially, but she intended to play hard and take no prisoners tonight, so in the end it would not matter. She picked up her hand for the first phase of the game. She watched him cast off five cards, and she in turn discarded only three. It was all she was allowed. They both checked their hands.

He declared.

"Not good," responded Angelica, the knowledge that she had beaten his first declaration sending a little rush of courage coursing through her.

"Point of seven."

Her heartbeat slowed its excited rhythm.

"Equal."

He declared again, and this time her heart sank.

"Good," she replied, in opposition to her feelings.

When he had finished his declaration and the first trick was laid, she began hers, but evidently she had not managed to gather a good hand with the measly three cards she had been allowed to discard and replace from the stock. Her declarations were met with either equals or not-goods, and then the tricks favored him six-fold. She was losing at the end of the first of six hands. Perhaps she could redeem her play?

But any hopeful thoughts along those lines were put firmly to bed with the next round. As he gathered the cards to deal, he caught eyes with her. In that moment, any slovenliness disappeared, and a streak of sobriety appeared in those eyes. His face became sharp and cunning as he dealt and drew the stock close to his elbow before play. A sudden unease began to grow in the pit of her stomach. He looked at her as if he knew something. More than that, now that he looked so awake, so alert, she thought she recognised him, but from where she knew not. She was sure they had never met before, not even in her other life, but still, there was something familiar in his face.

The next hand confirmed her fears. Something was wrong.

The way the gentleman moved his hands, quick even for a sober man, dazzled her eyes. He was fast and his play was hard. Something was amiss. Why did she recognise him?

Her opponent seemed to have gathered a golden hand. She did not do well in the declaration phase, nor with the tricks. The next deal followed, and she felt her courage ebbing with every wave of cards. Her opponent won another hand, and once again she nodded at the loss with a serene smile as though none of this were a great catastrophe. Something was not right.

She glanced across at the servant seated at the edge of the table, leaning forward in his chair, quill in hand, and scratching the score which beat Angelica's into a ledger. The lines of ink remained proud and glistening on the paper in the candlelight, taking their time to dry, taking their time in sealing her fate this evening.

Mr. Rivers was dealing again. He paused in his actions at the sound of a newcomer. He looked up to see a figure entering the room behind Angelica, and his face transformed into a wolfish grin. She recognised him then, and she knew where she had seen him—seated silently beside his friend at Mr. Russell's last night, his friend the Marquis of Ravensbough.

Angelica froze. Her hands clenched on the arms of the chair in which she sat. Her heart stopped beating for several seconds, and when it resumed, the steady beat was lost in a wild pattering of frantic beats. She dragged in a few gasps of air.

Without looking, she knew whom Mr. Rivers had seen behind her—she could feel the dark presence—but she would not be frightened of this man. They were in public. He would not—he could not!—do anything.

She saw John across from her. He was stepping forward, a hand moving to the pocket of his frock coat, but to her horror she saw a man move towards him. The man said something threatening, jutting his chin towards the figure behind her. John stepped back, his eyes firmly on his mistress, his hand not moving from his pocket.

Half of her wanted John to do something. Half of her wanted him protected. She couldn't think. It had been hard enough to concentrate tonight. She had thought she was in control, but now everything was spinning loose from her grip. She had felt the approaching man's presence first, and now the heavy darkness of his shadow was cast over her as he drew to her side.

"Good evening," said Ravensbough, his voice smooth and cutting. He sounded just as angry as he had been last night when he had left her. "Leave us," he said curtly, sending the servant scurrying from the table.

How had he found her?

As she looked ahead, Mr. Rivers replied—which was more than she could do. "Good evening, my lord, I was just getting acquainted with your friend."

"As you were with mine, Miss Worth." The Marquis stood between them, his eyes resting condescendingly upon Angelica. "One of the things an exotic creature like you is not used to in the underbelly of the capital are friends like my Mr. Rivers."

As the Marquis said it, she saw the flicker of a card move from the stock of cards into Mr. Rivers' hands. He had done it slow enough for her to see this time. Slow enough to know for certain that he was cheating.

"Uh!" The Marquis held up a commanding hand to Angelica, staying her before she could think of moving. "Think carefully about your next steps, my dear." He used the endearment sardonically, and yet there was still the light of lust in his eyes. She knew what he desired. "You wouldn't want another upset like last night and, unlike Mr. Russell's hell you frequent, this one is filled with...my friends... and I don't believe they have let any boys in this evening."

How she wished in that moment that Felton was here, beside her, protecting her, fighting for her. But she would not be so lucky twice.

"And it is filled with others as well," she said finally, trying to fight back, her voice unsteady, and speaking of what she was not certain. "I am well loved." In this moment she could only hope that she was and that those who loved her were here.

The Marquis laughed and ran a finger down her cheek, pressing hard on the sun-shaped patch at her jaw, making her flinch. A tear came to her eye as he rubbed her loose face powder between his finger and thumb.

"You are much desired, Miss Worth." He eyed the bruise he had made last evening. "Have you thought over my proposal?"

"I am at play." She tried to focus on Mr. Rivers, but the man was looking at his master like a dog panting, waiting for the next stick to be thrown. If she finished this game, she would surely lose to this card sharp.

"I know. I was informed of it when you entered. I have friends, as I have said, in many hells. It was fortunate this was one of the establishments. Isn't Rivers a good player?"

A good actor, she wanted to say—he had fooled her with his false drunkenness. But her fear kept her frustrations silent. He had no doubt fooled Joe the doorman too. Felton had been right—she should never have come gaming. This Marquis had stripped from her the wisdom and wit that she prided herself in possessing.

"I require an answer. What better way to pay off your debts than with yourself? I can think of infinitely pleasurable ways we can settle them between us. All you need do is become my mistress."

The word sent a wave of sickness through her. It disgusted her. *He* disgusted her.

"I cannot...decide it now." She tried to buy time by not giving him an outright denial.

"But why not? We are without your attack dog this evening. It is most gratifying. And you know full well that a second son cannot provide for you as I can. Leave his pathetic attentions alone and come into my keeping."

His brazen statements echoed her own thoughts from when she had first met Felton. She had leapt to the same conclusion—though in terms of marriage—that he could not support her. She had considered this sadistic Marquis more eligible than a second son with no prospects.

Her jaw was aching, her stomach felt sick, and all she wished was to go home. But the memory of Felton brought with it images of his courage. "I shall not answer your proposal," she said suddenly, a resurgence of spirit powering through her. "I tire of fencing. Shall we play?" If she was to be taken down, she would be taken down playing. What else could she do?

She glanced at John. He was still being held against the wall by one of Ravensbough's lackeys.

"You are making a mistake, Miss Worth," hissed the Marquis, all pleasantries evaporating.

Her eyes fell back to the cards which still lay face down on the table, and the patterns that decorated them dissolved before her. Images of the events at Mr. Russell's flashed before her eyes. The thought of Ravensbough's hands on her made the sickness in her stomach grow. She shook her head gently but the images did not go away. She flexed her jaw slightly and felt the pain from the bruise. She blinked away the feeling of being thrown into the wall, all her strength not even close to being a match for his.

Tears rose in her eyes, and the lump in her throat

constricted her breathing, making further speech an impossibility. Apparently the Marquis had signalled Mr. Rivers, and he declared before laying his card. Ravensbough was happy to watch her fall.

She declared. Then she answered Mr. Rivers' trick. She wrestled with the tears which had come so suddenly. She pushed back at them, forcing them away, forcing herself to remain immovable. She had never before felt such shame, but now it covered her like soot. She wanted a bath drawn—she wished to wash, scrub, scratch these feelings off.

"Your play." Her opponent pushed her.

She cleared her throat unsteadily. The threatening tears had gone, but they were replaced with a dark despair. She was not paying attention, and the card she laid failed her. She lost another trick. She could still feel Ravensbough's eyes upon her though she refused to meet them. She felt rather than saw his smile. She was losing, it was going wrong, and there was nothing she could do.

The game continued to deteriorate. She lost all of the tricks, then all the hands, then the game itself. Mr. Rivers laid the last trick with a fiendish smile, and just like that she had lost a thousand pounds. What would she do? What could she do? Rivers had cheated, and she could call him out, but John was being held at the wall, there were others here who would spread a scandal, and if she made such a move she could not be sure of the Marquis' actions.

"I will have to draw on my bank to pay the debt," she said in a monotone voice.

"At your convenience. The debt is owed to the Marquis of Ravensbough," said Mr. Rivers, rising to his feet and now appearing the picture of sobriety.

"I will await your payment and your answer," Ravensbough said with some satisfaction.

Angelica almost stumbled as she skirted the table. She

needed to flee from here. She could not be here, not with him. The poison of his presence was beginning to destroy her. What was the old proverb? "Fool me once, shame on you. Fool me twice, shame on me." He had made a fool of her again, and this time it was her own fault.

When she reached the door, she tripped again, and this time Joey caught her arm.

"You alright, miss? You played t'other chap to the one I was talkin' of. I meant the young pup."

If Angelica had been in her right mind, she might have realised how stupid she had been. As it was she could not even figure out how to ask for a carriage home. She turned to search for John and saw him coming towards her, a shiner on his face.

"John!" she gasped. "What happened?"

"Nothing. We must get home." He refused to look her in the eye and instead went straight outside to call a carriage. She followed close behind, terrified to be left alone in the hell.

She could not remember coming home. She could not remember the carriage journey, the walk to the servants' door or the climb of the stairs to the main hall. She was oblivious to Libby taking her cloak and hat and pushing a glass of brandy into her hand. When she finally became aware of her surroundings all she could say was, "We are ruined. We are quite ruined."

CHAPTER TEN

L ady Rebecca Fairing came over quite unexpectedly the next morning. In her usual unorthodox manner, she arrived through the servants' entrance at the back of the house. She had ignored her maid's suggestion that she be dropped at the front of the house like any lady of consequence. Her groom would need to walk the horses during her visit, and the back of the house saw far less traffic. Rebecca had seen it as the only reasonable entrance for her to use.

Despite her maid's protestations, Rebecca had propelled her into Caro's residence through a back door. Her maid had unwillingly led the way down the corridor, but she stopped short upon the threshold of the kitchen. Rebecca, who had been admiring the look of her new kid gloves on her hands, collided with her.

"Maisy, honestly! Whatever are you stopping for? I said I wished to be shown upstairs. With all your concern over propriety you are the oddest creature." As the last words left her lips her eyes caught on the very scene which had halted her maid's steps.

Caro was seated at the newly scrubbed kitchen table with

her maid Libby holding eight ounces of the finest beef anyone could obtain in London to her mistress' face. John, her manservant, was seated at the table nursing a freshly brewed cup of tea out of the China which was used when Rebecca paid her morning calls and issuing instructions to his wife upon the exact situation of the meat upon Caro's face.

All three persons looked to the intrepid Lady Rebecca at the same moment, and all three were rendered speechless.

Finally, still with a steak upon her face, the fair-haired Caro, who was looking quite the worse for wear, spoke. "Lady Rebecca!"

"Rebecca, please, my dear. I have already told you to call me it," said the brunette beauty, as though her sudden entrance were anything but eccentric. She plucked at the fingers of her gloves until she could release her hands and then waved them in the air as though to dismiss the bemused looks of the kitchen's occupants.

Libby took the steak from Caro's face and plopped it noisily into an enamel dish. After this she pottered towards the fire.

Rather than confronting her unexpected visitor, Caro settled on the most insipid question she could think of. "What are you doing, Libby?"

"Putting the tea on, miss. We have company. Besides, that steak could do with eating soon, so I must cook it if we don't want to waste it."

"But...."

"Now, miss,"—Libby leaned closer with a fierce whisper —"we both know that Lady Rebecca does not leave until she is satisfied, and there is much needed to satisfy her this morning." She removed the pot from the fire, and Maisy, bewildered by the presence of their mistresses in such a rustic atmosphere, came over to help her, taking refuge in menial tasks as a response.

"Impertinent, but quite accurate," said Rebecca. "Thank you, Libby. The first satisfaction I will receive is an explanation as to why you had a raw piece of dinner on your face when I came in." She pulled out a plain wooden chair from the table and sidestepped around it until her large skirts could descend gracefully into the seat. She laid her gloves on the table but kept the modish petite tricorn she wore firmly nestled in her powdered locks.

"Should we not go upstairs?" asked Caro a little faintly.

"I do not see why we should. You are already installed here and clearly need access to that choice cut of beef." Rebecca pointed a finger to the enamel dish. "And I deserve to remain here after gaining illegal entry to your property through the servants' entrance. No, here will do just fine for us both. The steak?"

After a moment's pause, Caro answered. "I injured my jaw."

"Ah, yes," said Rebecca, eyeing the purple bruise on her friend's face. "That looks monstrous."

Caro reflected that Lady Rebecca had not seen her since the Mires' ball. How different she must look now—pale and drawn, with dark shadows beneath her bright eyes and a look of anxiety marring her face.

"How did you do that?"

"I slipped on my shawl in my room"—Caro thought up the lie quickly—"and caught my chin on the wall sconce." At least she could be partially truthful—her friend deserved that much.

"And am I to think you look so ill due to a broken heart?"

Caro stared at her, her brows puckering in bewilderment. What did her friend mean?

Rebecca folded her hands. "Must I be more obvious? I mean the pain the Marquis of Ravensbough has caused you."

Caro gasped. Her blue eyes flew wide open, and her face turned impossibly paler. "What?"

"Caro, you look shocked, my dear." Rebecca half-rose from her chair. "Whatever is the matter?"

"Mistress,"—Libby's gray eyebrows arched, and she widened her eyes as if conveying a deeper meaning—"it seems that a *singular* explanation may be in order."

Rebecca looked from the maid to her mistress and back again. Singular? A bruise on her jaw? A steak on her face? Such marked distress over the Marquis of Ravensbough?

She had been at a small breakfast party when she heard from her aunt that Miss Angelica Worth had been involved in some kind of affair with the Marquis of Ravensbough. All Town spoke of it. It was not known exactly what had happened, but everyone was certain that the Marquis had some claim on Angelica Worth. Felton had been mentioned, but no one was sure of his involvement apart from that he had been there—Rebecca expected nothing less of the reckless gentleman. Whatever had happened, Rebecca had known it would upset Caro. She had seen how interested her friend had been in the Marquis, and to have him fall to the lures of her half-sister....

"Libby!" Caro almost cried out her servant's name, and then as if remembering herself added, "Please would you pour the tea. My jaw aches too much for me to do so."

The old retainer did so with a sniff and a huff. After finishing, she ushered her husband out of his chair, and they both went upstairs to the morning room with Maisy, leaving their mistresses in the kitchen to talk.

It was a most odd arrangement, and Rebecca remarked on it with a laugh before she turned her large brown eyes upon her friend in an inquisitive look. The kitchen was delightfully warm thanks to a recently banked fire beside which the now empty kettle stood. The floor, Rebecca noticed, had been swept clean, the flagstones spotless in the early light of morning which shone down through the high street-level windows. All in all, she had to admit, this little kitchen made a cozy little sitting room. She would prefer a little more space, but she was not above sitting here with her dearest friend.

As she observed her friend, she could see she was not well. There was conflict in Caro's eyes and an emotion akin to pain etched into the worried lines of her face. Rebecca wished with all her heart that Caro would speak to her, that she would confide in her as Rebecca felt she could in Caro—but even as she thought it she saw the doors closing upon Caro's face.

"I do not wish"—Caro stretched a tentative hand halfway across the table—"to bring trouble to your door."

Rebecca could see the effort this statement had cost her friend.

"I...." Caro looked away towards the flames in the hearth, and Rebecca followed her gaze, becoming as entranced by the dancing tongues of light as her friend was for a few moments.

Rebecca sighed. Caro was not ready to share the broken heart that burdened her, and Rebecca knew she must respect her wishes. Still, it frustrated her that Caro felt the need to protect Rebecca from her half-sister's disgrace when she was in such obvious pain, when she needed comfort. Rebecca did not care about the scandal, only about her friend. It was painful to watch Caro in such distress and hold no power to help.

"I shall make a bargain with you," said Rebecca, freeing Caro from the struggle of what to reveal. "You shall tell me whatever it is which weighs so heavily upon you when you are ready, and not before. Nothing you say to me shall change our

friendship, dear Caro, nor what others in Town have to say."
She reached forward to clasp Caro's waiting hand and smiled
at her friend.

Caro hesitated and then smiled in return. "I do not
deserve you as a friend, Rebecca."

"Nonsense," said Rebecca, waving her hand as if it did not
matter. "I know you would tell me if you thought it good, and
I appreciate the protective feelings you have towards me. Now,
are you to come to Astley's Amphitheatre tomorrow? I understand my aunt sent around an invitation for you to join us."

Caro touched a hand to the bruise on her chin. For a
moment, Rebecca thought she would decline the invitation,
but she surprised her by accepting it with good grace. Apparently her heart was not *so* broken that she could not leave her
house.

St. Saviour's dock in southeast London was thronging with
ships and workers. It was always busy. Inbound ships stacked
high with cargo from the colonies and the West Indies were
waiting to gain entry via the Neckinger to the safety of the
tidal dock and unload their cargos of sugar, molasses, and
indigo.

James Worth's ship had been waiting a day already, but
thanks to the connections of his former business partner, he
would be the next to land. He would miss Mr. Everett's help,
but the man had decided to pull his investment, too excited by
new opportunities in the slave trade to be bothered about the
sugar, molasses, and spices from Asia in which James traded.

He rubbed a calloused hand over his ruddy face and
looked again towards the entrance to the docks. On either side
of the waterway, slap-dash timber-framed buildings hung at
precarious angles. Men from the ships already landed were

milling to and fro, barrowing cargo from the vessels to warehouses on the Thames or to markets already awake and bustling.

James had not slept the night before last, thanks to a choppy Channel crossing, and now he was feeling it. Tiredness tugged with tiny hands at his eyelids, begging them to close, but he had to wait until his job was done.

He was already missing the heat of the West Indies, and when he had left his cabin this morning, he had done so with several layers of clothing. But even three shirts and a frock coat more suited to merchant's work than to a ballroom could not recreate the heat of the land he had inhabited for the last two years.

"Come by!" called a man holding papers at the dock's entrance.

James felt the great girth of his ship move as the captain swung the wheel and the men below began to row. The sails had been furled yesterday, and as soon as they were close enough a smaller vessel would come before them and they could pull their oars in too, ready to be towed into the dock. He sighed, pleased they would be docking today—he had worried they might miss the tide again.

After half an hour the ship was docked, and the men, all starved of land and good food, were scurrying down the gangplanks like rats. James was not far behind. He pulled a canvas bag from behind some barrels and slung it over his shoulder, walking across the deck in his practical leather boots, worn and supple.

"And to London we go, eh, Mr. Worth?" said Captain Jameson, descending the steps from the wheel onto the deck proper.

James had refused to take his father's title, and he was happier for it. Anything to distance himself from his father was a blessing. And from the rest of his family as well.

"Yes, Jameson, I hear it's a great and monstrous thing these days." James had not been in Town for two years, and before that he had barely been to London, still being at university until his father had reneged on the fees.

"Aye, so it is. Do you know what you want done with the cargo?"

The ship was full of the fruit of James' labour—sugar, molasses, and barrels of Madeira that had been traded on that island for half James' supply of indigo dye.

"Instruct your men to leave the cargo in the warehouse on the west side of the dock. The buyers will come with papers in the next few days to pick it up." And in the next few days he would be gone again, leaving London and all his bitter memories of England behind him. Would a few days' time be enough to find another investor now that Mr. Everett had deserted him?

"As you like, Mr. Worth, and a good year to you. I doubt I'll see you again until your foot hits the golden shores of the West Indies."

"Yes, true," said James. His tanned face broke into a smile. He would be catching any ship bound for the islands for his return journey as merely a passenger.

He grasped Jameson's outstretched hand. The almost toothless captain might look terrifying but he was one of the best sailors James had met. He regretted being unable to travel back with him.

"Godspeed," said James and turned on his heel, canvas bag on his broad shoulders, heading down the gangway to solid ground.

At least, it would have been solid if it were not covered with waste and soiled cargo which had been unfortunate enough to fall from the barrows. James had seen worse. He strode out in spite of the muck and headed for Shad Thames and eventually London Bridge. He would be staying north of the river at the Grand Hotel. Everett had directed him there. It was a newly opened hotel and was proving popular among the Ton at present, making it an ideal location from which to find a new investor.

For now, all James wanted was a hot meal and a bath. Two months on the sea had salted his skin so much that he could probably be preserved for winter! He caught a hackney once he reached London Bridge. It had been easy to follow the river to the bridge, but he did not know the rest of the way from here.

From the window he watched passers-by, the boats which flocked on the Thames, and the Tower of London rising like a white ghost of past centuries. The more people he passed, the more he noticed how their clothes differed from his. Many wore the silks he had seen shipped into the West Indies before being taken north to the colonies. He saw coats with many capes, jackets less full in the skirts than his, cuffs not as deep as his. He was out of fashion.

But what did it matter? He would not be here for long. Then again, how could a moneyed investor take him seriously if he looked as though he belonged half a decade before? Perhaps he would go shopping. He was not fantastically wealthy, but he was certainly independent—independent enough to be renting rooms at the new Grand Hotel, to buy himself a new set of clothes, and to purchase an enormous steak dinner when he arrived.

He reached the hotel situated near Covent Gardens in a little under three quarters of an hour and descended the steps of his carriage to stand beneath its impressive façade for a few moments. If he had not been so tired, he would not have bothered to look. Appearance hardly meant anything to him. He knew what mattered, hard work and common sense—that is what had caused him to rise from a lowly assistant to a merchant with a ship full of his own cargo in two short years.

As it was, however, he did pause beneath the grand building and admire it for a few moments—until the hackney driver climbed down and thrust his canvas bag unceremoniously at him. No doubt he thought him some common urchin from the docks spending his few pennies on a pointless journey.

James turned his piercing blue eyes upon the man.

"Here is your fare, and I suggest, for the sake of your business, that you go about treating your customers with a little more courtesy."

The driver looked annoyed, but when he saw the overpayment in his hands, his face altered considerably. "Yes, sir, quite right, sir, and if you be needing me, sir, I will wait just down there for you, sir." The middle-aged man tugged furiously at what was left of his forelock on his balding head.

"That won't be necessary." James could do with a walk later after having only a deck to walk for the past two months. As much as he loved the sea, it was a pleasure that ran down to his very toes to be on solid land again, at least for now.

In an unusual act of consumption, James took two rooms, a bedroom and adjacent sitting room ideal for doing work while he was here. He also ordered that hot steak meal to his room and commanded a bath to be drawn. He offered payment in advance, not liking to be beholden to anybody, and was soon installed in his well-furnished rooms.

His dinner disappeared in a matter of minutes, every mouthful of hot, tender steak making his mouth water as it neared him on the fork. While he ate, the bath was drawn, and once the servant had disappeared, he took great delight in peeling off his grubby clothes, garment by garment, before descending into the hot depths of the tin bath.

He awoke sometime later, the water lapping at his nostrils as he breathed in—he had sunk deep into the bath in his slumber. He stretched luxuriously and then leapt from the tub and vigorously toweled himself down. He rang the bell for a razor and a mirror and shaved, getting rid of the stubble which had been unlooked to on the rough seas when using a razor aboard was hazardous.

He redressed in clothes from his canvas bag and enjoyed some coffee and fresh toast before leaving as suddenly as he had arrived. He did spare one backward glance, for the soft bed which he would enjoy later, but shutting the door briskly he descended to the hotel hall. Now that his cargo was safely landed he needed to fulfil his sole task—finding an investor.

Of course, the one thing that did not feature in the well-thought-out plans of James Worth, was the scandal currently enveloping London in its salacious tentacles. He had only to enter one of London's exclusive clubs—under the patronage of his friend Everett's name—before he heard tell of the infamous gamestress Miss Angelica Worth, of the fortunes she had lost at the tables, and of her philandering with the Marquis of Ravensbough.

Upon hearing each recounting of the affair, James became more and more suspicious of the principal actress in the tale. The name Worth struck him as odd and unfortunate—but she was raven-haired, not claiming the fair hair natural to his sister. Besides, his sister was most probably still in Sussex kept by whichever man it had been that had offered her such a position of security two years ago. Even now the shame felt hot and thick upon him—that his sister, a lady of quality, should throw everything away for a few guineas, and that she should have the audacity to offer them to James to help their fortunes after their father left them with nothing!

He had not wished to delve into the gossip surrounding this Miss Angelica Worth—the similarities to his past caused pain—but apparently every investor he met with had that exact desire. They recounted the tale with relish, from her entrance to London's hells, to her notorious wins and losses, to the heated affair between herself and her lover, the Marquis of Ravensbough. She was the subject that all London talked of.

"She is a great beauty," said one corpulent investor. "Hair as black as a coal. I would ask if she was kin to you, being a Worth, if not for the difference in her colouring. She is no relation, I suppose?"

The fat financier was devouring a great steak and ale pie that James would be footing the bill for. As James watched gravy from a large bite dribble down the man's cheek, he found himself hoping the investor would choke.

"Absolutely not," he replied flatly.

"I can understand your disdain." The investor began waggling his fork at James. "But trust you me, if you saw this woman you would not look quite so haughty, I assure you, boy."

James gritted his teeth. This man was not worth the gristle he was currently ingesting.

"And her half-sister, old Lord Worth's daughter, Miss Caro Worth, she is a golden-haired angel. I wouldn't mind a kiss from that woman either." He stabbed a piece of beef mercilessly.

The colour drained from James' face. "Miss Caro Worth?"

"Aye, she has been in Town these past six months, not that she'd ever be seen in company with the likes of Miss Angelica Worth."

Caroline was here? She was in Town? It struck him like a blow to the gut.

And who was this Angelica Worth who used his father's name to gain entry to gaming hells? He knew his father had no bastards—it had been a pleasant revelation in the unpleasant settling of his father's entrenched estate.

"You are sure you are no relation of the gamestress?" The man paused eating and squinted at James.

Some kind of mischief was afoot, and James knew Caroline must be the architect. But her games would not affect him. He would be cursed if he let his sister's immoral actions drag him down.

"I would no more be associated with a woman who has thrown away her virtue with so little regard than I would be by one who is titillated by such vileness." James rose, his broad shoulders stretching the seams of his outdated coat.

"Or of Miss Caro Worth?" said the man. He watched James begin to move away. "What? No business discussion? You've been wasting my time, you young whelp!" The man shoveled another gravy-soaked slab of pastry into his mouth. "You shall not last, my boy."

"As you please, sir." James bowed stiffly and left. In the past two years he had risen from a lowly merchant's assistant to a West Indies merchant in his own right. He was nobody's boy, but he knew when he needed to fight and this was a battle best left in retreat.

When the affair was mentioned yet again by another investor, James was quick to rebuff any assumption of relation. He could not afford to be tainted by this scandal. It would ruin his chances of securing financial backing. He had no desire to meet his sister again either, for it was clear to him, that though he knew not what she was about, she had not changed her ways. However, if he was to leave London with his business name unscathed, he was beginning to feel compelled to visit her...if only to dress her down, to warn her off whatever evil path she now trod.

It had been easy when he was on the other side of the Atlantic—there had been so much for him to do he had barely thought of her except in a few of his dark moments when he had remembered their father and the aftermath of his death. But now when they were once again in the same country, the same city, he could not ignore the tug at his heart, nor the indignation her actions caused. If he could see her, give her the sermon she deserved, warn her off any more scandals until his business had been transacted, he could disappear again to the West Indies with a new investor in tow.

On his third night in London, after hearing of the affair for the fourth time, he resolved over dinner that he would confront his sister. The only problem was that he could not afford to call on her at her house, even if he could find out her address. It would be unseemly and impractical considering he had already denied the relation. A public arena would be best, and his plans were furthered when a fifth potential investor invited him to Astley's Amphitheatre the following evening. Rumour had it that Miss Caro Worth would be attending in the company of Lady Rebecca Fairing and Lady Etheridge.

He would be able to warn his sister off whatever game she was playing and to drop a word in the ear of those ladies of quality whom she was no doubt deceiving about her reprehensible past. Then he would confirm a new investor and leave for the West Indies. Let his sister be her own destruction. She would not be his.

CHAPTER ELEVEN

Tobias Felton was not his usual self. Viscount Felton had noticed as much when he sat down in the window seat of the apartments his son had let for the Season. His pale gray eyes drifted between the bustle of the square outside and the distracted figure of his son inside. His second-born was leaning forward on his chair, shoulders tense, brow knotted as though he were attempting to work out some great sum. On a chair near him sat Lady Felton, watching her son as attentively as her husband, though with that kindly look only a mother's eyes can bestow, even on a child who has tried every nerve possible.

There had been no drunken greeting, no wry jokes at his father's expense, not even the kind words which Felton always reserved for his mother, no matter the circumstances. At first the Viscount had been surprised, then pleased at the seeming sobriety in his son's manners. Now he was growing concerned.

"I have not seen you since last week," said Lady Felton. "It is delightful to have you all to myself, for I swear, I meet others in Society who see you twice as much as I do!" Lady Felton smiled but did not receive such a look in return. Her son was still staring into his hands.

"Perhaps I should make these morning calls a regular feature of my week's events if it will gain me your attention."

"I do not think you have had his attention this last half hour, my love, though I do not think the fault is yours." The Viscount rose, making a tour of the room with his hands clasped behind his back in his customary fashion.

"I think you are right, John." Lady Felton leaned over and placed a hand on her son's arm. "Tell me, what so captivates your thoughts as to rob me of your conversation?"

Felton looked up, his words finally breaking through his pensive thoughts. "I apologise, Mama, it is nothing." He had thought his father had come to deliver the final blow that would sever his financial dependence upon them, right at the moment that he wished to use those finances for another who needed it—but they had not mentioned it yet.

"Oh, how cruel! You mean to say that *nothing* is more interesting than my conversation?"

"Nothing is more interesting to me than you, Mama," said Felton, suddenly coming back to himself, his eyes lighting with their usual amusement. "Tell me," he said, sitting forward and taking Lady Felton's hand in a warm clasp. "What was it you said to me?"

"Oh, it is of no consequence. What plans have you for today? Your father has promised to take us all to Astley's this evening, and I wondered if you would deign to come with us?" A twinkle appeared in her eyes that matched the diamonds peeping from her ears.

"My plans, my plans are...." Felton released her hand and lay back in the brocade chair, drawing his hand up to rub his chin.

"You see, my dear, not concentrating enough for a simple

answer." The Viscount waved a long arm in a gesture of exasperation. He rounded upon his son and faced him. "*Nothing* is what you say? I beg to differ. It must be *something* that causes you to be so cast down in the dumps that you are incapable of holding even the most basic of conversations. Really, Tobias."

Felton sighed while the older man continued to watch him from beneath his hooded eyelids and his mother peered over from her chair.

"I face an unorthodox situation," he offered finally.

"Another? I should have thought you used to them by now."

Felton glanced sideways at his father, a little of the mischief reappearing in his green eyes.

"It cannot be gambling debts," said the Viscount, "for you have asked for no money."

"John, allow the poor boy to speak."

The Viscount bowed toward his wife in acquiescence and then looked back to his youngest son.

"This particular situation is quite different from my previous experiences."

"Really?" said his father. "You intrigue me. In what way?"

"It involves a woman," said his mother.

Felton started at that, but he shouldn't have been surprised. His mother had always been able to read him. Sometimes he felt her intuition was better than his own at putting its finger upon his exact feelings.

He nodded, the movement more of a jerk. "There is a woman."

His father sighed but was silenced halfway through the exhale by a look from his wife. Lady Felton might have been small, but she was nonetheless a formidable woman.

Felton carried on in the silence that was created. "She is in an awkward predicament, but though I have tried to help her, the situation has simply become worse."

"What on earth did you do to make it worse?"

At his father's words the humour left Felton's face and he bristled. "I assure you, my lord, my actions in no way worsened her situation."

The depth of feeling in his words made Viscount Felton check himself.

"In fact," Felton carried on, his blood heating, "I tried to correct the situation, but she was too headstrong to take my advice. Now she has ended up in a worse situation from which I will find it infinitely harder to extricate her."

"That sounds frustrating," said Lady Felton, casting another hard look in her husband's direction to stop him from mentioning the irony of the situation.

"It is!" Felton leapt up from the chair and began pacing.

"And is there naught that can be done?"

"I am yet to come up with a solution."

"And can we not know the girl's name?" demanded the Viscount. "Or the situation, for that matter? What quality of woman is she?"

Felton's eyes blazed as he turned them upon his father. "Of the highest quality, Father, you will be happy to hear, a woman that I believe even Frederick would approve of—not that I shall ever subject her to such a distasteful meeting if I can help it."

"He is your family, dear," said Lady Felton gently. "Have you offered for her?"

"Not yet. But she is dashed headstrong—I doubt she will accept even if I were to. No, I must content myself with helping her...everything else shall have to wait." He tapped a finger on his chin.

"Is the lady known to us?"

"I am inclined to think not."

"And you really cannot tell us the business in which she is embroiled?"

"If I were to do so, I would break a trust."

His mother looked at him a little strangely then, as though she hardly knew the son to whom she was speaking, but the look was followed up with the most munificent of smiles.

"And it would paint an ungenerous picture of a creature whom I believe has been treated most ungenerously by her family," he added.

"This tale becomes more and more intriguing," said his father. "I almost think you are attempting to describe yourself with some poetic license."

Felton chuckled, finally finding the humour in his father's words.

"You may think it, but you would be wrong."

"The more you speak of her so compassionately, the more I wish to be part of the solution," said Lady Felton. "Can you not think of what she will try to do next in her headstrong manner?"

"I do not like the sound of it, boy," said Viscount Felton, cutting off his wife.

"Another scandal to muddy the family name," Felton said sardonically. "Have no fear, my lord. I shall not cause you to send me to the continent again at any point soon."

"Your father hardly means that. Is it really that serious?"

"It is a boiling pot of liquid atop a tripod above a flame, and soon one leg of the tripod will give way." Felton rubbed a hand over his eyes and suddenly looked far wearier than his father and mother had ever seen him.

"Then I can only suggest you stop the hand that plans to remove a leg of the tripod," offered his father.

That was exactly what Felton intended, but until he struck upon a proper plan, he must settle for merely ameliorating any damages such as the loss he had heard Angelica had made at the tables last night.

"Mother," said he, as if none of the conversation had gone on. "I should be delighted to attend Astley's tonight if you shall have me."

Astley's Amphitheatre was aglow with the light of hundreds of candles. The stuccoed ceilings were displayed in all their ornate glory, and every spectator's face was lit with excitement as much as by candlelight. Balconies rose in three stories above the arena, each with rows of seating and some with their own boxes separated from either side.

As the show commenced, spectators peered over the edges of their high prisons, trying to get close enough to the riders who stood on the backs of their cantering horses in order to touch their outstretched hands. The crowds responded to each feat of equestrian acrobatic prowess, with awe, excitement, and anxiety, delighting at the skill on display before them. The orchestra played to the prancing of the horses' oiled hooves—dancing phantoms from some mythical era, come to the arena for one night to reimagine their classical glory.

In spite of the tumultuous series of events that had preceded the evening, Caro was enjoying herself. She adored horses—she always had—and she missed riding immensely. It was a great joy to see such amazing riders doing things she could only dream of. They were so in tune with their horses it was mesmerising. Each small movement sent the beast forward or sideways at its master's will, and the riders who rode two horses, a foot on each, were moving in a rhythm that made them look as though they walked in water, their feet rising alternately in slow undulating movements.

"I fancy that man down there has more of an athletic frame than all of the classical statues from Greece," said Lady

Etheridge, fanning herself gently against the warmth which rose easily to their second level balcony.

"I would hardly think you would notice, Aunt," replied Rebecca.

"Well, you certainly have, child," her aunt replied with some alacrity. "For I have seen you staring at young John Astley for the past quarter of an hour."

"It certainly isn't my fault that he chooses to wear those buckskin breeches as a second skin." Rebecca's dark eyes flashed as she rose to her aunt's challenge.

"I do not know what I shall say to your mother when I restore you to her. You shall be a woman of irreconcilable morals, I have no doubt. Imagine speaking of a man's breeches! I hardly knew to look so at a man at your age."

"I find that impossible to believe, Aunt, utterly impossible."

"Well, I said I *hardly* knew—that is not the same as *not* knowing. There was a young man, one of the hunting set at Melton Mowbray when I was a girl. He had the finest set of legs that I've ever seen on a man and could take his horse over a six-foot hedge as though it were a twig on the floor. I will not regale you with stories of Lord Etheridge's legs, but suffice it to say that they would not have been put to shame beside your young John Astley there.

"Ah," exclaimed Lady Etheridge, looking to the first level balconies opposite. "Speaking of fine legs, I see young Felton has arrived with his parents. Tell me, has he been causing you problems since last I saw you, Miss Worth?" Lady Etheridge fanned herself vigorously.

Caro had been allowing the conversation to wash over her. It made her feel somehow safe, somehow normal, the knowledge that some things in her life had not changed. At Lady Etheridge's words however, Caro sat up straighter, her blue eyes darting to the balcony opposite. As she did so, Felton looked up from his seat and caught eyes with her.

"He was watching for you." Lady Etheridge halted her fan, closing it in one movement and tapping it gently against her chin. "I understood from my niece that you were far more taken with a certain Marquis. I can't help but wonder—if he were here tonight, would you be gazing into his eyes instead?"

"Aunt, please," begged Rebecca.

"Well, I speak the truth, do I not? You have set your cap at Ravensbough? Though I suppose most of Society has."

"I had," Caro responded, not wishing to bring that man's face to mind. She had done her best to ignore the impending doom he meant to bring upon her. "Though I am not sure I still have any interest in that direction."

"The affair with your half-sister? Yes, it is a bothersome business, mostly because I cannot find out from anyone the exact details of the story. Apparently the only other person present is the one who was staring at you from that balcony just a moment ago."

"Mr. Felton?" asked Caro, her jaw beginning to ache.

"Yes, but Aunt, he was just there gaming."

"We don't know that—I heard he was involved in some way. I have a mind to ask the man myself."

"I don't think Felton would have anything scandalous to relate," said Caro suddenly, partly from a fear of Lady Etheridge asking him and partly because she felt some urge to protect his name.

"Do you not? But he has insulted you many times, and Rebecca tells me he has said some very saucy things to you."

"Aunt!" Rebecca turned sheepish eyes towards her friend. "I swear to you I thought her silent as the grave."

"One day, my dear, but at the moment I choose to use your information at my own discretion."

"I am your niece. Surely you should preserve my confidence!" said an exasperated Rebecca. She turned her eyes back to the spectacle. "I say, look at that horse dancing!"

Lady Etheridge ignored her niece's chastisement. Her beady eyes followed the acrobats alongside her niece's, but still she carried on with her interrogation.

"What is it that has changed your opinion of the man?"

"I have found that since my first meeting Mr. Felton he has become...." She struggled to find the right words. She could not say a hero, but perhaps a savior?

No, he was not a savior. He was a man who told her without reserve she was beautiful and that he wished to kiss her. He was a man who barged into her house without propriety just to see that she was well. A man so determined to find out the truth that he ignored the dictates of etiquette. A man who refused to hold the truth over her as some kind of bargaining chip.

"I meant to say, he seems to be a good sort of gentleman." It did not do him justice, but she hardly knew how to speak of a man who had shown her such compassion and had displayed such strength on her behalf.

"Well, I doubt he has been called as much before by many, but I agree with you—that boy might be the highest order of rapscallion, but he has a heart that cannot be faulted. Unlike, I hasten to add, a certain Marquis whose name made you jump so."

Caro wanted to deny being startled, but that would only cause more questions. She remained silent and waited for Lady Etheridge to carry on. At this point, John Astley's breeches must have gone from the arena for Lady Rebecca began to listen to the conversation once more.

"I do not blame you for the reaction, if you have heard what I have. He is known to have accosted your half-sister at a gaming hell some days ago."

"Accosted?" exclaimed Rebecca. "I thought they were

having some sort of tryst. Aunt, I heard it from the Countess of Goring."

"And when did you start holding Lady Goring's information superior to my own? No, Lady Goring is mistaken. The gamestress was accosted by the Marquis, and apparently received a mark on her face from his violence. He was halted, however, before he could do anything too vile, and I'm told that it was the man of the faultless heart, young Mr. Felton, who separated the two. It was that gentleman who escorted Miss Angelica Worth to her carriage at the end of the evening."

"But I heard it was a tryst," disputed Rebecca. "Many people are saying so."

"So the Marquis would have Town think, but even loyal tongues wag upon occasion. I had it from my maid who is seeing the valet of one of the gamers who was present."

"My goodness!" Rebecca's hand went to her mouth, the story too debauched to appeal to her delight in saucy tales. "It is too horrid." She looked towards Caro, and as she did, those large dark eyes of hers caught at her friend's chin, and then, Rebecca's fingers dropped to touch her own chin at the point where she had seen Caro's bruise yesterday morning. A crinkle appeared between her fine brows.

"My maid has always been helpful with the truth in these kinds of delicate tales. It seems this Marquis is hardly worthy of your affection after all, Miss Worth."

Neither Caro nor Rebecca responded—they only stared at each other.

"Town is divided on the subject," pronounced Lady Etheridge. "Some assume the Marquis was forcing his attentions on Angelica Worth, some think a love triangle is the answer, while still others think it simply a quarrel between two lovers and a third party happened to come by."

Caro finally spoke. "I have heard nothing to confirm the

two latter ideas, Lady Etheridge. I do not think them true at all."

"Do you not?" Lady Etheridge's shrewd eyes watched her.

"How would you know?" asked Rebecca. In her voice, Caro could hear a yearning for the truth, and an unspoken question that Caro was not sure she dared to answer.

Before she could speak, the curtain at the rear of their box drew back and a man entered.

"Ah, Felton, we were just speaking of you a moment ago," said Lady Etheridge, pleased that another cook had been added to this overcrowded kitchen. Her eyes looked knowingly between each person.

Caro's colour rose and her hands twitched in her lap. Felton was here! And Rebecca was still waiting for her answer....

"All good things, I hope," said Felton in his charmingly relaxed manner, offering a bow to the women. "I was actually hoping to steal away Miss Worth for a few moments. I have something to discuss with her."

Caro looked between Felton and Rebecca, not knowing who it was safest to be with in this moment.

Rebecca made the decision for her. "You cannot speak with her alone, Felton—however *faultless* you are, it would be unseemly." She was coming back to her commanding self. "I shall attend on you both if you will release me, Aunt?"

"Of course, my child, but you will miss John Astley's next act if you are too long."

Rebecca nodded to her aunt and rose, placing a firm hand on her friend's arm and guiding her out of the box. Following Felton, they found an alcove in the corridor behind the box which gave enough concealment that they might converse unseen and unheard if they placed their backs to the arena.

Before either Caro or Felton could speak, Rebecca charged ahead in a whisper half-panicked, half-frenzied. "I'm no bluestocking, but I am able to piece bits of a story together when I must. I feel half insane for thinking it, but I've just heard that story from my aunt about the gaming hell, and then you"— she pointed to Felton—"appear in our box to speak to my friend...."

She paused, and in that moment Caro hoped beyond hope that Rebecca would not desert her. She could not bear to carry on without her plainly speaking, plainly shocking friend.

"Tell me the truth—are you Angelica or are you Caro? A black wig would be easy enough to don."

Felton, who up until this point had been a mere observer, finally intervened. "Caro, whatever have you been saying in my absence?"

"We shall come to you and your heroics in a minute," chimed in Rebecca, determined to get her answers before she was cut short. Her dark eyes confronted Caro. "You are one and the same, are you not?"

Caro's lips parted to speak, but her friend needed no confirmation to be convinced. "To think what that beast did! And you said not a thing. Oh, if only you had come to me before! Caro, is what I have heard true? Have you lost as much as three thousand? There is no time to lose—we must formulate a plan."

"A plan would not be needed," said Felton grimly, "if she had merely obeyed my direction and refrained from gambling again. Now her losses are greater and all owed to the Marquis. That man has more sharps for friends than a milliner has hat pins. It will be harder to right this now—no matter how fine the plan."

There was a pause and Caro finally spoke. "Plan?" Tears sprang to her eyes. She knew not where to look, what to think, what to say.

"Don't upset her," said Lady Rebecca, clucking like a mother hen. "Caro, dear, I shall get a kerchief, and then we

shall right this in spite of Mr. Felton's melancholic attitude."
Lady Rebecca left their conspiratorial huddle and disappeared
down the corridor into the box.

Felton turned back to Caro, and it was at that precise
moment, that James Worth made an appearance on the scene.

CHAPTER TWELVE

T he sight that greeted James Worth in the alcove of the corridor at Astley's Amphitheatre confirmed all the prior judgments he had leveled against his sister.

"Caroline," he said coldly to the back of the man in whose arms his sister appeared to be residing.

The couple moved apart and James saw that no limbs were entwined at this present moment—a lucky happenstance. He was not sure whether to be relieved or further disgusted. They had certainly been sharing an inappropriate closeness. At the sound of his interruption, two sets of bright blue eyes, one fierce, the other fearful, caught at each other.

"James?" whispered Caro.

Caro knew that voice. It was a voice she had not heard in two long years but one she had thought of often. A voice that had filled the world of her childhood. A voice she could remember scolding her without mercy shortly before it had disappeared from her life. Her body flushed cold and hot, a mixture of joy and fear overpowering her senses.

"James?" she whispered, half in pain, half in hope. In the storm of life which had broken upon her, a bright star had suddenly appeared beyond her bow. Would it light her way enough to steer a course to safety? She reached out her hand.

James stepped back as if repelled by the thought of contact.

"James?" she asked again in disbelief, seeing the youthful face of her brother disguised in the ruddy lines of a man of thirty. She had been observing his face and figure so intently that she had lost contact with his eyes, but on regaining it, she could see they still held the contempt they had displayed at their last meeting.

"James?" echoed Felton, clearly peeved that he did not know this intruder and, worse still, that he had chosen to come into their company at such a crucial moment.

"Yes." Caro did not look at Felton. "My brother."

"And apparently the brother of an illegitimate sister too?" said James coldly. "What immoral hijinks have you been performing whilst I have been away, Caroline?"

She had forgotten what it was like to be called by her full name. James had always referred to her so, even when they were children, and he did so now with no hint of the endearment she had hoped to hear. Why was he here?

"I see that you are in the same state as when I left you." His bright eyes moved suggestively between his sister and Felton. "You bring yet further scandal upon our family name without thought to consequences. Imagine my surprise when I berthed in London to find out I had not one, but two sisters roaming these streets, and one an infamous harlot and gamestress by all accounts? Is this your keeper, your protector?"

Caro could see Felton stiffening under the accusations which James was heaping upon them.

"I assure you, I am no such thing, though apparently there is a vacancy in that department which I assume you created— you are Miss Worth's long-lost brother?"

"Brother!" exclaimed a recently arrived Rebecca, a kerchief dangling from her raised hand. Caro took it. "Your brother is here? I thought him halfway across the world."

"Who is this woman?" demanded James, clearly flustered by being increasingly outnumbered.

"This woman," replied Rebecca, drawing herself up to her full height, "is Lady Rebecca Fairing, and I shall thank you not to take such a tone with me."

Caro was pleased to see James looked cowed at that. He shrunk a little before Rebecca's imperious manner and offered a belated bow.

"Such manners," said Felton, a little amusement in his voice.

"Indeed," corroborated Rebecca.

"You need your fan at the ready, Lady Fairing."

"Quite."

The absurdity of the situation finally dawned on Caro, and she emitted a high-pitched laugh.

"This is no laughing matter, Caroline!" barked her brother, regaining the authority he had lost momentarily before Rebecca's onslaught. "Your immorality has cost me one investor, and I shall not have it interfering with any others. Cease your antics, at least while I am in London, and we shall not have to speak again."

"Investor?" queried Rebecca. Had it been Felton who asked, James would have declined an answer, but Lady Rebecca seemed as if she would not brook any such denial.

"I run a trading company out of the West Indies."

"And you are only just come to London?"

James began to look uncomfortable at all the questions, as if this was not at all how he wanted this interview to go.

"Of course he is," said Felton, "for his sister was as surprised as we at his arrival. Are we to *enjoy* your company long in London? Or for that matter, this evening? As much as I love an alcove tryst, this is becoming a little busy."

Caro almost laughed again but was quelled by the frustration building in her brother's face.

"Who is this man?" demanded James. "Are you the Marquis of Ravensbough?"

"The Marquis of Ravensbough!" repeated Rebecca. "Of course he is not. How could you say such a thing?" She waited for no answer. "This is Mr. Felton." She looked at James' unfashionable clothes with something less than admiration. "You really haven't been in London long."

Felton put his hand out in greeting, but Caro was disappointed to see James turn up his nose at the gesture.

"I would more like to make the acquaintance of a dog on the street."

"I assure you my paws are cleaner." Felton shrugged and dropped his hand.

"Caro," said Rebecca, turning to the only silent person in the gathering. "Does he not know what has happened? For him to ask if the Marquis were in your company...he must be told."

"I do not want to know," replied James shortly. "All I came here to say was that Caroline should desist in her efforts to destroy our family name. It is making life difficult for me to say the least."

"Difficult for you?" Caro could barely speak above a whisper.

"Tell me," Felton cut in. "You are quick to accuse and rebuke, and though I care nothing for what slanders you lay at my door, I do for those you lay at your sister's. Where were you, pray tell, to defend her honour? The honour you chastise her for losing?"

James received the challenge with crimson face, hands shaking, teeth clenched. "I am not my sister's keeper," he ground out.

"So said Cain after he betrayed Abel."

"You darn cur! I will not be held accountable for her foolish decisions. Caroline,"—he turned to her, his eyes as cold as his voice—"I warn you. Following father's footsteps will see you ruined—or, more so than you already are."

He swung around to face Lady Rebecca. "My lady, I apologise for my language, and I suggest you take my advice and sever all ties with my sister before she ruins your reputation as she has hers."

With that James swivelled on the wooden heel of his leather boots and left.

"You should not have done that," said Caro after her brother had disappeared down the corridor.

"Why? If your father left you penniless upon his death, then he left you both so, and it seems to me that your brother is doing well."

"Penniless?" Rebecca looked shocked. "Caro, why did you never say? I thought—"

"That she was a woman of means? As did we all." Felton sounded annoyed. "But what she has failed to communicate is that her father died in the ignominy of gambling debts and she was left destitute by her brother. Why else would she have turned to gaming?" He turned to Caro. "You would not be in such a coil now if he had not deserted you—I have no doubt of that."

Caro did not have a response to that. It was true. There

was a part of her that yearned to be reunited peacefully with her brother, but at the same time, the shame he made her feel sparked indignation within her, and Felton's remarks were only fanning the flames.

"You should go." Caro turned to Rebecca. "My brother is right—if you continue to associate with me you will be ruined."

"Nonsense. That is the word my aunt uses when confronted by something she does not like, and as far as I can tell, though it is hard to understand all that has gone on, none of this is your fault. I do not like your situation, my dear, but you, on the other hand, I am very fond of. I must admit I am a little hurt that you felt you could not confide in me, but I shall not have your brother dissuade me on that count. Now, I do not mean to be flippant, but we must simply forget about your brother's return to London. It is neither here nor there in your problems. We must hark back to this plan we were in the midst of formulating before he arrived."

"You speak with such wisdom, Lady Rebecca," said Felton with a smile, "that I could embrace you."

"I would rather you didn't, however charming you may be. You should expect intelligent thoughts from an intelligent woman. Do you have any solutions?"

"Yes, I had one—for Caro not to game again until the scandal had died down. But as you know, she did not lis—"

"Oh, I do dislike people crying over spilt milk. Let us not look to the past but to the future."

"Why on earth do either of you care?" cried Caro suddenly making them both look round. "My brother himself has disowned me. You barely know me apart from the simple facts that I am a liar and a compromised woman. Why don't you believe him? Why would you care about me?"

"I always care about beautiful women," said Felton without pause.

Rebecca's brow furrowed. "My dear—"

"No, give me an answer!"

"Lady Rebecca, a moment." Felton's tone was compelling. Rebecca hung back a moment while Felton leant forward to whisper in Caro's ear. "I know that you are no one's mistress because of the look of fear upon your face at the Marquis' advances."

She coloured deeply, the heat on her cheeks so intense that she was sure Felton could feel it.

"If you were an immoral woman as your brother claims, I doubt you would have rejected such an illustrious man."

He came away from her a little and spoke so that Rebecca could hear once again.

"We can both see that you are a woman of honest character who has been pressed into a situation not of her making and has survived as best she could."

"Hear! Hear!" Rebecca came forward and took Caro's hands. "I should have cast you off as a friend long ago if I did not believe you one of the finest creatures. Other women my age are not quite so understanding of my blunt words and impetuousness. Who else would put up with me?" She chuckled.

The sound caused Caro's sombre face to crack, breaking into a smile. Against her wishes, tears stood proudly in her eyes.

"Mr. Felton?" The curtains to the women's box had been drawn back, and the formidable Lady Etheridge was staring at their gathering. "You have caused both of these women to cry," she said dryly. "You must be losing your touch, my dear boy, though not your looks I see." She unfurled her fan and wafted it gently towards the diamonds that rested elegantly on her neck. Her brows rose pointedly, and her mouth curled into a satisfied smile.

None of the party knew quite how long her ladyship had

PHILIPPA JANE KEYWORTH

been waiting for them. Caro had the distinct impression that she might have been listening for some time.

"Alas, yes," said Felton. "I'm afraid I am boring them both to tears, but I thank you for the compliment." He bowed, grinning.

"Well, stop it," she said, snapping her fan shut and pointing it at the young man. "I will not be gracious enough to allow you to rectify your ill behaviour, for you have had them for too long. Young Astley is back in the arena, and I am missing my companions."

"Of course." Felton bowed again to Lady Etheridge and then turned to his two female companions. "I shall call on you tomorrow Miss Worth, and perhaps I can trouble you to join us, Lady Rebecca? You are always such an amusing conversationalist."

"Amusing and *intelligent*," replied Rebecca. It was clear that the plan they wished to formulate would have to wait until the morrow unless they wanted yet another party added to those who knew the truth about Caro Worth.

"You are persistent, Mr. Felton, I shall give you that. Good evening." Lady Etheridge inclined her head and then beckoned the women back into the box.

"If I did not know any better, my artful niece," said the older woman as Rebecca's full skirts moved past her, "I should believe that there was some mischief afoot that I did not know about."

"I don't know what you mean, Aunt." Rebecca paused as she retook her seat. Then, from the corner of her mouth, without turning her head from the arena, she said, "But if I should chance to come across any mischief, you shall be the first to know before the Countess of Goring."

Her aunt smiled. "Very well. I am drawing my own conclusions. I so dislike becoming involved unless it is absolutely necessary. Stories are far more interesting if one has not played a principal role in them, so I shall leave you to play your part for the time being. Unless, of course, I deem it necessary for me to step into the breach in the stead of my sister."

Lady Etheridge took her niece's hand and patted it gently. "In the meantime, my child, let us enjoy young Astley's legs—they are looking at a fine advantage on the top of those Spanish horses."

CHAPTER THIRTEEN

C aro had been thinking on it all night. She knew that there was only one way to protect the honour of Rebecca and Felton, as well as the futures of Libby and John. The hackney passed through several streets known to Caro before stopping part way down one she had never been to before. She alighted at her destination, the windy day sending gusts against her red dress and fluttering the veil covering her face with its powdered and patched bruise. The first of her red shoes touched the pavement quickly followed by the other, and when Caro retracted her hand from the driver's she paid him and sent him on his way. She watched the carriage turn onto the busier street of Piccadilly leaving her alone in Clarges Street, a haunt made infamous by the person she intended to visit.

She felt profoundly alone without Libby chaperoning her, but it was necessary to protect the maid. She did not want the Jew King to know anyone else who would benefit from the loan she intended to ask for. That way, if she reneged on the payment, he would not come looking for them. Just for her.

Besides, her alter-ego had never needed a chaperone—it

was one of the advantages of being a ruined woman. She used to find it liberating, but in this moment, with her life on the rocks being pounded by a storm, she felt lonelier than she ever had before. She had not told anyone where she was venturing, and the caring words from Rebecca and concerned remonstrances from Felton felt very far away today.

She placed her hands in the fur muff and turned from where the carriage had disappeared into the busier street, beginning her walk to John King's abode. She had heard of him many times from the gamers she had won against. He was a moneylender and broker to the aristocracy, and she knew that many a man visited his house in Clarges Street to ask for loans after running too deep the night before. She had even known Lord Avers to do it, and the memory of his friendly face made this visit, despite her better judgment, seem like a good plan. She was sensible of the astronomical interest rates King would charge, but it was the only way to cover her debts and come out from under the Marquis' power.

On either side of the road stood large stone edifices, some built from red brick, others covered in crisp white facades, and all with small sets of steps leading up to pristine front doors. She looked for the door behind which King resided. It would be a short interview. If pressed, she might well have to show her face to him, but she had covered the bruise in enough powder that it did not show. She would ask for the money, put up whatever furniture was worth anything of value in her house as collateral, and receive the money. She hoped she could pay him off quickly. In fact, she had spent the majority of her wakeful night convincing herself it was possible. But the strength of her conviction could be measured by her unsteady step and faint breathing.

And yet, what other choice did she have? Her breath came stronger now. She must be resolute if she were to survive, just as she always had been, ever since she had been left abandoned.

It made everything so much worse that James had come back to London at this exact moment. Although his remonstrance had lit a small fire of indignation in her chest, she did not wish him ill, and this time there was at least some truth to his complaints. She *was* acting a dishonourable role, and it *was* impacting his business transactions.

It was a misfortune far outside of her intention, of course. She had only wanted to sustain herself and her household on the money from men who took their lot in life for granted so that she could secure her future. There had been no intention of damaging others in her plan, and now her very person endangered the reputations of those she would call friend—Rebecca, Felton, her own brother.

The thought steadied her step and strengthened her resolve. She *must* do this. After she saved Angelica from the flames, she would turn back to caring for Caro Worth's identity. She would pay off the Marquis as Angelica and hope it would be enough to stop his advances. She could only pray that he would not force himself on her further once the money was in his hands. But even as she prayed it, she knew how false that hope would prove—the bruise on her face was proof of what lengths the Marquis would go to possess her.

These sombre thoughts brought her a few yards from the steps that led up to King's house. She was about to go up to knock on the door when she heard footsteps behind her and laboured breathing. No doubt it was some banker late for work, a servant hurrying home from an errand, or a shop boy sent with a package for delivery. She had no desire to be recognised here, even as Angelica, so she refrained from turning her head. She moved over, her skirts rustling against the railings which enclosed King's house, and waited for the footfalls to pass. But pass they did not. Instead, the feet fell in step beside her.

She caught sight of the end of a cane flicking forward and backward, but that was all until she heard his voice.

"Why, Miss Worth, whatever brings you to this part of Town?"

The question made her jump, but the voice made her scowl. Her step faltered. She sent a frantic look to King's door —it was still within reach.

"Are you in a hurry? Can you not tarry with me a moment that I may bid you good morning and earnestly try to dissuade you from this unwise course of action?"

Caro turned her veiled face toward the interloper with a great deal of reluctance. "Good morning, Mr. Felton. This matter is not your concern." Even with the veil on she avoided his eyes. She did not wish to see the feelings which lay there. She could tell by the tone in his voice that he was more than concerned, that he wished to be here, that he wished to help, and she could not bear that she was betraying him again. "How could you even know I was here?"

"Lady Rebecca and I have been waiting for you for over an hour already. We were paying you a morning call as promised, Miss Worth. A wise person told me to think of what you would be likely to do next. I surmised from your worries last night over our involvement that you would try to solve this problem yourself, and as you are in debt to the Marquis, it did not take a fortune teller to realise you would seek out a moneylender."

"Well," said Caro, her hands sagging within her muff and a sigh escaping her, "you are quite the investigator. Apparently you know my feelings better than I do."

"Yes," he replied with a great deal of smugness. "And although you say it is not my concern, I think it odd that your step should have been so unsteady."

"The wind is up. Perhaps I shiver so much that my step falters."

"I do not think that the cause."

Fed up with these games, Caro was roused to sharpness. "Mr. Felton, please let me alone. This is the course open to me, and I shall take it."

"But you do not understand—"

"Nor do you!" Caro's words struck out like a knife, the frustrations she had felt at his interference over the last several days coming to the surface. "How can you possibly understand the predicament I am in when comfort and fortune are your privileges? Your high and mighty words are no currency for debt collectors. How am I to pay Ravensbough and his friends in order to protect myself? With your good intentions?"

"You attack me as if I were Ravensbough myself. All I have ever done is offer you help."

"But why?"

"I hardly think that is the question to be asking. Why not accept it?"

Now he seemed hurt, and for all Caro's frustration she began to feel a little guilt.

"What do you propose then?" she asked, giving in to the pained look upon his face.

The wind buffeted them both as it blew between the rows of tall buildings. It loosed some of his unpowdered hair from its ribbon, and he reached up his free hand to tuck it behind his ear.

"That you do not borrow money you could never pay back. That we take a hackney to your home now to meet with Lady Rebecca and think of another way out of this scrape."

"I cannot. I must go in to Mr. King's." Caro moved to sidestep Felton, but he moved as well, blocking her passage.

"I shall not let you, even if it means shouting down these streets and exposing your identity to anyone that may be passing."

Caro's mouth dropped at these bold words. "You wouldn't—"

"Dare? I assure you, madam, and I am sure several others would too, my actions are sometimes far from proper, especially when pushed to extremes."

"You are abominable!"

"And you are stubborn." The mischievous glint returned to Felton's eyes. "But let us not quibble." He moved to the edge of the pavement and raised his hand. A hackney that had been idling before returning to his stand took up the opportunity and roused his sleeping beast.

Caro remained where she was. Her hand had slipped from her muff, and she was too distracted to replace it. The clattering of hooves came closer. All the while, Felton faced Caro, his hand still raised, his eyes focused on the face behind the veil. When the carriage drew up, Felton greeted the driver, opened the door, and drew back to offer Caro a hand up. With no other option left to her, she huffed loudly, flinging out her arms in irritation and refusing Felton's assistance into the carriage.

Once the last of her skirts flourished through the carriage doorway, Felton took a deep breath and launched himself in after her. He fell into his seat, sent the driver on his way, and settled in to what was to be a most awkward journey.

"A good morning to you once again, Lady Rebecca." Felton executed a rapid bow as he entered the morning room before turning scrutinizing eyes upon Caro. "I would bid you another good morning, except that you do not look as though you have had a good morning thus far."

"You know I have not," said Caro, flashing venomous eyes at him.

"How ungentlemanly of you, Mr. Felton," said Rebecca. "I expected better."

"I have no idea why."

"There you go again, berating yourself, when I know as well as Caro that you are a hero."

"Enough of that nonsense—unnecessarily flattering a known cad is almost as bad form as telling your hostess she is looking anything less than beautiful."

Despite the situation, Caro's answering blush caused a twitch at the corner of Felton's mouth.

"Was she where you thought she would be?"

"Yes."

"I am right here," cried Caro in exasperation.

"Yes, and thank goodness for it. You needn't have tried to go to a moneylender, Caro. We will figure a way out of this."

Caro looked less than persuaded.

"It would have added trouble upon trouble if you had made it to the Jew King." Again Felton's tone flipped from amused to stern.

"Very well! I was wrong...according to you!"

"Perhaps you should be a little less hard on her, Mr. Felton. She is becoming upset."

"I am still here!"

"I would be too," Felton said, his harsh tones at odds with the softened expression in his eyes, "if I had thrown myself into the territory Miss Worth entered two nights ago." Now that they were safe away from Clarges Street, he seemed more and more agitated.

"What, a debt? Surely that is not such a bad thing? We must merely find a way of coming up with the capital. Between us all, we might."

Felton ignored Rebecca and fixed his attention wholly on Caro. He rose and stepped closer to her, but she could not bear to look at him.

"Why did you not do as I advised?"

Only one reply came to Caro's mind, but with it came shame and it bade her not speak. Could Felton not take his pick from the reasons she had shouted at him outside of King's house? Did she need to repeat them?

Felton, with a look of hurt upon his handsome face, turned back to Rebecca.

"Her debt is far worse than you know, Lady Fairing."

Caro felt a need to tell the truth stifled by the silence her shame forced on her.

"I heard it is run up to five thousand already," said Lady Fairing in a way that challenged Felton's superior tone. "Have you that amount or close to it in your yearly allowance?"

"No, I regret that I have spent through it and more since coming back to Town, and my father is soon to cut me off."

The admission should have shocked Caro, but the battle for justification was still warring within herself and the need to explain herself was winning out.

"It is not just a debt," said Caro quietly.

"Not just a debt?" echoed Rebecca.

They thought that money would untangle the knot, but they had to know the truth. They had to know how impossible the situation was. Her need to speak finally overcame the shame the truth brought.

"He asks for...for myself in payment."

Caro coloured so deeply she might have matched Angelica's red gaming dress.

Rebecca's mouth formed the shape of an "O" but made no sound.

"Devil!" exclaimed Felton.

"He will not relent, no matter how much I pay him. So you see, no matter what you do, I am ruined. Going to the Jew King was only to give me time to stave off the Marquis...I am ruined."

Caro stood up, walking over to the mantel to shake off their stares. She put a hand on the wood—the support seemed inadequate. Dizziness flooded her mind, and numbness crept over her extremities.

"Are you well, dear?" asked Rebecca, watching the unstable swaying of her friend. "Here." She held out an arm to Caro, and when the fair-haired woman did not respond, Felton took her firmly by the elbow and sat her back down.

"Get the housekeeper to fetch coffee," commanded Felton as Caro collapsed against his chest.

"Not smelling salts?" said Rebecca with raised eyebrows.

"Whatever! Just get her something!" Felton barked out the words while his hands cradled Caro's face, tipping up her chin. Lady Rebecca disappeared, leaving, for once, to do as she was bid.

"We can fix this situation," murmured Felton to Caro. Her eyelids began to flutter. "Where is the strong, indignant woman who makes a pastime of insulting me, eh?"

He let go of her face, but she fell back against him.

"I shall not stand for this. You are a fiendish woman, and I shall not see you becoming goosish now!"

His words did a good deal to bring her to her senses. She coughed a little and when she came fully back to the present was utterly embarrassed. Pulling out of Felton's arms as quickly as she could, she tried to stand. He would not let her and pulled her firmly back down.

"You may not wish to slumber in my arms, but I shall not let you fall to the floor either."

She barely had the strength to nod, but she sat still as she was bid, noticing that Felton did not remove his hand from her arm. It rested there, warm and sure, and in spite of herself she liked it.

Libby and Rebecca came in with coffee, the former carrying the tray, the latter directing its location.

"Thank you, Libby," said Caro, using all of her strength to speak. "I am quite recovered. You may go."

"Yes, miss, but here is a letter arrived just a short time ago. I had no wish to disturb you, knowing you was putting the world to rights with Mr. Felton and Lady Rebecca, but as I am here." She came forward and placed the letter in Caro's hand.

"Thank you, Libby."

A look from Rebecca prompted Caro to explain that Libby and John knew the whole.

"I suspect I was the last to know," said Rebecca, huffing into her cup of coffee and making the liquid lick up the edges. "I suppose it's no matter. Are you feeling better?"

"Immensely better, and immensely foolish. I hate to swoon in company." She ignored the look Felton was giving her and drank the warm, bitter liquid before turning to the letter.

"It is from your aunt, Rebecca, and it is...very cryptic. She asks us to meet her in the coffee room at the Grand Hotel where she is currently awaiting us." Caro looked up, the letter hanging from one hand, a puzzled look upon her face.

"There is more. I see a second sheet," said Rebecca.

Caro read it, turning pale.

"What does it say?" asked Felton.

"A new scandal has broken, and by now, according to most of London, Angelica Worth is the mistress of the Marquis of Ravensbough."

"What!" Felton thundered. Caro could see the veins standing out on his temples.

She continued to read. "The Marquis has told all his acquaintance that any debts Angelica Worth owes are now his and that the altercation in the hell was a lovers' quarrel."

Even as she said it, pain and fear contorted her face. "He has trapped me by the rumours. It's only a matter of time before I will be reeled in to his clutches. Everyone believes him.

Lady Etheridge has more news and begs me attend her, for the sake of my reputation as Caro Worth."

"We shall all go," answered Felton, already rising.

"An odd rendezvous to say the least, Lady Etheridge," said Felton, looking up at the stuccoed ceiling of the hotel and then across the regulated lines of rectangle tables up and down either side of the great room. None of the party were staying here at the Grand Hotel, and it was quite out of the way of Lady Etheridge's Town house north of St. James'.

"Odd?" said Lady Etheridge. "Your impertinence is less than endearing, Mr. Felton. Although I must say I have been most interested to see you again after all I have heard winding its way through the streets of London."

Felton bowed and helped seat his companions at the table butted up against the foot of one of the Corinthian pillars which separated the windows. He offered no apology for his statement, and Caro acknowledged the truth of it. It *was* an odd place to meet, quite out of the way—was there something more to the choice than Lady Etheridge was admitting?

"Ah, Miss Worth and my dear Rebecca, please partake of some cold ham, bread, and sweetmeats. I thought you had probably not eaten, and what I have to relate must not be heard or dealt with on an empty stomach."

"My lady?" questioned Caro, not ready for another set of surprises after the past few days. She wished Lady Etheridge would state her business this instant rather than keep her in suspense. "Please tell me the whole of what your letter gave the half."

"I shall, all in good time, but please do take a seat, dear girl, for you look as white as a sheet and thin as a rake. I shall see you eat at least three slices of ham and bread and five of those sweetmeats before I speak to you."

Caro looked around the table, surveying faces instead of the food spread before them. "Am I to believe that you have heard tales of my illegitimate sister or of myself?"

"Both," replied Lady Etheridge, a knowing look in her eye. She held Caro's gaze for a moment and then wiped away the look and repeated her entreaty.

"I do mean it—eat."

Caro reluctantly decided to obey, and though she had not felt hungry when she arrived, when she nibbled at a slice of bread and butter with ham atop to please her ladyship, she was surprised to find herself suddenly ravenous. She devoured the required three slices of bread and ham, pausing only to wash them down with large sips of coffee. The only waiter present refilled her cup. Lady Etheridge had commandeered the waiter for their table—she would not be attending the counter for her drinks as these younger patrons seemed in the habit of doing.

Caro, having finished her ham and bread, needed no second bidding to begin with the sweetmeats and, in a matter of moments, she was finished with those also. The taste of honeyed almonds mingled pleasantly with the coffee.

Lady Etheridge rewarded Caro's efforts with praise. "I declare you have quite changed colour, my dear—none of that snow white complexion you came in here with. I half thought you a ghost. The food and coffee has done you good."

As if to spread the compliments around, she turned to the only gentleman present. "Mr. Felton, I know I have already remarked on it at Astley's Amphitheatre, but I really do think you have become quite handsome with age."

"He needs no more encouragement to act entitled, Aunt," said Rebecca with more than a hint of temerity. "He is quite a saucy gentleman already."

"I thank you, your ladyship." Felton's eyes twinkled as he grinned at Lady Etheridge, happily ignoring Rebecca's words.

"If I were twenty years younger, if only—but alas, I must resign myself to watching you young people chase after each other without a sensible thought in your heads."

"Sense is overrated, my lady, where there is amusement to be had."

"Do you see, Aunt?"

"Devilish man!" said Lady Etheridge. "You have not changed a jot, though I perceive perhaps a little wisdom in those emerald eyes of yours, especially if you have been assisting this young lady as I have heard.

"And you, Miss Worth, do you value sense? I imagine you do if my letter brought you here today. I told Rebecca I would not become involved unless I thought the matter needed me, and so it does, I find. But let us not talk in here—it is far too hot for my constitution by this fire and...ah!" Lady Etheridge looked over Caro's shoulder, recognition lighting in her bright eyes.

Whomever she saw she made no attempt to hail them, however, and so Lady Etheridge carried on. "A walk in Hyde Park is always agreeable this time of day—shall we? My carriage awaits us, though it may be snug."

She swept a gloved hand toward the door and directed her party out of the establishment. Just before they exited the coffee room she leant toward a man at the welcome table, his quill scratching at the parchment before him.

"You will deliver my note. I believe the recipient has recently returned."

"Yes, Lady Etheridge."

The carriage ride was less than conversational, and they arrived at the destination as they had left their last, puzzled and silent.

"May I, madam?" Felton offered his arm to Lady

Etheridge who took it in a perfunctory manner, only the corner of her mouth betraying the pleasure she felt in being offered a handsome young man's arm.

Rebecca and Caro fell in with one another behind the others. They had only walked a short way before Lady Etheridge declared, "Excellent! Now let us find ourselves a bench off the main promenade, and I shall relay all to you."

Caro felt her heart flutter, and Rebecca responded to the twitch of her hand upon her sleeve by squeezing it tighter beneath her own.

"Perhaps, madam, you wish to tell me first?" Felton asked, turning his back upon Caro and Rebecca in an attempt to persuade her ladyship.

"Preposterous! You may be a young blade, but I have it upon good authority that Miss Worth is perfectly capable of dealing with her own affairs. You shall do very well as her assistant as you have done until now!"

Felton looked not a little amused, and Caro was torn between indignation at Felton's forwardness and shameful pride at Lady Etheridge's words. She had felt in control, in complete control of everything until Felton came into her life. Now she could hardly lay claim to capably dealing with her own affairs.

"Here is the very spot," said Lady Etheridge pointing to a bench. She swung the full layers of dress that hung elegantly from her bodice in a *robe à l'anglaise* style and seated herself. Even as an older woman she maintained an attractive figure. The others stood before her in a half-circle, ready to listen.

"Now, you read in my letter that, according to the Marquis, your alter-ego has become his mistress?"

"Her alter-ego?" queried Felton.

"Now, do not try me with your games. I may be old, but I assure you, dear boy, that I am no fool. Rebecca has, of course, given away more than she ought, but only at my coaxing."

"What, I? Hardly! I am as silent as the grave."

"Not where your worry for your friend is concerned. First I hear the story of Miss Angelica Worth's losses and the affair with the Marquis, and then my own niece is coming to me asking for money to aid her friend Caro Worth—what was I to think? I say again—I am no fool."

"Rebecca, you didn't?"

"And why shouldn't I? But it was to no avail, for Aunt does not have the funds to save you. I had thought her silence on the subject as it came to nothing could be assumed. Aunt, you really are being unbearable today."

"I pride myself on it, but that is not the topic of our meeting today. I asked you here—though not you, Mr. Felton. You appear to just be a hanger on—"

He smiled affably at that.

"—because," Lady Etheridge continued, "Ravensbough is besmirching your name, or at least the name you game with. He substantiates his claim by saying he has been footing your gambling debts."

"So you wrote to me."

"And so it is true. His name is in your debtors' ledgers, and by that he has gained his power over you."

"But I am not his mistress."

"But with such power he plans to force your hand," said Felton grimly. "The debt will be forgiven"—he turned to look at Caro—"only when you are given in payment." Felton's tone was too dark for polite conversation.

"Something must be done about that wretched man." Lady Etheridge stated unequivocally.

"Yes, indeed," replied Felton.

"It seems to me that your alter-ego Angelica has become a liability," said Lady Etheridge. "Is she necessary?"

"It is how she supports herself," Felton replied on Caro's behalf.

She looked at him then, and he caught her gaze, the look in his eyes telling her that he had heard her arguments before. If he had not appreciated her financial straits before, he did now.

"Of course, the gaming." Lady Etheridge waved a hand to clear her thoughts, ready for another idea.

At that moment a stranger happened upon the party from behind, and thinking he wished to pass by the bench, Felton and the two ladies moved out of the way. Lady Etheridge, who from her seat on the bench had doubtless been watching the man make his way down the path, had other plans, however.

"Ah, Mr. Worth! Come join us in devising a way to extricate your sister from the mess in which she currently resides, for you are as much a part of it as any of them."

Caro, Felton, and Rebecca all looked in turn, as shocked at Lady Etheridge's invitation as the man who stood before them.

"Me?" queried James, his lip curling in disdain.

"That is obviously why I left a note for you to meet us here." Her ladyship seemed genuinely baffled by James' surprise.

"Lady Etheridge!" Caro gasped.

"Yes?" replied her ladyship, the picture of innocence. "Here is the brother you kept secret, among other things."

"You cannot deny it, Caro," Rebecca said, but then took her eccentric aunt to task as well. "Aunt, you *have* been busy."

Lady Etheridge banged her cane on the gravel of the path in response, like a judge bringing a court room to order. "I heard you arguing at Astley's. At least, *you* did most of the arguing, young man." Lady Etheridge eyed James Worth. "And I declare it high time you called a truce. You youngsters need to be set on a path out of the woods in which you've lost yourselves."

"I am not aware we have met before, but, Lady Etheridge,"

said James, trying out the name his sister had used, "I am not lost in any woods, I can assure you."

She gave him a long, hard stare and finally replied. "Very well, but if your hard head should give way, and I suggest you let it, you could be of assistance in this situation." She nodded briskly at the still perplexed gentleman.

James bowed stiffly to all members of the party. But when he rose, he continued to stand there instead of taking his leave, saying nothing. An awkwardness descended upon the gathering as the young people sent furtive glances at one another.

Finally, Caro spoke. "Are you taking your leave of London, James?"

A flicker of confusion passed over her brother's face. "Not as yet," replied James. "I apologise," he said, coming back to his normal commanding self. "I believe I interrupted your conversation, but I wonder if I may have a private conversation with my sister?"

"It is inconvenient, sir, for we were in the midst of contriving a plan, and rude as well, I might add, as you have not deigned to help in the matter, but I suppose your claim of blood entitles you to it."

"Aunt!" Rebecca chastised her again, no doubt realizing that her own forward manner was as tame as a lapdog compared to Lady Etheridge's audacity.

James looked quizzically at her ladyship but said nothing.

As Caro stepped away from her companions, Felton laid a quick hand upon her arm. "Do not let his rebukes lead you to folly."

"It has already been proven that it is *your* rebukes that will do so," she shot back at him in an angry whisper.

The words hit their mark but failed to provoke the response Caro had been wishing for. A grin broke out upon Felton's face, and he slipped her one of his famed winks. "The fair-haired beauty with the barbed tongue—I surrender to you." He lifted his hand from her arm.

The brother and sister bowed and curtseyed to the remainder of the party before walking down the path and leaving the others far behind.

CHAPTER FOURTEEN

I t was not until they had walked quite some way that James
spoke. It was just before the fashionable hours of four and
five, and the park already hosted a large number of prome-
naders. They skirted several parties, keeping to the smaller
pathways, finally finding a secluded spot appropriate for the
subject at hand.

"You were formulating a plan with Lady Etheridge? What
was it for?"

"You do not know? A miracle—apparently everyone
knows!" Caro had intended to stay calm, but the ludicrousness of the situation made it impossible. All her lies,
constructed over many months, had been exposed in a matter
of days. How had things careened so wildly out of control?
When would the rest of London find out the truth?
Tomorrow no doubt.

She cast a sidelong look at James. She had thought of him
often since Astley's, of how she had missed him, and those
feelings had been mixed with sadness and frustration at his
stubbornness which had kept them apart. He had looked up
to her, and his idealised view of his sister, especially in contrast

to their wastrel father, had only built up the pedestal from which she might fall.

And fall she had. True, it was not in the way he had assumed. It had seemed suspicious, the high sums she had earned playing loo at card parties, but she had never been any man's mistress—no matter that James thought otherwise. Not that she had not been tempted once or twice in her more desperate moments. The idea of riches and security were appealing, but she could not break her principles so thoroughly. Once broken, those could not be mended—she had seen as much from others she had come across.

But James had been too young and hurt to hear the truth after their father's death. After seeing the worst of Lord Worth, he assumed the worst about her. And now, in the years apart, she could see he had grown harder, more black and white, with no room for understanding and compassion.

"You would not like to hear of the plan, or the need for it."

They walked a little further.

"Caroline, I can see in these years apart that things have not been easier, that they have gotten worse." He cleared his throat, looking straight ahead. "I have thought upon our last meeting."

She wanted to say she had too, that she had thought of him often, that she wished all this unhappiness to go away and for them to love each other again, as they had in their youth, but she maintained her silence, afraid that she might fracture the moment with her words.

"Every time I have thought of it I have felt ill over it."

So had she. Caro felt a glimmer of hope.

"I have come today to ask you one last time to turn away from the life you are choosing to lead. Come back with me to the West Indies. The place I live is far different than England, but it could give you a chance to start again, to resist the temptations you have succumbed to here."

He was going to go on. He did, but the words sounded farther away to Caro, washing over her in one long gurgling tide. The beginning of her brother's proposal had given her immense hope, a new beginning, but the end showed her exactly the man he had become—hardened and self-righteous.

Did he know what dire straits he had left her in two years ago? She, a woman with no fortune, no way of gaining a respectable income or match. Why else had she spent two long years cultivating this life for herself? A life she had worked hard for, a life she would not be giving up so easily, neither to a brother who did not know her, nor to a Marquis who only wanted to own her.

"I thank you for the kind offer, sir," Caro interrupted, alienating herself from him with the form of address. "However, you and I hardly know each other and, I believe, we would not fare well together."

James was startled. "But I am your brother."

"And so you are, but you gave up any pretensions to kinship when you left me two years ago, abandoned with no help." Caro spoke all these words calmly, a feeling of release finally descending upon her.

The same could not be said for James whose steady steps had faltered.

"How dare you! I came with an olive branch, and you throw it back speaking the words of that cad Felton to me! Am I to leave you then to your whoremonger, the Marquis of Ravensbough?"

Thankfully, most of the crowds had either passed by or disappeared down other paths. The raised voice of James Worth was lost amid the wind.

"And that is why," said Caro, her temper finally flaring, "we would never get on. You choose to believe the worst of me without allowing me defence or explanation. I may ask how you presume to bark orders at me when you choose to know nothing of me or my life. What brother abandons his sister at the hearsay of townspeople?"

James flinched, his stern face rapidly fracturing with shock and what Caro thought was shame.

"Am I then," said James after being forced speechless for a moment, "to believe you are *not* the mistress of the Marquis, as all the gossip says?"

The question offered the opportunity to finally redeem herself before her brother. Caro felt overcome. The stress and pain of the past few days flooded through her being, and tears began pricking at the backs of her eyes.

"How could you think that of me?" she asked in a hoarse whisper. "I am a maid, James, as I have ever been. Any money I have now is from the tables and from no man's pocket. The only gift our father bestowed upon me was the talent for cards, and look where that has got me." Several tears trailed down Caro's round cheeks.

The raw emotion on display before him seemed to rock James to his very core. All the sureness, the certainty he bore that kept his manner firm and foreboding began to fall away. His shoulders, so strong and proud, slumped in defeat, and the hands clasped behind his back came forward, flitting quickly on and off her arms in a manner of comfort.

He took a handkerchief from his brown frock coat pocket and offered it to Caro. She accepted it, dabbing her face and unintentionally revealing the bruise on her chin.

James frowned, but before asking any questions, he led Caro to a nearby bench. She arranged her large skirts to sit, and he sat down beside her. For a moment, he struggled to speak, and when he did his voice was low. "I did not know."

Caro did not look at him. She was silent for some time before speaking. "I am only happy you are here."

James smiled, the first real smile Caro had seen, and it

reminded her of him as a boy, fresh-faced and excited by the world, not determined to shun it.

"Libby and John are still with me, you know," she said, knowing it would please him.

"They trusted in you," he said, the statement implying much more than it said.

She did not respond to that but instead turned the conversation from herself.

"John is still as silent as ever, and Libby still makes it up for him. She is not above scolding me even though I am grown."

They sat there silently together, remembering the past, their youth, and the lives they had once spent together so long ago.

"My offer still stands—you may come with me to the West Indies, Caroline, and John and Libby as well."

A frown puckered her brow. "I cannot." She did not divulge more. If word of her booking passage to the West Indies reached Ravensbough, she highly doubted he would sit idly by and allow her to leave...but this moment was too precious to sully with the Marquis' evil.

"Has it to do with that mark?" James pointed to the place where her tears had washed her face powder away. His voice darkened. "Did someone do that to you? And what is your affiliation with the Marquis if I was so wrong?"

Caro touched her hand to her jaw feeling the exposed bruise. "I cannot be seen like this." She rose abruptly.

James got up to follow. "Caroline, tell me the scrape you are in, and I shall do my very best to right it."

"That is what we were trying to work out when you came upon us."

"Well, come on then," said James fetching Caro's arm into his own and pulling them into a quick walk. "You had best tell me the whole, and we shall confront the problem together."

Together. That was what James, her brother, had said.

Caro could hardly believe it, but she went with him all the same.

"I confess I have longed to try Libby's beef stew again."

She laughed. "So you shall."

His strength and sudden resolve carried Caro along. The wounds of their shattered childhood remained, but a bridge, however fine and delicate, had been built between their two lives.

In the distance, Caro could see Rebecca waving as they approached. Lady Etheridge lifted her cane in salute. Felton's arms were crossed and a pensive look upon his face, but when he saw her returning, he resumed his air of amused nonchalance. Caro had no doubt that as soon as they reunited with their party enmities could be laid to rest, explanations could be given, and a solution to all her problems could be contrived among them.

Lady Rebecca had insisted upon Caro's attendance at her aunt's card party. It would be a good opportunity for her to circulate in a dignified manner and thus quell the rumours growing about her alter ego. It must be seen that Miss Caro Worth was impervious to whatever scandal might surround her half-sister. Caro had no wish to be out in Society after the adventures of the last several days, but when her brother came out in favor of the card party to strengthen her good reputation, she gave in and agreed to go.

James, after learning the whole truth, was no longer brushing off his relation to her but openly declaring it. More than that, he was taking it upon himself to raise the money for the debts to Ravensbough for which he was in part to blame. The debt payment would stave off the Marquis until they could think of a plan to stop his advances—and at least the money was their own, not belonging to any moneylender.

Caro's relief at James agreeing to take on her debts had been great. She finally felt able to rest, and she slept for many hours until James arrived with his cases and trunks from the Grand Hotel to take up residence at her home for the foreseeable future. With the situation turned out so happily, Caro had no need to think upon or worry over her affairs immediately, only a party to attend to save face.

But though her own problems did not trouble her at this moment, the actions of Felton did. When she had returned to her party at the park and related the happy story of her reconciliation with James, Felton had remained silent. While James had unfolded his plans to sell off a part of his business in order to settle Caro's debts and to take up residence with Caro until a solution was found, Felton had refused to give his opinion. Whatever was troubling him, Felton had not been himself.

She had tried to catch his eye several times, but he would not allow it. It frustrated her. She had wanted him to rejoice with her that there was now a solution to her coil, that his reputation and Rebecca's had been saved, that all would be well once again. She had wanted to convey her gratitude that he had stopped her from going to King's that morning, from making a foolish decision which could have cost her this happy outcome. She had wanted to thank him for saving her honour, for defending her against violence at the risk of his own person, for persisting in the most irritating way imaginable. He had helped her in so many ways, but he had not looked at her once after James had returned.

As she stood in Lady Etheridge's drawing room, looking for Felton, she felt the need to thank him more keenly, for before long she would be gone from these shores and leaving him to his amusements and carousing. If all went to plan, she would be leaving London, her debts paid, both her names cleared, and would be heading for the West Indies with James. James had asked her again to start a new life with himself, John, and Libby for company. No more lies. A fresh start. And she had not yet shared the news with anyone.

That was why she was looking for the man who had saved her. He was her one hesitation in accepting the new life that lay before her. In recent weeks she had grown accustomed to his appearing at her elbow at the most inconvenient moments —offering an amusing and wholly inappropriate comment, saying something to cause her mask to slip a little, and then adding another word which would pierce through her armour and expose the truth in the way only he could. Despite her attempts at keeping him distant, he seemed to know her quite thoroughly. It would have shocked her past self to know now how much she would miss him.

"Here you are." James appeared at Caro's elbow and handed her a glass of Madeira. "Not as good as the stuff which I brought over, but adequate."

"Thank you," she said, taking it and sipping the sweet liquid. "But you had better not mention that to Lady Etheridge."

"Oh, but I shall. However else am I to grow my business if I cannot blow the horn of my own prowess in matters of taste?"

"My!" Caro smiled. "You have come far from the little boy who turned up his nose at his first sip of ale."

The corner of his mouth creased. "Aye, so I have." His bright eyes took in the rooms. "This is quite a swell of respectable Society. I see Lady Rebecca is no stranger to such popular parties." His tone was steady as ever, but his eyes were alert and keen as he looked over to Rebecca who stood talking to people of all shapes and sizes with an easy intimacy.

"She has been a great friend to me in a Society which judges by reputation rather than relationship." Caro spoke in wistful tones, too occupied by her own thoughts to see the look of interest in her brother's eyes.

"You will miss her?"

"Yes." She would miss Rebecca's plain speaking. She would miss her humour and the little female intimacies they had shared on points of dress and toilette. She would miss how steadfast a friend she had been in the face of all the vicissitudes Caro had undergone. To some degree, Rebecca had been the only one, aside from John and Libby, with whom Caro could be herself. How could one quantify such a relationship into a single feeling of missing her?

"Lady Rebecca." James bowed as Caro's friend moved towards them. The skirt of his newly purchased jacket, a far more fashionable garment than any he had worn thus far, flared toward the back, the point of his dress sword moving with him. "You are looking very well this evening."

"Thank you, Mr. Worth," said Rebecca, curtseying herself. "As are you. What a brilliant blue that coat is!" Rebecca, whose boldness before James had thus far been tempered by events, was now in full force. "It quite rivals the eyes your family lays claim to."

"I...thank you. They are inherited from our mother," he replied a little unsteadily. The compliment, spoken with such casual assertion and accompanied by the fine brown eyes of Lady Rebecca, was enough to fluster even the most resolute of men. When James' confidence finally returned, he had the good sense to escort Rebecca to a card game of her choice and partner her.

"A couple in the making, no doubt." Felton was at Caro's elbow, appearing in his usual fashion, and though he smiled his tone was somewhat flat and his eyes without their customary merriment.

"Rebecca and James?" queried Caro, her heart fluttering at his appearance but her head determined to carry on sensibly.

"She would certainly be a match for his serious nature with her raucous humour." As if hearing the far-off words, Rebecca burst into rolling laughter, her eyes sparkling while James smiled with a distinct look of admiration in his eyes.

"And you are to be made quite eligible again." Felton's voice turned oddly husky. Caro's heart continued its rapid beat.

"Will you finally make the match you craved?"

"Oh yes," she said, suddenly desirous of lightening the mood. Her tone turned mischievous. "I shall be hanging out for a husband of title and fortune." She waved her hand at the crowd. "None of these...." Her boisterous words trailed off as she realised to whom she was speaking. "I am sorry," she said suddenly, "I did not mean."

Felton's face had turned hard, but he brushed off her apology. "No need. My father says the same—younger sons are useless. I must admit, I had hoped...I had planned...." He didn't go on. "But it is no matter. You are reunited with your brother, and no doubt you will be married off within the Season."

The words were spoken with such bitterness it shocked Caro. Coarse talk she had become used to in gaming hells, but Felton's words were not coarse—they were raw with unspoken emotion. It grieved her to see him in pain, and she felt a corresponding ache to his sorrow. She swallowed. As long as he was already angry she might as well tell him her news.

She tried a rallying tone again, hoping this time to choose better words. "It is possible, however, James shall be searching for my potential husband in the West Indies once we have left London."

The words hung in the air like raindrops suspended, their full impact still to come.

"I am to bid you goodbye?" His eyes were inescapable, the tone disbelieving.

Caro cringed, hating the look on his face. She had spent enough time with this man that she could discern when he hurt—when he clutched a wound no one else saw, hiding the trails of blood and shrugging off attempts at compassion.

"I only go with all the gratitude my heart can bear towards you. If not for you...." She faltered, her hand raised, her gloved fingers touching the embroidery of his coat for a brief moment. "You have saved me, sir...Mr. Felton,"—she corrected herself, a small wan smile accompanying her misty eyes—"and I shall never, as long as I live, consider the man who has shown me what a true gentleman is, to be useless. Saving a life from ruin can at least be added to your list of accomplishments. Perhaps you should tell your father that." She smiled again though a lone tear had found its way down her cheek.

"Caro, I...." began Felton. His finger came up to touch her cheek and then catch in a curl of her golden hair. His voice was thick and his usually overconfident tongue halting, delaying over the words.

That hesitation cost him dearly.

Across the room of card tables, a commotion gained the attention of most of the players. The ornately carved door-frame of the fashionable London house welcomed a most unwelcome visitor to the party. At least, he was unwelcome by five of the guests—the other twenty or so gawked, their eyes alternating between the newcomer and Miss Worth. Shock turned to relish as a scandal began to unfold before their very eyes.

It was a splendid thing indeed for the people of London Society to be thrown into the midst of an ongoing scandal. Any respectable gentleman or lady would of course deny the excitement—it was unattractive to appear preoccupied with the *on-dits* that crossed the bounds of propriety—but when such a tasty morsel lay before them as now, it was impossible to feign disinterest. The respectable Caro Worth was about to meet her bastard sister's keeper.

Lady Etheridge, whose duty it was to welcome new guests, should have been flummoxed by the arrival of a person she had not invited, but it was not in the nature of this formidable woman to be flummoxed. She rose gracefully, and in no degree of hurry, and greeted the late arrival with clipped severity. "Lord Ravensbough." She offered him no curtsey or even a nod. "I marvel at your ability to find a party to which you were not invited, being the fashionable man in London that you are. But, as you are here, I suppose you shall have to join us." She made no effort to speak to the Marquis' companion, Mr. Rivers, who entered behind him.

Several of the waiters and maids paused in their duties to smirk. Their mistress' punctilious rudeness was no surprise to them. None of the guests remarked on Lady Etheridge's comments—she was well known for her honest speech—and the Marquis of Ravensbough appeared to take no offence. He was all amiability as he took her ladyship's hand and flourished a bow over it.

"You are too kind, my lady. Fortunately, I am come with a guest you did invite—ah, there she is, Miss Worth." The Marquis dropped Lady Etheridge's hand and walked towards Caro, his face an open smile beneath which lurked dark intentions.

Caro hardly knew what was happening. Her face was stricken, and as he neared, her breath became ragged and her heart raced. The ranks drew in around her. Felton placed himself slightly before her, his shoulder in front of her and his body facing the latecomer. On her other side, her brother's strong presence reappeared. But despite the reassurance of these two men, her breath continued to shorten, and all the muscles in her body froze as they were.

As the Marquis approached, the attention of the rest of the room was diverted to an ornately plastered alcove in the corner as someone struck up a tune on the spinet. Felton thanked Lady Rebecca's quick thinking and her quicker fingers which beat mercilessly on the keys, forcing all attendees to listen to the noise and ignore the meeting of opposing forces.

"Ah, Miss Worth," said Ravensbough, now denied the undivided attention of the audience he had desired but finding pleasure in his purpose nonetheless. "Such a kindness to invite me this evening." He was trying in vain to gain access, but Felton would not give ground. "My confidant, Mr. Rivers." The second gentleman did not respond to being presented.

As the music grew louder, James' temper grew hotter. He thrust a foot forward, leaning into the Marquis. His height rivaled that of the aristocrat's, but his fair hair was an ironic contrast as light vied with the dark.

"You darned cur! If ladies were not present, I'd have you whipped in the street for the dishonour you have brought upon my family."

Felton put a restraining hand upon James' elbow.

"Me, dishonour your family? I believe you have it quite wrong. You are the long-lost brother, I presume? It appears you are quite unaware of your bastard sister's gambling debts. She has been the one dishonouring your family. Oh," said the Marquis, lounging on one foot and delicately plucking each finger of his white gloves to reveal pale, long-fingered hands, "the trouble out of which I have had to dig your poor half-sister—you should be thanking me."

"I should strike you where you stand!" ground out James.

Felton's hand tightened on his arm. He could not let James give the game away, the dual identities—it was all that protected Caro, and already James had alluded to the way things really stood with his accusation of dishonour. The Marquis seemed not to have noticed yet. He was enjoying the conflict he caused too much at present.

"In front of all these people?" queried the Marquis, a delighted smile licking its way over his lips. "I shouldn't think your family's reputation could afford it." He had a stranglehold over the Worth siblings, and he knew it.

As he watched the pleasure of control course across Ravensbough's face, Felton himself began to lose patience. "What do you want, my lord? You can see that the sister who owes you these debts is not present. Why come with false stories of being invited here by Miss Worth?" The line between Caro and Angelica must be sharply drawn, and Felton must be careful to tread it precisely.

"How do you know I was not?" asked the Marquis in lazy tones.

"I did not invite you." Caro finally spoke up though her voice was small and her hands shook behind Felton.

"Ah, the virtuous sister speaks, and as I came to converse with her, not her guard-dogs, I am pleased."

Caro's breathing came fast. Ravensbough's figure loomed large behind Felton's shoulder. They would not leave her—she could not bear the thought of being without her so-called guard-dogs.

She could see Ravensbough's dark jacket and those pale hands with their claw-like white fingers. She could remember them clamping around her arms. She screwed her eyes shut to destroy the image and then flung them wide open again, afraid he would make a move when she was not looking. As she did, her blue eyes looked into the darkness of his and took in all the lust and malice that lay there.

"What do you want of me?" she heard herself asking, though she could not feel her lips moving.

"*Of* you? Well, it is quite simple really. I wish you to tell your sister that I expect her to come to me for the payment of her debts, in one form or...another. I have been waiting long enough for her reappearance, and I grow impatient."

"And if her half-sister does not choose to see you?" asked Felton, cutting in.

"Then,"—Ravensbough's eyes turned impossibly darker, and his face contorted with malice—"I shall ruin this sister." He pointed a long white finger at Caro.

"How can you?" Felton countered. "Her reputation is spotless."

"My word against some common little doxy with a wastrel dead father? I think we know who the Ton will believe. With one sister fallen, Society will easily believe the other is not far behind. A few choice words sprinkled by myself and Mr. Rivers and the rumour mill will do the rest of the grinding for me. Just imagine the damage it will do to your little business, tradesman." He looked at James whom he—or Mr. Rivers—had apparently researched thoroughly.

"You would not dare!" raged James.

"And tomorrow I shall be calling in those debts I kindly hold for Miss Angelica Worth, for she has failed to keep up her part of our bargain. No doubt my creditors will chase the gamestress to my door, or perhaps you"—he looked at Caro—"if the creditors cannot find her. One sister or the other, bastard or not, it does not matter to me. They are equally agreeable, and I will not settle for nothing."

"You cannot do this," said James. "We are her protection and shall not fail her."

"Not protection enough from Society's tongues. Do you really think you can protect your respectable sister from the vicious lies that will spread through Society? I warned Angelica Worth, as Mr. Rivers is my witness, and now I am being kind enough to warn you."

No one replied.

"I expect to see one or the other in Duke Street tomorrow. If a Miss Worth arrives by evening, I shall forbear from calling in the debts."

The threats laid, the ultimatum given, Ravensbough replaced his gloves, smiling all the while and allowing short bows in farewell. To any outsider, the group looked as though they had enjoyed a friendly conversation.

"Alas, a former engagement takes Mr. Rivers and me from you, my lady," said Ravensbough, bowing to Lady Etheridge on his way out.

"As you were not invited, I can hardly promise that your company shall be missed," replied Lady Etheridge, pursing her lips and following the Marquis of Ravensbough's departure with her beady, but relieved, eyes.

As she looked back at the party to whom the Marquis had been speaking, she could see something was wrong. Yes, something was very wrong indeed.

CHAPTER FIFTEEN

The card party, thanks to some uncharacteristically inhospitable words spoken by the hostess, broke up at a reasonably early hour. Lady Etheridge sent her servants around to fold away the card tables and remove the glasses scattered about the room, and then turned upon the stragglers from the party—Felton, James, Caro, and Rebecca—who were standing about in various attitudes of despair. "To the drawing room," she ordered, sending them ahead of her and only pausing long enough to ask her butler to send up the good brandy. She was certain her young companions stood in need of it.

Upon entering the room, Felton, James, and Rebecca grouped together about the fire in intense discussion whilst Caro stood further off, staring at the dark green drapes drawn against the night outside.

"Now, an explanation of what has happened, if you please," commanded Lady Etheridge. "It has been most irksome having to entertain my guests when something has happened unknown to me. I have never wished one of my own parties to be over so soon before!" She took a seat by the fire which still burned well in the grate, fed by her attentive servants, and spread a hand, beckoning them to draw near and begin.

James, bursting with emotion, disclosed the whole, including every insidious threat the Marquis had uttered. A short silence followed the exposition, and then, as if the gates of Hades themselves were flung open, chaos ensued. A cacophony of dismay, indignation, and rash solutions filled the room. Only one voice was not among the chorus. Felton's tenor quickly dropped out as he stared at Caro's small and defeated back.

The room was less well-lit than the card room. Shadows leaned in from the corners, creeping close, waiting to envelope those within. Caro looked as though she were fading into the darkness. Her fire, her spirit, had taken too many blows.

As Felton separated himself from the arguing group, he could feel the despair that overwhelmed her. Her escape to the West Indies had not been something he wished, but better that than the look of weariness in her eyes. As he came to stand beside her, he could see that her clever evasions, her artful cunning, her careful planning had all ceased, and in its place was only a look of brokenness.

She stared ahead not turning to greet him. He did not expect her to. Standing shoulder to shoulder, he reached out a tentative hand till his fingers found hers and her cold hand was taken in his own, hidden behind the folds of his frock coat and her evening dress.

"We shall find a way out of this," whispered Felton, a hoarseness in his voice. "I shall not leave you forsaken."

"I wish that you would," she said, not removing her hand from his.

He felt her fingers tense and then tighten, as if thankful for the contact, before she drew the hand up until she could hold it in both of her own. "You should leave me now, Mr. Felton."

She addressed him formally, and he felt himself loathing it. "You have been all that is a gentleman to one who is less than a lady, and I thank you for it. Though I may not have shown it, I hold in my chest a grateful heart. But you must leave me now —I am to fall by way of a scandal, and I would that I did not take you with me." Her hands trembled still clasping his tightly, and then she released his hand as though that settled all matters, however reluctant she was to let go.

Felton's jaw flexed.

"I am not jesting, as is my habit, when I say that you are wrong. My leaving you will do neither of us good." He jerked away from her abruptly before she could reply and went to rejoin the group gathered about the hearth.

The hubbub continued as Caro found herself walking slowly about the room. She went forward and then came back again, her mind half-absent, her body acting unconsciously. Why would Felton not leave? What did he hope to gain? The only answer she could find was one she did not believe. He *did* not. He *could* not!

She glanced at him, taking in the strong chin of his profile, the easy curve of his mouth, and the brilliant green of his eyes. His hair was tousled and coming loose on his shoulders. As she looked at him, she felt a stirring in her stomach. A warm ache filled her senses, but she pushed it away.

She was only harm to him, and she found herself caring too much for him to want to cause more. She felt her heart fracture again just as it had when she first determined to leave him for the West Indies.

"We must leave now—tonight," said James.

Felton's voice came in hard. "A foolish action. Creditors— some, not all—shall cause you trouble through their related businesses in the West Indies. Your business would flounder, Mr. Worth. You could not support yourself let alone her."

"You don't know the state of my business," James replied stiffly.

"Indeed he doesn't," said Lady Etheridge, "but the man does have a point, Mr. Worth. You would be taking Caro's ruined reputation with you. The West Indies may be far off, but they have a Society of sorts, and the *beau monde* of the Indies is only ever a few months behind London news. If only you had escaped before tonight! I would have counselled you so if you had shared this plan. The Marquis could have ruined Angelica's reputation, but not so easily Caro's."

"It was a family matter." The stiffness was still in James' limbs and voice.

"No doubt he would have destroyed both regardless," said Felton.

"I do not understand why he must be so heartless," said Rebecca, wringing her hands and showing a little of her vulnerability beneath the confidence that always cloaked her.

"Neither do I." James' awkward manner softened.

"Some men have maddened with the reason of this age," said Felton, "rationalizing any deed that causes pleasure regardless of the damage it causes others." Caro saw him looking her way as she paced the room. "And he lost against Caro—both in game and in heart. The Marquis does not like to lose—I have heard as much of his character before, though I had no idea he would go to such lengths to destroy a lady with connections to quality."

"It will not damage him to destroy Caro," said Lady Etheridge, with more insight than most, "which is why he does it so willingly. He has too many friends in Town and can never be ruined as a woman could be." She looked sharply at Felton and then James. "Wishing and hoping does nothing to the past. We must find a way out of this coil."

"Indeed!" James exclaimed enthusiastically if a little curtly. The zeal soon died away however, as no plan presented itself in his mind.

The group lapsed into thoughtful silence, tapping fingers, scratching chins, wringing hands. Some eyes stared into the hearth, looking to the fire for inspiration, other eyes were directed towards the stuccoed heavens, whilst still others roamed from figure to figure, hoping that another had contrived a plan which boded well for Caro.

A few words passed between Lady Etheridge and her niece, words producing comfort rather than any ideas. The low murmur hid the looks that passed between James and Felton, and the ladies barely noticed when the gentlemen struck up a conversation in a corner of the room, separating themselves from the women for a time.

The candles burnt low in the wall holders. A servant came in to bank the fire and paused to ask if anything was needed. When he left, Lady Etheridge coaxed Rebecca to sit down and take another sip of brandy. She looked at Caro sympathetically. "She simply stands. Will you not ask her to sit?"

"She will not," said Rebecca.

"She should."

"Look at her face; she believes she is the one to blame. She has caused all this—or so she thinks."

Lady Etheridge pursed her lips and adjusted herself in an agitated manner on the sofa. "Society may think her actions debauched if they were made public, but Society has a way of being inexplicably stupid sometimes! She has done a great many things through necessity and has managed to keep her virtue— with no one to turn to, mind you—until now. If Society accepted rather than shunned a strong woman, Caro Worth would be a fine example. Whatever happens tomorrow or in the future, you shall not hear reprimands of Miss Worth upon my lips."

Rebecca's deep brown eyes filled with admiration at her aunt's powerful words. "Nor mine." She took hold of her aunt's hands, feeling the soft, wrinkled skin. "But what shall be done?" she sighed.

Lady Etheridge nodded toward the corner where the gentlemen were still deep in conversation. "I believe," said Lady Etheridge, a sudden, almost imperceptible smile appearing on her lips, "that that particular gentleman has no intention of seeing her ruined."

"No, thank goodness, although he still seems a trifle frosty —it is good they are friends again after all these years estranged."

"Oh, no," whispered her aunt, "I was not speaking of her brother. No, indeed, *he* will do everything within *his* power to protect her, and I suspect he shall not let her go so easily to the West Indies afterwards."

Rebecca, whose eyes for this sort of happening were usually very acute indeed, stared at the corner wide-eyed. She had become distracted by all the dramatic events of the past few days, and while she had wondered before about Felton's affections, those thoughts had been swept away in worry. Now that she looked afresh upon him, she saw what her aunt saw— a determination, and it was a determination born undoubtedly from love.

"I wish you would stop acting the fool and just marry the girl," said Lady Etheridge with enough force to make Felton splutter on the brandy she had provided him with.

"Don't be so wasteful," she chastised him, taking the glass out of his hand and setting it down on the sideboard. "That was my husband's best French brandy. Roderick often sat and drank a glass with me in times of need. Young people today are quite unappreciative of the better things."

"Lady Etheridge, what do you mean?"

Felton stood with her ladyship by the sideboard in the card room. The tables had been packed away, and the rest of the gathering were still in the adjoining room, but her ladyship had asked for his help in bringing some liquid courage back to the others.

Felton had thought it odd that her ladyship refused to call a servant for the task. He also thought it odd when she had demanded he immediately drink the glass she poured for him before they returned to the others. Now he understood a little of her motives.

"Oh, don't be so coy, young man. I do detest people treating me as a senile old woman. I have as quick a wit as any person of one-and-twenty, and in case you are quite as unobservant as you are obtuse, I am not blind."

"Obtuse? Lady Etheridge, what you suggest is—"

"Scandalous? Come now, young man, you are quite as well versed in scandalous talk as I, and you know that people like us are inclined to say things which have truth in them. We hardly ever bother saying things that are just ridiculous—though it has been known. The notion of you marrying a woman you clearly care for in order to save her is rather clever."

"And how," said Felton, gaining his bearings and glancing back to reassure himself that the others were still a room away, "will that save Caro?"

"Urgh!" Lady Etheridge finished pouring the rest of the drinks and took up a glass herself, sipping at the amber liquid. "They call *me* old! Tell me, is there anything between your ears, Tobias? I know your mother, and I am quite sure she and your father have excellent minds—how could you have ended up without one?"

Felton couldn't help smiling. This woman's wit was as wicked as his own, and her idea called up feelings which had, up until now, been held in check, tempered by circumstance. What was it he would have said to Caro this evening had the Marquis not arrived and spoiled things? Even as he suppressed the answer to that question, he knew very well what it was.

"My lady, I bow to your superior mind." And he did so, mockingly, causing the woman amused irritation.

"So you should, you cad, but I was in perfect seriousness. I only came in here that I might avoid the censure I would otherwise have drawn from my niece at being so plainly spoken. So I say it again without fear: you must stop your dancing about the matter and offer for her."

"I fail to see how marriage to a younger son of no fortune could save her. Besides, I am unsure that she would...." For the first time since he could remember, he felt the heat of embarrassment in his cheeks. "What I mean to say is...."

"You are unsure she returns your regard?" Lady Etheridge's sharp eyes were upon him as she finished his sentence. "That woman is bewildered by the situation she finds herself in, yet she remains one of the most striking women of my acquaintance. The ability to drag herself up from the depths of despair and build a life from nothing is remarkable. I doubt we shall see another woman like her in our lifetimes. Hardly the sort of woman to pass up, don't you think?"

She eyed him over the rim of her brandy glass, taking another sip. Then he watched her draw back a little, making a slow circle of the card room to the music of humming voices in the room next door. He did not know a great deal about Lady Etheridge. She was an acquaintance, one whom his father had always called an eccentric and whom his mother always enjoyed.

"My late husband always said of me that I was quite the

oddest creature." A faint smile played about the older woman's lips as she echoed Felton's thoughts. She skirted a chair, passing worn hands over the back of it, carrying on her journey around the room. "And so many people thought it an insult. I think it was dear Roderick who made me known as the eccentric most people see me as today by saying such things. But they never heard the statement that accompanied it."

She had made a circuit of the room and was coming back towards him now. The brandy glass was drained, and he wondered if some of it had gone to her ladyship's head, if that was why she intended to tell him a lover's secret which had up until now been locked between two souls alone.

"He also used to say that it was not in spite of my eccentricity that he married me—quite the contrary—it was because of it. He married me because he would not find another woman like me in his lifetime."

She discarded her glass, removed his from his hand also, and took both his hands in her own. She looked deeply into his eyes, hers older and wiser than his, wishing to impart something which she considered so very important. So very sacred.

"And as eccentric as it may appear to intervene, I cannot stand silently by and watch two people whose lives are made to intertwine, veer in opposing directions. This is a crossroads, young man, one which shall dictate the rest of your life. It is a turning point, and the course you sail by afterwards will never be the same.

"Ah, yes, the marriage will not solve Caro's problem completely—you, despite what I have said, have brain enough to work out the finer details—but I will tell you, it should start with you marrying that girl."

Felton was captivated by this woman now. He was enthralled by the sharp eyes, the handsome, lined face, her imperious figure, the truths she exuded with such beauty, and the perplexing message which overhung all.

She looked up at him, the feeling almost bursting from her eyes. "Roderick and I spent the happiest twenty-seven years together that any human being could spend with the soul of another." She suddenly released him and turned away. "We may not have been blessed with a family—everyone has their own battles to wage on this earth...no paths run smooth—but we were always with each other, always happy. Do not let that opportunity pass you by, or more fool you."

The end of her speech came in a clipped tone, the tone that all Society knew, the tone that spoke amused and shocking truths. She swept towards the bell and pulled it, beckoning a servant to come and carry the tray of drinks through to the adjoining room.

Their moment of confidence was over. She had bared her own truths to him, regardless of her own pain in recollection, to advise him. A plan began to form in Felton's mind. The pieces of the puzzle were coming together. He knew what to do.

CHAPTER SIXTEEN

"I have a plan, but I will need your permission." Felton spoke to James in low tones.

They had parted from the group after obtaining the courage-filled drinks, which Lady Etheridge's servant had brought in, and now stood conversing quietly so as not to be overheard.

"Permission? I wish I could easily give it for whatever you can think of to get us out of this cursed coil...however, the fact my permission is needed is concerning." James' brow furrowed deeply, and his bright eyes cast a serious shadow. What was this fellow driving at?

"I would not give it so readily if I were in your position either." Impatience sounded in Felton's voice. "Hear what I propose."

James hesitated. "You have been of such service to my family that I can't help but trust you. I will hear you out."

Felton seemed struck by this pronouncement of trust. He continued to outline his proposal. "It requires a false-hood, but one small by comparison to previous lies used." The man paused, as if debating how to put it. Then, shunning caution, he spoke directly. "I wish to marry your sister."

James, whose serious face had been eager for revelation, grew even more sombre. "You wish to marry, Caroline?" He looked across the room to the figure of his sister and lowered his voice even further. "I had wondered over your interest in helping her...but why? When she is in such a predicament surely a man of your stature—"

"—should run?" Felton looked almost amused. "I have had no intention of doing so for some time, despite your sister's best efforts at encouraging my desertion."

James' gaze remained steady. "I cannot give my permission for something Caroline does not want."

"What Caro wants and what she admits she wants are two very different things. I mean no offence by what I say next." Felton paused and directed a look of earnestness to James. "You have been gone from England for two years. I have been intending upon marrying your sister for some time now. I ask your permission as it is correct and you are here, but I should have done so without it if you had not returned. I believe, in the absence of your presence, your sister has become increasingly lost. If we can but persuade her to marry me, we can enact a plan that will set all to rights, protect her, and serve my somewhat selfish ends by allowing me to marry a formidable woman with whom I have fallen in love."

"Persuade her?" James believed in the man's earnestness. Felton's eyes seemed honest in the feeling they portrayed. He cared for Caro. But his own sister's heart was harder to read....

"I cannot presume to know your sister's feelings for certain. I hardly think she would admit to them for fear that her troubles might affect me. Her selflessness is one of her more frustrating qualities, I have found, but just as my heart is sure of itself, I have a strong hope in hers."

James was not entirely satisfied, but Felton's plan seemed

worth exploring. "And if she agrees and I give my permission, how does that get her and our family out of this scrape?"

"We will have to spread abroad the story that we have been engaged for some weeks secretly, waiting for your return from the West Indies before we announced it to Society. We have been seen much in each other's company which will add verisimilitude to the story, and Rebecca can vouch for it as Caro's friend."

James felt an innate aversion to the public nature of such a plan, but he could see its value. "It could work, but it relies on two factors; first, that Caro will say yes to you, and second, that Ravensbough believes you."

"It is the former I have more fear of," Felton replied lightly with a forced grin. "Like I said before, your sister is formidable."

"But you realise what you are asking of yourself? You risk much—you are sure of your feelings?"

"The task I take upon myself is no task at all; my certainty is complete. I will fight for your sister until her safety is gained whether you agree to this plan or not. Her welfare is my uppermost concern. It has been for some time," Felton added, almost to himself.

James listened in silence as Felton unfolded the remaining details of his plan. He was used to measuring situations, to making decisions of business, but never had they involved hearts, happiness, and an entire life. Felton was watching him intently—no doubt he could see James' mind at work, weighing the circumstances and evaluating the costs. James had only known Felton a few days, but in that time he had proved himself not only valiant but honourable. Lady Etheridge trusted the man—she seemed to hold an indulgent place for him. Even Lady Rebecca, who was a plain-speaking and sensible, if somewhat passionate individual, seemed to trust Felton thoroughly. Could James also?

He had seen the looks that passed frequently between Felton and his sister. He had plumbed the depth of feeling in Felton, but he was not sure he had the same insight into Caro. James looked for Caro in the room and saw she was already engaged in observing the gentlemen. What was that in her eyes when they looked at Felton? She had surely already shown a partiality towards him, as the man himself had said; she shunned help usually, but she had accepted Felton's.

Then again, how far could feelings enter into the subject? The situation was grave, and Felton's plan was the only solution that presented itself to save the Worth family's honour and to rescue Caro from destruction.

Finding resolve at last, James turned back to Felton. "You will promise to love my sister and put her happiness above your own? I could not agree easily without such a covenant. She has suffered much at the lack of care that has been shown her." James tried hard to hide his pained expression.

If Felton saw it, he made no indication. "I promise."

"If you do not, I shall feel justified in forcing Ravensbough's fate upon you, and though I may look like some poor merchant,"—he leaned in dangerously close to Felton, his eyes suddenly alight with the same fire Caro's frequently showed— "I trust you will believe I am fully capable of bringing you to justice on my sister's behalf."

Felton seemed to repress his amusement at James' warnings and voiced his understanding with solemn tones. The men shook hands, the plan finally agreed on, and turned back to the ladies present to tell them, at least in part.

"We have come up with a solution," announced James, his tone less than celebratory.

"Subject to your consent of course," added Felton, his green eyes flicking over Caro.

Caro nodded and drew near, finally acquiescing to Rebecca's request for her to sit.

"What is it you suggest?"

"Caro, the heart of your predicament is your reputation, not the debt," said James, deliberating upon each word and speaking with the clear-cut pronunciation that so reflected his character.

"We are suggesting the casting off of your gamester alterego. Angelica Worth, as Society now knows her, must disappear."

"Disappear?" queried Rebecca.

"Yes, to the continent perhaps," supplied Felton.

"But how will this solve the problem if the Marquis of Ravensbough has threatened to ruin Caro also?" asked Lady Etheridge, an impatient look in her sharp eyes.

"Caro Worth will be above reproach." James hesitated. Caro shot him a glance, waiting for the rest of what he was to say. "Caro Worth will have been secretly engaged to marry Mr. Tobias Felton these past weeks, and when that is come out and the news of Angelica's flight, Ravensbough will have no power over you."

"Engaged!" exclaimed Caro, shooting up from her seat, eyes blazing, the woman that Felton had come to admire so much. Gone was the frail and defeated creature and in her place stood some kind of Amazonian. "I am to marry?"

"Felton, yes." James' tone was more certain than before. He did not intend to give any ground. Felton's plan was their best chance.

Caro turned on her would-be fiancé. "I am to marry you? This is ridiculous."

Felton bowed ironically, imbuing his words with sarcasm. "Aye, Miss Worth. I am no Duke or elder son, but I am a solution to your present predicament."

"I can't marry you. James, how have you forced this upon him?" Caro's eyes flashed at her brother before she rushed over to Felton.

The late hour was beginning to show, even upon her beautiful features. Her hair was coming loose from its fastenings, and her dress was wilted. But her eyes—oh, how her eyes shone! They pleaded with Felton and in an undertone, so did her words.

"I told you to go. You want no business with me—this plan will ruin you."

Felton could feel her breath warm upon his face.

"It was Felton's idea," James said, not hearing Caro's words. "And it is the best chance we have to save your honour."

Her eyes widened at first and then they narrowed.

Felton, predicting the explosion Caro was about to let loose, saw only one way forward. He spoke quickly and in soothing words, even putting his hands on Caro's arms. "You need me to extricate you from this coil, and when it is done we may break the engagement—we must only wait for a safe amount of time to pass."

James shot Felton an alarmed look which the young man happily ignored. He kept his gaze upon Caro's blue eyes, firm and reassuring, willing her to trust him.

"I cannot enter into such a falsehood."

"My dear." Now Rebecca stepped forward. "I realise your hesitation, but—and do not be angry, my friend—you are no stranger to deception." Her words were bold while her eyes were soft and coaxing. "This particular falsehood can save you and, as Felton says, may be undone at some later date. Though it is all quite in the style of romance," she added quietly with a small smile.

"My niece is quite right, as are the gentlemen," said Lady Etheridge. "Angelica Worth must be sacrificed to the continent and Miss Caro Worth sacrificed to this young cad." Her eyes twinkled, their gray matching the powder of her curls. "I trust he shall not be found without virtue."

"You are too kind, ma'am." Felton grinned back, bowing ironically again.

"Urgh!" Caro threw her hands up in the air, exasperated by what she perceived to be madness surrounding her. "You plan and you jest whilst I have not even given my consent. I may trust your word to release me, but I can hardly entrust myself to a plan that shall surely cause your reputation's destruction! You will be shunned by polite Society for entertaining such uncivilised company."

"And what do I care for those who would dare hold such an opinion of me?" Felton said in mock-challenge. He could feel her objections beginning to weaken. "One benefit, which I have only realised lately, of being a younger son in an aristocratic family is that you are almost expected to be a disappointment, whether in your poor-choice of career, your shocking lack of fortune, or your choice of an infamous wife."

"There you go again, jesting," huffed Caro, stomping about the room, the short train of her *robe à la française* sweeping in her wake.

"Seriousness was never my forté, Caro, as well you know." The teasing grin was suddenly wiped from his face, leaving sombreness in its wake. "However, I speak in all seriousness now; I am offering a way out of this scrape. If not for yourself, then for your brother, your family name, and your friends, I charge you to accept this plan."

Caro looked from the earnest face of Felton to all the faces surrounding her in eager anticipation. Rebecca showed compassion, Lady Etheridge a certain amount of sharpness, and James looked solemn indeed.

"Very well," Caro said at length to a cacophony of relieved sighs.

With that, the slow motion which seemed to have come over the house, lifted. Everything now hastened like an errand boy. Rebecca offered to stay with Caro, but her aunt advised against it until the scandal had died down, and Caro agreed with that piece of wisdom. James reassured Rebecca that he would look after Caro now that he was lodging in her Town house.

Felton reluctantly seized on this moment as a suitable time for departure. Caro had not been able to take her eyes from him since agreeing to the plan—what was she thinking? Felton did not know. He showered affectionate but hurried goodbyes upon everyone present, his presence only lingering when he kissed Caro's gloved hand.

Then, as Rebecca bid good night and Lady Etheridge unceremoniously shooed the people from her presence, Felton departed, darting quickly out of the door and into his waiting carriage, leaving Caro utterly confounded and destined to be more so on the morrow.

"To what do I owe this unprecedented pleasure?" Viscount Felton asked of his younger son. "For surely this early hour was not known to you before today."

Felton allowed a smile onto his lips and resisted the urge to correct his father by saying "to whom," for it was a *whom* that had brought him here today.

"I concur," was all that Frederick offered. Felton, unappreciative of the offering, did his best to ignore his elder brother.

The Viscount clasped his hands behind his back. "Your mother and I can well recall our last conversation. Are we to hear the result of your actions on behalf of the mysterious woman you spoke of?"

There was a certain eagerness in his lordship's face.

Felton's mother, who was seated resplendently upon the chaise longue, rose to offer her hand to her son. "Oh yes, my dear boy, do tell us—your father and I have been discussing it since our last visit with you, and we have both been very anxious to hear the outcome."

"Mama," Felton came to his mother and kissed her proffered hand. "You are looking as well as ever."

Lady Felton, a good ten years younger in age than her husband *was* looking well. The *robe à l'anglaise* she wore was made up in a particularly becoming pink floral cotton, and the lappets of a matching cap rested upon her head of natural curls. Laughter lines lay about the sides of her ladyship's gray eyes, and that ever present twinkle, which she had passed on to her younger son, could be seen as she gazed upon him.

"I see that my life has become as interesting as the newspaper columns to my parents," Felton teased, smiling at his mother affectionately. He kissed his mother's hand but refused to sit as she offered, preferring to remain standing for this interview. He had chosen an emerald green suit for the occasion. It was an outfit he knew his mother liked, and he needed all the goodwill he could gain.

"Well, newspapers do report the best scandals," replied his mother in equally mischievous tones.

Viscount Felton sighed, no doubt awaiting this silliness to end. Frederick merely looked toward the fire, as he always did —he had not inherited the spirited nature of their mother by any means.

"It is on the business of scandal I come to you," said Felton, his tone turning serious.

"Of course it is," said Frederick.

"At such an hour?" demanded the Viscount. "What on earth have you been doing this early in the morning?"

"No time of day matters to him, Father. Even in the

respectable surroundings of the eccentric Lady Etheridge he finds mud to spread on our family name."

"Hush, Frederick!" implored the Lady Felton, desiring peace between her two sons in the place of the antagonism.

"In answer to your question, my lord," Felton, carrying on as if his brother had not spoken, "it is not what I have done but what I intend to do."

The Viscount's face was like a storm, ready to break, the thunder colours gathering to turn their glowering gaze upon those below. "Anne, perhaps you had better leave us." It was more of a command than a suggestion.

"I certainly shall not! And you needn't speak to me in such severe tones, John. I am quite able to hear the troubles of our son."

"Troubles indeed!" exclaimed the Viscount, knowing that trying to remove his wife from the room would now prove futile. She was as stubborn as a mule when she wished it. Yet another of her endearing traits she had managed to pass on.

"Out with it, boy! What trouble are you intending to cause?"

Felton took a breath and exhaled, bracing himself for the onslaught. "I am going to marry."

The plain statement caused even his imperturbable brother some shock. Frederick's jaw dropped several inches, and he stared open-mouthed at Felton.

Felton's parents met his news with silence. Neither the Viscount nor his wife could quite comprehend what they had heard. They stared in surprise at their son before eventually turning to one another, as if they might derive an explanation from there.

It was his mother who finally spoke. "Did I not say to you, John, he is in love—did I not?"

"In love?" scoffed his brother, to which no one answered.

The Viscount refrained from speaking for a few moments,

and when he did, instead of responding to his son's news, he corrected his wife.

"I believe that's what *I* told *you,* my dear." He rubbed a hand over his face, his fingers massaging the puffy skin beneath his eyes, and when he let the hand fall, it knocked the side of his wig causing it to go askew. Before he could correct it, Lady Felton was upon her feet and gently coaxing it into place, murmuring something to her husband as she did so.

"Married?" queried his lordship as he waved his wife away from him. "I never would have thought you likely to gain the sense to marry."

"Sense is overrated, I grant you, my lord. However, in this lady's case, I am wont to make an exception."

"And what lady is this?" asked the Viscount, beginning to circle his son with planned steps.

"Yes, what lady?" echoed his elder brother, never too far behind his father.

"Miss Caroline Worth, my lord. I asked her brother's permission just last night."

"You did, did you? And what of the arrangement? She has no title, but does she have a fortune? And what was this business she was caught up in only days ago? Is it settled?"

"It will be, my lord." Felton paused, a mischievous grin appearing on his lips before he took command of his countenance. "I have merely to fight a troublesome duel, and then I shall be wed to my betrothed at her earliest convenience."

This time, rather than silence, Felton's provocative words conjured indignation with a hint of incredulity.

"I knew it!" Frederick's voice was raised in triumph at his brother's embarrassing entanglement.

"A duel! What the blast do you speak of?" shouted the Viscount.

"Perhaps our son is a trifle disguised," offered Lady Felton, gesturing towards her husband to still his now-manic pacing.

"I would not be surprised," said the elder son. "He is undoubtedly drunk as a wheelbarrow."

"Frederick, that is not helpful," said his mother, chastising him.

"I assure you, madam, no drop of alcohol has passed my lips this morning," replied Felton with equanimity.

"I'll be dashed dead if I let him speak such folly before you regardless of his state," shouted the Viscount, simultaneously speaking to wife and son.

Felton bit back a hasty reply.

"Shall I remove him, Father?"

"I ask you," said the Viscount, ignoring his eldest son and striding closer, aiming a condemning finger, "to tell us plainly. What do you speak of?"

"I speak, my lord, of a duel I must fight in order to defend my future wife's honour. A slur has been cast upon her name which, if gone unchecked, will do irreparable damage to her reputation."

"I doubt the virtue of her reputation very much if a duel is necessary in the first place."

"Miss Caroline Worth?" remarked Felton's mother. "Is that not the girl with an illegitimate gamestress for a sister?"

The Viscount swung round at this. "Anne! I declare you know far more about our son's dreadful behaviour than I thought. You almost sound pleased. Are you happy he is causing such troubles?"

"Oh, my dear," said Lady Felton, not getting up but raising her hands imploringly towards her husband, "you know I am as displeased as you; however, our dear Tobias has never quite trodden the perfect path. Should we not be happy he has found himself a wife and will defend her honour like a gentleman?" She swivelled in her chair, suddenly thinking of something pertinent. "But you will not kill the gentleman, Tobias? For then you shall have to go off to the continent, and that will be a most turbulent start to married life." She shook her head against the potential future.

"I only wish to gain satisfaction and with it an end to his slanders, Mother," answered Felton with a tone that was for once soothing rather than antagonistic.

"Oh, good."

The Viscount let out a cry of anguish at his wife's calmly spoken words. "Good? This is too much! Have you both gone mad?"

"No, Father, but I can assure you I am most certainly in love, and no manner of persuasion will sway me from my current course. My only purpose in coming here this morning was to apprise you of my bride's identity and give you fair warning of the duel."

"Oh, how very thoughtful of you, my son," snapped the Viscount. "Most respectable sons would not gad about fighting duels!"

"Indeed," corroborated Frederick, solidifying his position.

"My lord—" Felton's tone and expression became one of all earnestness and his words those of honesty. He ignored his brother and came to the pacing Viscount, forcing him to stop, and bowed low before him. "You have been wishing to teach me responsibility these many years. Well, I finally have a desire to take some upon myself. I have found a woman whom I wish to take responsibility for, and I am aware of the task, the work needed. I have disappointed you in many ways, but if you can, I would ask for your blessing."

The speech was well-spoken and, in its own way, beautiful.

Lady Felton stayed very still, awaiting her husband's answer.

"My blessing? You troublesome child, how can I give you such a thing when you are to fight a duel?"

The words were worse than a physical blow would have been at such a moment. Felton's jaw clenched tightly and his body went rigid. He bowed, first to his father and then to his brother and mother. The latter's face wore a mournful expression.

"I understand, my lord," said Felton coldly, his voice laced with bitterness. "I am sorry to cause you irritation, but I must do what I believe right. I only hope that one day you may relent and meet Miss Worth, for a stronger, finer woman I have yet to encounter. Until you forgive my actions, I shall refrain from imposing my disappointing presence upon you.

"My lord," he said, his voice barely above a whisper. He bowed again, bid them all good morning, and left. In his wake a gaping hole remained. It was as though a part of the atmosphere had been taken away.

Lady Felton sat very still, but soon a few silent tears were falling from her eyes. She pulled a handkerchief from her pockets in the midst of the capacious floral gown and dabbed gently at the tears.

"I am sorry, dear Anne, that he should upset you so. I cannot think what has come over him, but I fear he is going to be lost forever after this business."

"Oh!" cried Lady Felton, standing hurriedly and patting out her skirts beside her vigorously. "It is not our son that upsets me but you!"

"I?" exclaimed the Viscount.

"Yes, *you*, husband. How will he ever win your approval when he does just as you ask—he finds a wife and decides to act as a grown man—and still you will not be satisfied?"

"I shall be happy when he does not cause such a ruckus!" said her husband indignantly.

"And you, Frederick," continued Lady Felton. "You are just as bad! Not once has he chastised you when you have fallen, but you are constantly at his throat for every mistake he makes. Imagine that from an older sibling who knows more of the world than he can!"

"Anne...."

"He has always been unconventional, John," she said, not allowing her husband an inch. "And to think I may never see my daughter-in-law, all because you are so intent on casting him off!" Lady Felton was raising her voice now, her anger overcoming her sadness.

"And what would you have me do?"

"I would have you fix it!" cried out his wife before taking a few deep breaths and calming herself down.

"Can you not see, dear John, that our boy is in love and, better than that, it is to a woman who brings out the gentleman in him. For once let your heart rule your head and make this right." She finished by clasping her husband's hands between her own and squeezing them tight. She placed a kiss upon his cheek and then on the cheek of her eldest son and left the morning room.

CHAPTER SEVENTEEN

F elton stepped down from his family's Town house to be greeted by the first few heavy drops of what would prove to be a heavy downpour. The skies were burdened with gray above, hanging so low, they threatened to catch themselves on the chimneys of London's buildings. The sun hid itself behind the clouds, and in swept a cool wind, making Felton pull tightly the Garrick coat his valet had insisted upon. He hugged the railings cutting off the houses from the street, his fractured thoughts skipping over his feelings like the raindrops scattering themselves upon the cobbled street.

He had expected better. He had hoped for at least a little support when he had stated his intentions. He should not have hoped, have longed, for approval, or for even a satisfied word from his father. His mother understood. Perhaps she sensed what Caro felt—perhaps she knew what it meant to be a woman in need of a protector.

Felton flicked his cane out before him, the clatter and scratch a welcome sound. His frustration would not abate. A duel could not have come at a better time. If it would not affect Caro negatively, he would happily kill that wretch of a man. For a moment a part of him wanted to, if only to anger his father—why worry about making matters worse when there seemed no hope of salvaging the Viscount's good opinion?

Stupid! He flicked out the cane again, this time catching the metal tip upon a groove in the paving slabs. The splintering of wood could be heard. He had used more force than he realised. The cane split, only a few shards of wood connecting the two halves.

"Curse it!" He stopped, endeavouring to straighten out the piece of polished wood and only succeeding in tearing the two halves completely asunder. He held them, one in each hand. It would have been comical had they not reminded him of Caro and himself.

What was he thinking? Would this plan even work? Did he need to abandon it now, see Caro and her brother off safely to the continent and take no backward glances? He had felt so sure yesterday—he had felt so certain. Caro was so broken— he had wanted to mend her, to keep her...but did she want him?

He felt like shouting, like crying out. He needed guidance —he needed confirmation from God. If his father cast him off, what good would it be marrying Caro? What could he offer her? Neither money nor title. Only himself.

He was walking again now, the two halves of his cane still in each hand. He turned a corner into another street, making his way to his next port of call—but would his resolve hold? Was he still going to do this? The image of the broken, splayed piece of wood was still before him and in his mind.

He wanted Caro—he wanted her body and soul. The notion which had been birthed at the card party and encouraged by Lady Etheridge had only been confirmed by the thoughts that kept him awake all last night. His pace quickened, the steady stamp a marching beat. He wanted her. He wanted to save her, and he wanted her for his own. She was the only woman he had ever wanted in this way, to this degree. He rounded another corner—he was almost at the hell.

He wouldn't kill the man. He wanted a life with Caro, with his father's blessing or not, and he could not give her a life if they were running away from the gallows. All he wanted was satisfaction.

The downpour which had begun with a few heavy drops now came thick and fast. If he could not gain his father's approval, he would at least be sure not to let Caro down. Once he had fought this duel, he would persuade her, beg her if needs be, to marry him. She loved him—he was sure of that, even if she was not. They would marry, but first Felton needed to gain satisfaction.

As he rounded the next street corner, he saw James come into sight, waiting outside the hell, his sombre attire at odds with his demeanour. He was pacing back and forth, his hands perpetually clenching and unclenching. Felton watched him reach into his pocket twice to check his watch. Apparently, Caro's brother was as anxious as himself over the whole affair.

James had been waiting outside the hell for the past quarter of an hour. As Felton came into sight, he finally felt somewhat calmer. He was about to unleash a tirade of uncertainties, like a list of ailments, upon Felton, desiring a dose of encouragement in return, but the expression on Felton's face stopped him.

The young gentleman looked murderous. At first inspection, his hand seemed to be carrying two sticks for beating, and his purposeful stride would cause anyone to think twice before engaging in conversation with him.

"Felton," said James, taking a step back. He felt that

bidding him good morning was not appropriate under the circumstances.

Felton caught himself, as if remembering something. "Caro—how is she?"

"Worried," replied James, relieved that he was not on the receiving end of Felton's mood. "I left her at home expecting Lady Rebecca. Lady Etheridge will call in the afternoon. Hopefully she can maintain calm when the news breaks—half of London shall know by teatime. This is the part of the plan that I find the most repulsive, I hasten to add."

Felton nodded grimly.

"Felton?" James removed the look of distaste on his face. "I realise it's a bad time to ask this, but—are you any good with your sword?"

Felton's mouth broke into a grim smile. "Good enough. Let's go inside and be done with this."

James touched his arm as he began to move off and gestured to the sticks in his hand. "Not an appearance which will benefit our situation."

Felton shook himself. "Ah, my cane has seen better days, it appears. Best I leave these outside"—he dropped them by the railings—"lest I beat Ravensbough senseless when I come upon him."

It was said with a hint of humour, and suddenly James was happy he was with this man. He would certainly not wish to be against him.

The interior of the hell was even darker than outside. The inner doors were manned by an impressive servant whose height would dwarf the majority of the persons entering. Felton, without his broken cane, still had his Garrick and hat to bestow upon the man, but he refused the servant's request for his garments.

"I shall not be staying long." Then, as if realizing he must present an affable appearance in order to gain entry through the two bolted doors to the room above, he said, "We are just come to pay a debt held by our friend the Marquis of Ravensbough." Felton looked to James for confirmation.

The merchant nodded. "He should be expecting us." A hint of irony could be heard in James' voice, his indignation rising.

"'E's not told me to expect you," said the doorman. "Mind, 'e 'as been in a glee mood all morning. Says 'e's waiting for a message for an arrival at his 'ome, one 'e's been expectin' for some time." Evidently Ravensbough's drunken state was encouraging loose lips. "But I knows you, Mr. Felton, so your entrance is no worry. Who be your friend?"

The doorman with the large scar on his face leaned closer to James, though the smaller man did not back down. A sudden desire to defend his sister's honour gave him strength. If all Caro had spoken was truth, of which he had no doubt, the blackguard within these walls must learn that retribution awaited anyone who laid a hand upon his sister. He had lost her for two years through a misunderstanding—now he would show how wrong he had been, how much defending her honour meant to him.

"James Worth is my name," he replied, confidence in his voice.

"Worth...no relation to Miss Angelica Worth by any chance?" asked the bruiser, his face suddenly softening.

James was slightly taken aback by the ruffian's changed attitude. "Yes."

"Ah! I've been missing Mistress Worth. No sparkle, not without 'er."

James was about to take exception to this comment when Felton stepped in.

"Joey, I presume?"

The servant nodded.

"Miss Worth speaks very highly of you indeed." Felton spoke warmly, offering a hand to the man. Joey took it, his own coarser hand swallowing Felton's.

"Which is why," Felton continued, coming closer and lowering his tone, "I shall tell you I am about to cause quite a ruckus."

James felt alarm at this. Was Felton trying to sabotage the plan?

"I am here to call the Marquis out on Miss Caro Worth's account."

"Oh," said Joey, his face looking thoughtful. "Oh, I sees. Well, I guess 'e is owed a debt after his treatment of Miss Angelica, though I don't know what 'e's done to Miss Caro Worth. I 'ear things," Joey murmured, knowing he should not be speaking so. He was paid for his discretion as much as his protection. "And I ain't one to speak ill of my betters, but what I 'ear of 'im ain't good." He paused, releasing Felton's hand, and then stepped aside to allow both the gentleman passage.

Felton nodded his thanks. "Good man."

They banged upon the doors and were admitted through one set and then another, the bolts scraping back as though the doors scratched an itch on their other side.

"You remember what we decided?" asked Felton, turning mid-step before the final threshold leading through to the gaming rooms.

James nodded. He had rehearsed the plan in his mind constantly since they had devised it at Lady Etheridge's.

As they stepped through the doorway leaving the last of the hired men behind, the room opened out either side and before them. James could see the walls of Monsieur De Sauveterre's establishment were mostly hung in wood with any gaps taken up by jewel green paper whose flocked surface reflected the light of the scattered candles in regular patterns. The heavy brocade curtains were pulled shut, and above, a plaster-moulded ceiling was lost in places to the dim light. The hell was like a cave, harbouring all manner of evil in its dim depths.

James had limited experience with such places, but he recognised that the men at the various tables were serious gamesters, those for whom pleasure had become a habit and habit had become a need. This extravagant itch played on their minds like drink, intoxicating them with wins, forcing them to play again and again for bigger stakes to satiate their appetite more fully. Just as his father had done. A twinge of guilt lanced at James when he thought of Caro being driven to a place like this.

The tables were not full, and Felton pointed out Ravensbough to James almost immediately upon entering. The Marquis was playing whist at a table by one of the windows. It allowed him, whenever he pleased, to tweak the curtains open and look at the street below. He was watching for someone, no doubt a messenger who would never come, hastening to inform him about the arrival of a woman who was safe elsewhere.

He did not look for James and Felton, however, which made James think he had missed their entrance. He could see Ravensbough's partner nervously perspiring, eyes darting at his cards and then at his opponent, hoping he had the better hand. He could remember his father looking so at the private gaming parties he had organised. How James looked forward to putting this world behind him once and for all!

Though there was a general lack of spectators in the establishment, the Marquis' table had attracted two men who lounged just behind the noble himself. If Caro had been here, she would have identified one of the gentleman as the card sharp Mr. Rivers—the man who had tricked her with his pretended inebriation and won, along with Ravensbough's help, three thousand pounds from her.

Felton wasted no time. James followed him as he headed directly for Ravensbough's table. Felton's step did not falter. His Garrick coat flared out behind him, raindrops flying off the sides and spattering players as he passed.

"Ah," called Ravensbough, seeing Felton and James approach. "Good evening, or is it morning, Felton? I never can tell in these cursed dark hells." He leant back in his chair, his dark eyes moving over Felton's form and briefly flitting to the man following behind. He could not have appeared more relaxed—as though he were not blackmailing a woman, as though he had not handed down an ultimatum that could ruin a life.

"I have not come to exchange pleasantries, Ravensbough," spat Felton, all the fury that had been gathering finally being given a focal point in the Marquis' face.

"Oh, then why are you here?" asked the Marquis laying down his cards and leaning casually back in his chair, his dark, attractive features made ugly by his thoughts.

"I am come to speak to you about Miss Worth."

The Marquis' thin lips curled up into a smile.

"You have dishonoured her name."

The Marquis let out a bark of laughter. "I say, Felton, you have developed a *tendre* for the female gamester. Well,"—he looked briefly at his well-polished nails—"I saw her first. You are too late to offer for the position of her keeper."

The young gentleman stepped closer. James could see his arms shaking with fury. His face soured as he prepared to say what they had agreed. Both James and Felton knew there was only one Miss Worth they could save.

"I am not speaking of Miss Angelica Worth—I am

speaking of Miss Caro Worth, a lady of quality and one whom you have dishonoured."

"Dishonour the sister of a whore? Tell me, Felton, just how is that possible?"

James watched Felton leap forward, his fingers gripping the folds of the aristocrat's cravat, his hands sinking in about the Marquis' throat. The two men either side of the Marquis made to stop Felton, but Ravensbough raised a hand halting them.

Felton's breath came fast, saliva flicking out from his mouth, his breath hitting Ravensbough's face.

"The woman you have sullied and will sully with your words is my betrothed. I should kill you right here for what you have done."

"And yet you cannot." The Marquis emitted a wheezing laugh. "So just what do you intend to do?"

James touched Felton's arm, and the young gentleman threw the Marquis back in the chair, releasing his cravat and with it the chance to throttle him using that garment.

"What do I intend to do?" Felton asked rhetorically. "I intend to call you out." A crease appeared to the left of Felton's mouth. His upper lip pulled back revealing a white crescent line of teeth, and his green eyes glinted at the sight of the Marquis' surprise. The hair that had freed itself from Felton's ribbon was loose about his ears making him look half-mad as he stood smiling at the aristocrat.

But, even with his sanity questionable at this precise moment, James saw before him an impressive man. To sacrifice and defend for one's own blood was commonplace, but what Felton was doing for a woman of whose affection he could not be certain, was something more than honour—it was selflessness. Felton loved Caro—James had no doubt of it.

James stepped forward, his hand upon the hilt of his rapier. "I second Mr. Felton."

The Marquis flinched in his chair, his eyes darting between the two gentlemen who stood shoulder to shoulder. James' statement was confirmation that Felton's must be taken seriously.

"Who shall be your second, Lord Ravensbough?" asked James. "I shall call on him later today to arrange matters for tomorrow."

"Tomorrow?" cried the Marquis indignantly.

"Yes, tomorrow," said James. "Tomorrow your indecent words shall be dealt with according to the dictates of polite society which is more than you deserve."

"A charade we shall have to suffer," concurred Felton. "Now do you find it in you to accept, Ravensbough? We need your second."

With this hint at Ravensbough's potential cowardice, the Marquis snapped. "Of course I bloody accept! That chit's sister is indebted to me—if I should have to exact that debt through the seduction of another sister I will do so. And I shall have no qualms about getting you both out of the way before furthering my cause with the virtuous Miss Caro Worth, if you are both so intent on defending that fallen woman of yours—at least that is what I shall be saying of her soon. Odd that she should choose to marry a mere boy."

"We shall see how boyish I am when I face you with a sword tomorrow, dog. The lies you threaten shall not leave the tip of your tongue if I cut it off."

"Come, sir," said the Marquis, having regained his equanimity. "No need to resort to barbarity. We shall settle this as gentlemen. We shall meet you tomorrow. Rivers, will you second me?"

The man nodded.

"I do not believe I called out a gentleman, just a dashed cur." Felton did not wait to be reprimanded again. He swung around and strode away on a course for the door. James moved swiftly out of his way.

Before following suit, he bowed to Rivers and found out the name of his lodgings where he could call later to arrange the meeting. Then he bid the Marquis adieu until he should meet them tomorrow.

"What?" The colour drained from Caro's face. Her skin became pale against her hair and the shadows already existent beneath her eyes were thrown into a starker contrast.

Her hair was loose, resting in long tangled curls down her back instead of pinned up in the usual neat style Libby had perfected over the years. She wore her old open-fronted gown which was tied at the front but flowed freely over her figure.

She had not been able to face life this morning, but considering the circumstances, she had received no judgment from Rebecca for her unkempt appearance. Now, at this news from Lady Etheridge, she was quite incapable of anything at all.

"A duel," repeated Lady Etheridge. "The whole of London Society is ringing with news of it."

Caro fell back, the arms of Rebecca all that held her up.

"Come, Caro, you'll make yourself ill. Please be seated."

But Caro pulled out of Rebecca's arms. "Be seated? My brother and Mr. Felton are to fight a duel, and I am to remain seated? I cannot!" She strode across the room with more power than was normally evident in her slim frame and went over to the window. She threw it open, feeling the gusts of air push against her, and took in long breaths.

The clipping of horses' hooves, the creaking, lumbering roll of carriage wheels, and the chatter and shouts of passers-by invaded the solemn atmosphere of the room. There they all were, going on as though life were not crumbling beneath their very feet.

"This is insanity," Caro whispered desperately.

"It's not quite as romantic as I had thought it would be," said Rebecca despondently.

"Actually," replied Lady Etheridge in matter-of-fact tones as she took a seat by the hearth, "it's rather clever."

Caro swung round, firing a gaze of disbelief at her ladyship.

"Now, now," said the elderly woman, putting up a restraining hand, "hold your temper long enough for me to explain my words."

Caro did not reply but retracted her gaze and found solace in pacing behind the sofa.

"Do you not see, once satisfaction is gained in defence of your virtuous self, Ravensbough may no longer molest you? For he shall be proven undeniably wrong at the tip of an honourable sword. Then, after the duel is done, the engagement makes you impervious to future scandals if the Marquis is foolish enough to try again. As long as Angelica is lost to the continent, and we let it be known, you shall be free from this coil."

Lady Etheridge shifted in her seat. "Felton asked me to spread news of the duel and of your engagement amongst my network of gossips. The duel must be a public scandal, and your engagement already known of, if it is to clear your name of worse stories. To think—the young gentleman is eliminating one scandal with another and thereby clearing your name. It's ingenious."

"And if my brother is killed? If Felton di—" She found herself unable to ask the last question. "What then?"

"Oh, my dear, that is highly unlikely—all these stories you hear of men escaping to the continent after killing their opponent are far more excitement than is intended here. Felton must only gain satisfaction in order to prove your virtuous reputation to the world."

The idea of a flesh wound did little to ease Caro's anxiety.

"Felton? I thought you said it was James who challenged Ravensbough."

"On the contrary, it was Felton—he is your betrothed after all."

"As a pretence only. Why would he do such a foolish thing?"

Lady Etheridge's next words brought Caro up short in her pacing. "If you are truly ignorant of the answer to that question, then you are blind indeed."

Caro's gaze switched rapidly from the walls to the beady, knowing eyes of Lady Etheridge. She felt a faint warmth gathering in her cheeks like clouds gathering on a summer's day. Unable to respond to the accusation, she looked at Rebecca. Even that loyal companion's brown eyes had been set to dancing. She looked almost reprovingly at Caro as though to say she expected better from her skills of deduction.

"You are both mad!" Caro finally exclaimed, throwing her hands up in the air.

At that moment the door to the morning room was thrown open and in walked Felton and James.

It was the worst possible time. Caro was looking frustrated and worn, Rebecca was staring on helplessly, and Lady Etheridge was tapping a hand on the table at her elbow exclaiming, "Absolutely not, my child, we are quite right."

After all that Lady Etheridge had implied, the appearance of Felton sent a jolt of anxiety through Caro's body. She could not take much more of this insanity. She caught Felton's eyes for a pregnant moment before she pulled away and headed back to the open window, turning away from the rest of the room, cutting them out.

In those brief seconds looking into Caro's eyes, Felton saw something similar to embarrassment at his sudden entrance. The brazenness of Angelica and the confident independence of Caro had never given way to that emotion before, and seeing it on her face told him more than any words.

"Good morning, ladies." James bowed.

Felton nodded in agreement and executed a rapid bow.

"Ah," said James catching sight of his sister's trailing curls and rather indecorous state of half dress. "Perhaps we should wait in the drawing room."

"You most certainly should not!" Caro swung round in her brother's direction, having quashed whatever momentary embarrassment she had been suffering from. "A duel? What cotton-headed idea is this? Oh, how could you, James! You must call it off immediately!" And with that outburst she swung back round to the window and, though she remained silent, the shaking of her shoulders showed her to be crying.

Lady Etheridge and Rebecca remained in stunned silence, and only James spoke in response. "Caro, please calm yourself. This has been done in your name, and—"

Felton put a staying hand upon James' arm. The conscientious brother fell silent, and the other two women looked to him for instruction.

"Allow me a private word with my betrothed."

James hesitated but then offered his arms to Lady Rebecca and Lady Etheridge, escorting them from the room.

Caro seemed not to have noticed. Even the shutting of the door did nothing to calm the gentle shudder that had taken over her shoulders. Felton's brow furrowed, his heart aching as he watched her. It racked his chest and hurt his throat. He wished to rush forward, to comfort her, to quiet her. Instead, he made his way to her slowly, quietly, not wishing to scare her away when he knew her vulnerability would make her timid.

Her form was outlined by the white afternoon light from outside. The wind pushed against her, as if ushering her back inside. Felton could see she was shivering. As he came to her side, he saw one of her hands was pressing against her collar-bone as if to still the sobs. Her other hand was covering her mouth, to quiet the crying. Her eyes were flooded by tears—she looked but did not see.

"What is done," said Felton in a soft and firm voice, filled with desire to comfort, "cannot be undone. I did not do it for you, whatever your brother may say. I did it for myself, for I am a selfish man who cannot bear the pain I feel when I see you so." He raised a tentative hand, weaving his fingers gently through her hair before his palm felt the smooth warmth of her tear-stained cheek. He released a sigh of longing. "I would see you happy again."

He pulled a handkerchief out of his pocket and, whilst his right hand still held her cheek, gently wiped her tears. He paused and then drew her face towards him, his lips soft and warm on hers, his kiss speaking far more than his words.

To his delight, she allowed him to kiss her for a few seconds. Then she pulled away, saying nothing.

"You shall be safe, secure, and happy."

Caro answered his sincere words with a small nod.

"We meet with Ravensbough tomorrow. Your brother seconds me. Can you settle for a younger son defending your honour?"

Caro used the handkerchief to dry her cheeks completely. "If there is one thing that I am learning, it is the worthiness of a man is not determined by his title."

Felton grinned a little. There was spirit to Caro's words, a sign she was still fighting, that she had not given up yet.

He tried to kiss her again, but a small hand on his chest pressed him back.

"We are not really engaged, Mr. Felton. You are too carried away. But remember, this will be over soon, and you will be rid of your infamous fiancée. Perhaps Society will be kind, and you will not be too badly shunned."

"My reputation has never been what it should be. Disappointing people is my way, as my father has found."

Caro folded the kerchief with decisive movements. A sudden fire lit in her eyes. "I may not understand you, Mr. Felton, but you have never disappointed me." She offered his handkerchief back to him.

"And I hope I never shall. I hope after tomorrow you will understand me completely. Keep it." He pushed the proffered kerchief back at her. Caro did not respond, accepting the handkerchief as a gift, that same gathering of heat in her cheeks happening again.

"Do not get killed, Mr. Felton," she said suddenly, a dark-humoured way of lightening the mood.

Felton had no intention of doing so—it was what would happen after the duel that he must live for. He would have liked to explain himself here and now, to kiss her again and tell her that these kisses meant far more than mere comfort or to lend colour to a false engagement—to tell her that he wished to do it again and again and again till he stole her very breath. But she was not ready. He respected her clear wish to change the conversation.

"Your care over my wellbeing is overwhelming."

"Where are you to meet?"

"On a common, Hampstead Heath, far enough away that the authorities will not find us. Your brother has already waited on Ravensbough's second. Any attempts at reconciliation have been refused. All details have been finalised. We are certain to meet tomorrow."

"I do not approve."

"I knew you would not—you are playing your virtuous self, after all." Felton winked, more sure than ever of Caro's feelings even if she was not herself.

"And if I were Angelica right now, I expect you would want me to encourage you to give the Marquis a good pinking?"

Felton chuckled.

"You can fight with a sword, can you not?" asked Caro.

"I am aware there is a sharp end and one must hold the other."

"Wretch!"

"We must go now—do not be too hard upon your brother. We shall call on you tomorrow after the deed is done."

"I cannot come with you?"

"No," said Felton firmly.

Caro acquiesced reluctantly. When they rejoined the rest of the party it was only to say goodbye. Lady Etheridge had another engagement, and both Felton and James were leaving to examine their weapons for tomorrow. James would be staying with Felton tonight in order to be ready to leave in the morning, and Rebecca had been given consent by her aunt to spend the night with Caro so that she would not be alone. The door closed behind the gentlemen and Lady Etheridge, leaving the friends behind, and for quite some time after they had gone, only silence reigned.

CHAPTER EIGHTEEN

F elton had been awake since three o'clock. He had not taken a leisurely breakfast, nor had he spent time lounging half-dressed about his apartments. He had risen and washed his face and dressed with efficiency. The clothes laid out by his valet had been rejected by the young gentleman. Instead, he chose black breeches and a loose old shirt. If he were pinked, he thought grimly, he did not wish to ruin a new one. He had no desire to don a waistcoat for precisely the same reason, and his valet brought him a plain woolen coat normally reserved for the country. His hair remained unpowdered, as usual, and tied carelessly with a leather thong.

He had picked out the sword he would take. It was the small sword he wore regularly. Its hollow shaft was sharp and flexible, perfect for a fatal thrust—not that he was planning on using deadly force today; however, the possibility that it might be necessary had dawned on him.

What happened if he was caught? What if he failed to parry effectively, was injured, and had no choice? What if his swordsmanship failed him and he was faced with the unobstructed point of Ravensbough's sword?

Answers to the questions failed him. He replaced the sword in its customary scabbard and went down to breakfast.

He was halfway down the stairs, his weasel-faced valet close behind him carrying his hardy Garrick coat and hat, when the bell sounded. It was early for the under-groom to be bringing the curricle round, Felton mused, but he could not blame the servant for being as skittish as he himself felt. He had elected to bring the curricle instead of the carriage—all the better to make a quick retreat if he were wounded.

Felton nodded to his manservant who scurried ahead to open the front door, but the expected under-groom did not materialise.

"I wish to see my son without the least delay!" said the stern voice. A large frame loomed in the doorway.

Felton stopped short, his back foot resting on the bottom step of the staircase, his right thrust forward taking the majority of his weight. He glanced up, his eyes piercing the darkness and making out the flushed features of his father's face.

"My lord?" queried Felton.

The Viscount looked over the shoulder of the manservant, avoiding the curls at the side of the servant's straggly bag wig, and took in his son's appearance.

"I shall speak to you if you please."

The authoritative voice and the way his lordship barged past the manservant and into the hall led Felton to one conclusion: his father was here to stop him. Felton's first instinct was to ask his father to leave, but his father's tone indicated that he would brook no such dismissal.

"If you will." Felton bowed and gestured towards the drawing room.

His father neither responded to the invitation nor thanked his son but rather strode past him silently. The drawing room had no candles lit; only a fire glowed warmly in the grate, but thanks to it being lately made, it burned bright and illuminated enough of the room for the two men.

Felton turned, inhaled a breath of sustaining air, and followed his father, bringing the doors to a firm close behind him.

"I have come here at this unchristian hour," his father began without ceremony, "at the behest of your mother."

There was a pause, and Felton took full advantage of it. "My lord, if you have come to persuade me into another course of action, I am bound to tell you, you shall fail."

The Viscount put up his hand. "I am not come for such a purpose."

"Well then, you know I have a pressing engagement and have little leisure time this morning. Can this sermon wait until later?" Felton was already moving toward the door.

"Gracious! You are so like your mother, stubborn and impatient. Hear me out—I shall not keep you long."

Felton almost ignored the plea, but he sensed that the urgency of his father's voice was born not from scolding but rather concern. He came back round to the front of the chair and sat down upon its edge. "Go ahead, my lord."

"Your mother requested I come and clear the air between us after our last meeting, and I..."

Felton saw him struggle for the next words. What was he thinking?

"...I agreed with her. I wished to come myself."

Felton was thrown back into his chair at this. He fell against the woven fabric, thankful for the horsehair stuffing which cushioned his surprise.

"I can hardly be expected to have been thrilled that you would be taking part in a duel, but I found myself, helped in large part by your mother's wise and blunt words, respecting your decision, though not approving of it. Your mother and I have tried, over the last several years, to make you understand and accept your responsibilities."

The Viscount's voice became, if not soft, somewhat wistful. His flushed face no longer looked angry and upset but rather kindly—very much like the father of Felton's childhood, before he and Frederick had grown to an age when responsibilities and the different duties of a younger and elder son had bred competitiveness and pressure.

"I have tried, though it may not have always seemed it, to do what would make you proud of me, Father." The Viscount's openness gave Felton the courage to say what he could never say before.

"I know." The Viscount had come to stand before Felton's chair and now rested a firm, unfamiliar hand upon his son's shoulder. "And neither I nor your mother have ever been more proud than when you took on the responsibility of protecting this young lady's honour. You said yesterday that it is the right thing to do—and so it is."

The sentiment of the situation rested heavily upon them both for a moment. They remained in silence, the Viscount's hand still resting upon his son's shoulder.

Felton, if he had not been in the presence of his father and very aware of it, might have shed a joyful tear at this admission.

"How this woman has managed to bring such a sense of responsibility out in you in the space of a few weeks after years of your mother and I trying, I shall never know."

Felton gave in to a hearty laugh. "No disrespect to you, Father, but you do not have this woman's face, nor her substantial charms."

The Viscount emitted a bass laugh, patting his son's shoulder and coming to face him properly. "Well, are you not expected in some obscure location? Be up and get about it, and then I shall meet this fascinating woman for myself all the sooner."

"Aye, my lord," said Felton, recognizing the intimate moment had passed and they were falling back into formality. "I await only my second. I shall send you news when the deed is done."

"Hang sending me news! I intend to attend! Should your sword point end up bringing the premature demise of the Marquis of Ravensbough—whom inexplicably your mother has found out to be your opponent—you shall need the weight I can bring to bear with the authorities."

"I mean to gain satisfaction by way of a superficial wound, but I should be grateful of your presence in case of other eventualities. I thank you, my lord."

The Viscount nodded stiffly, back to his usual straightforward self, and they came into the hall. At that moment the bell sounded a second time. It would be the curricle this time.

"Good morning." James had descended into the hall and stood waiting, neatly but plainly attired in breeches, sturdy boots, woolen frock coat, and simply-tied cravat.

"My lord," Felton turned to his father and stood aside for him to meet his second. "This is Mr. James Worth, my second and Miss Caro Worth's brother."

Both gentlemen bowed, a move seemingly out of place upon such an occasion and in the early morning. "He'll be watching the event today," Felton explained to James. "In fact,"—an idea came suddenly into his head—"may I ask a favor of you, my lord?"

"Name it, my boy."

Felton asked it quickly and his father agreed, surprisingly without qualm.

With all preparations made, weapons accounted for, and the curricle standing waiting, Felton stepped outside the door of his London home, followed closely behind by the other two gentlemen. The air was cold, seeping between the folds of his Garrick coat, and the sun's rays were scouting ahead over the horizon, sending small darts of light into a paling sky. This was the day, the hour drew near—soon, Felton thought, he would be duelling.

An hour before dawn, Libby came to rouse Caro, who was still wide awake. A carriage had drawn up to the Town house on the dark cobbled street, and the driver had rapped on the door until John had answered him.

"What is it, Libby?" asked Caro.

The old retainer entered the room, her face lit by the candlelight reflecting on the silver tray she held. Caro hesitated, thinking Libby was bringing her news. Thoughts ran rapidly through her head. Could it be a note about the duel? No. It was not dawn—they had yet to meet. What if it was from the Marquis? A new threat?

"Here, miss."

Libby placed the candle and tray beside the bed, allowing Caro to see that the only thing on its gleaming silver surface was a crisp ivory calling card.

"He waits in the carriage outside, miss. His tiger brought in the card."

Caro paused for a fraction of a second, afraid to pick up the card. Who would be calling on her at this hour? She took a breath, and like a flitting bird picking up seed from a path, her fine fingers seized the card from the tray.

It read in fine script: *Admiral Viscount Felton*. Felton. This was Felton's father? What on earth was going on? Caro muttered words beneath her breath that even her busybody maid could not hear. She replaced the card on the tray and threw back the bedclothes, making the candle on the tray flicker.

"Libby, I must dress at once, please tell his lordship that I shall see him downstairs directly."

"Beg your pardon, miss, but his tiger was most insistent that you rise and be in the carriage as quick as you can."

Caro's mind flitted here and there trying to discern the meaning of this. She paused only for a moment before rapid animation overtook her frame. She rose with haste and snatched up her chemise and stays.

"Libby, wake Lady Rebecca and tell her to dress. I can dress myself—I have done it many times before. Go!" She waved shooing hands at her maid and watched the old woman disappear through the adjoining door to Lady Rebecca's room.

After a quarter of an hour, dressing with more swiftness than she had ever needed to employ, Rebecca appeared through the door into Caro's room. "What in heaven's name is going on, Caro? I thought the carriage you ordered wasn't to be here for another hour."

"It isn't the carriage I ordered. It is Admiral Viscount Felton." Caro went to her side table and took the card from the tray again, thrusting it towards Rebecca.

"Felton's father? What does he want at this hour? Oh! Perhaps—"

Caro cut Rebecca off before she could finish her epiphany. "I don't know, but he begs us to go down into his carriage. He wishes to take us somewhere."

"To the duel! Oh, this is too delightful—don't you see? Felton must have known we would try to find the duel. He has sent us safe passage."

Caro cursed and blessed Felton's knowledge of her. "Are you sure?"

"There is only one way to find out," said Lady Rebecca, drawing on her gloves and swinging her cloak about her. She raised the hood until her face was half-obscured by shadows and took up one of the veils handed to both women by Libby.

Before Caro left the room in the wake of Rebecca, she turned to her maid. "Libby, belay my order for a carriage for this morning." She could have sworn the shadow of a smile marked the old woman's face, but she did not waste time wondering over it.

Before long both women were pattering down the stairs and out of the open door at which John still stood. They were greeted by a small, wire-framed man whose high muffler made him look like a highwayman on Caro's doorstep.

"Misses." He tugged where his forelock would have been if not for the hat pulled low about his ears and then walked immediately towards the carriage.

The women looked at each other and then followed. The tiger opened the door of the carriage.

"Thank you, Jedidiah," said a deep voice from the dark interior of the waiting vehicle.

"Ladies," the man greeted them without leaning forward. "Has Tobias' tiger apprised you of the situation?"

"No, my lord," responded Caro.

"Jedidiah is not one for words, but we must be quick. I am charged with taking you to view the duel between my son and the Marquis of Ravensbough. Apparently, Miss Caro Worth is as stubborn as my youngest son when it comes to following commands, and he does not trust her to remain at home!" The man in the carriage chuckled. "Well," said he, finishing laughing and wondering why neither woman had moved. "They duel at dawn and we cannot be late!"

They travelled north out of the city for close to an hour. With the sun now rising, the visibility was improved, and Felton made easy work of streets empty of all but shopkeepers. Felton drove his horses forward, the momentum sending the long panels of his coat flying back off his knees, exposing him to more of this early morning weather. The noise of the curricle on the road as well as the solemnity of the situation caused Felton and James to maintain a tense silence throughout the journey's duration.

Felton navigated the dirty streets with skill, frequently splashing through puddles, until the buildings thinned about them and the road widened. It was a full three-quarters of an hour by the time Hampstead Heath was reached. His father's carriage, with its slower progress, would take longer still to get there. The sun was now pinking the sky, overcoming the previous stark white rays it had shot upwards. Dew hung heavily upon the landscape, the smell of damp soil and wildlife reaching both gentlemen's nostrils as they sat in the open curricle. This haunt of highwaymen had never looked more idyllic.

Felton steered towards the meeting place agreed upon. Since James had limited geographical knowledge of London and its environs, he had chosen the spot himself. It was off the main road down a cart track that slowed their progress. The small glade opened before them as they approached. The grass was green and long in the clearing, its dew-laden lengths wetting the horses' hooves and fetlocks and flicking from the carriage wheels. The trees and bushes provided ample cover from the road, preventing any passer-by from seeing the flash of blades and reporting them. Up above, the sky lightened still further, and Felton gave it a quick glance, his awe at the beauty of this place juxtaposed awkwardly with knowledge of the bloody deed to be performed.

He climbed down immediately as the curricle came to a halt, and, in the stead of his tiger, pulled blankets from the back of the curricle to throw over the horses' steaming frames and ward off the inevitable chill. The action made him think fleetingly of Caro. Was she cold in his father's carriage? When would she arrive? What would she think of the encounter about to happen? What would she do after this was over?

"Ravensbough." James cut into Felton's hurried thoughts. He gestured to a carriage coming up the track behind Felton's father.

The arrival of his opponent sent a jolt of fear through Felton. He felt ashamed at such a feeling, but the possibility of imminent injury or death made it impossible to ignore. He tightened his hand which held his horses, so much so that the leather of the reins bit into his fingers and his knuckles were forced white.

James climbed down to stand beside Felton.

"Before this happens, please know how grateful I am for what you have done to protect my sister's honour."

Felton spoke through gritted teeth. "Thank me when we are both still alive in an hour." His eyes were hard and his jaw set.

James made no comment on this and moved to the next order of business. "I need your weapon to present for inspection."

Felton nodded, pulling out his blade and handing it hilt-first to his second. Ravensbough and his second were descending from their carriage, and James brought the sword over to them for examination.

Ravensbough's expression was as cold as the morning's air. He was dressed entirely in black, though he did not take after Felton in simplicity of attire. His black coat was embroidered heavily with silver, and his powdered hair, powdered face, and perfectly placed patch attested that he had spent many hours at the dressing table. The care to which he had gone with his appearance made Felton wonder if such attention to detail was mirrored in his fencing technique. He hoped not.

James came back a few moments later, the blades having been checked and agreed upon between the seconds.

"He greeted me as though we had come to a private ball!" said James, his tone exasperated but low.

"Let's hope that means he is unjustly confident."

"His second looks like a tricky fellow, hardly a gentleman."

"Tricky is an apt assessment. And knowing that Ravensbough's sense of honour is non-existent, we must not disqualify the idea that these two have hatched a plan."

"Do you think they mean to rush us?" asked James in shock. "Surely they will abide by the code of conduct?"

"I wouldn't rely upon such an assumption. If his second rushes in to kill me when I am knocked down, can I rely on you to—"

"I shall give my utmost," replied James without hesitation, his chest broad and his head up.

Felton nodded. "Let us hope we can laugh at this tomorrow. God be with you." He grasped James' hand and shook it with vigour.

"And with you."

With that, the two men entered the field alongside their opponents.

James cleared his throat. "Mr. Felton has called Lord Ravensbough out on a matter of honour this morning: to defend his betrothed's name against slanders from Lord Ravensbough. All attempts at reconciliation have failed, and now satisfaction shall be gained on this field. The weapon is the short sword, both checked and agreed upon, I, James Worth, act as Mr. Felton's second whilst you, Mr. Rivers, act as Lord Ravensbough's second. This is a matter of honour and is expected"—James looked from Felton to Ravensbough, lingering on the latter—"to be dealt with honourably. Attend upon your weapons and commence."

The gentlemen each drew their weapons, and the seconds retreated to a safe distance.

Felton faced Ravensbough, and for the first time that

morning, looked him in the eyes. Those dark orbs were hard and cold, and a sardonic sneer marked the Marquis' mouth.

"If I did not expect better, I would say you are bewitched by that woman," Ravensbough's voice taunted as he raised his blade.

"Why expect better? Nobody expects better of me."

"And yet you are to wed. Though, I am sure her virtue shall be gone by the time you get your chance at her—her sister owes me a great debt, and in her absence I shall take my dues once this farce is over with."

Angry heat flamed inside Felton's chest at the thought of Ravensbough's hands on Caro—of the hands that had already touched her, hurt her.

"And if I win?" Felton questioned, raising his own blade.

"Oh, you shall not!" Their blades touched, and Ravensbough rushed forward without warning.

Felton parried the attack, sidestepping as the Marquis lunged, beating off his blade with a slash to the left. Then, Felton went straight into attack himself. He swung about, his back foot coming down at a right angle so that he was now facing Ravensbough again. His front foot lunged forward.

The attack was ill-timed. Felton had been too eager. The Marquis had pushed an immediate daring lunge in order to assess Felton's response, and he was now ready for the response. Ravensbough parried and managed to slash Felton's fingers on his sword hand. Though the blow was light, Felton felt blood flow and the sting of open cuts.

Felton stepped back several paces, giving himself time to assess the damage to his hand and becoming warier. Despite the adrenaline running through his blood and the cold of the air biting at his limbs, his uncertainty had departed the moment their blades met. He remembered his training, and though he had let slip a foolish move, he now felt confident. The first cut was over with. He was ready.

CHAPTER NINETEEN

"Which of you is Miss Caro Worth?" asked the Viscount who had borne the initial silence in the carriage but could no longer.

Caro did not respond immediately.

"I thank you for the use of your carriage, my lord."

"Ah, so it is you! I apologise for the oddness of our first introduction. My son was insistent that I come to escort you, along with his man, for your own safety and propriety. I understand you have a similar disposition to my headstrong wife." He laughed, that same dry, bass chuckle. "I am Admiral Viscount Felton." He inclined his head and extended his hand towards Caro.

She took it tentatively in her gloved hand. The tumbling of the carriage wheels could be heard below the Viscount's deep voice.

"I am to offer you my congratulations, my child. Might I be permitted to see my future daughter-in-law's face?"

Caro gently pulled up the veil but replied, "You may, my lord, though I shall not take your congratulations. Your son has failed to explain we are not to marry—he only uses the engagement as a pretence to protect me."

The Viscount, who was much struck by Caro's features even in the dim light of the carriage, smiled. "You are very beautiful my child, and I highly doubt my son has any intention of letting you go. I have never seen him so much in love." The Viscount chuckled.

Caro's hands played with the veil in her lap, and she found herself unable to look the Viscount in the eye.

"I am sure you are mistaken, my lord."

"Much like my own wife—just as forthright. You shall suit him well. Let us pray that he will come out of this ordeal as the husband you deserve.

"And as for you," he said, turning the conversation from the grim tone it had developed as he turned to the other veiled occupant of the carriage, "am I speaking to the delightful Lady Rebecca Fairing?"

"You are indeed, my lord." Rebecca took his hand easily. "It is a pleasure to see you again, if under such circumstances. I trust Lady Felton is well?"

"She is as well as ever, I thank you. And your aunt?"

And so the conversation carried on. Caro was left to her own thoughts. The fear in her stomach growing with every turn of the carriage wheels. Almost an hour later they were nearing their destination, the telltale slowing of the horses signaling they were coming upon their goal. The wilds of Hampstead Heath beckoned, and on the green clearing, they could make out the small figures of four men.

Before the carriage even stopped Caro burst through the doors, ignoring the other occupants and disregarding what the Viscount might think of her. The tiger had expected as much, thanks to a rather accurate description of Caro's propensities from his master, and he was just as quick, leaping down from the halted carriage in time to catch the escaping woman in his wiry arms.

"Get off me!" Caro cried.

"I have my orders, miss," replied the tiger in a common accent, still holding the struggling woman.

"And they include man-handling me?"

"They include keeping you safe at all costs," the tiger replied calmly in the face of Caro's panicked words, "and I obey my master's orders, not yours."

"But I cannot see."

"You will see if I let you near, but I shall only do so if you give me your word not to run off."

"Yes! Yes!" said Caro, impatient to be rid of his restraining arms.

"Listen, miss—if you don't heed, the distraction you cause may mean my master suffers a blow—maybe fatal." The tiger's words were grim and without a hint of exaggeration.

Caro stilled at once, her face transformed from impatience to anxiety.

"My dear, let us do as Mr. Felton's man says," said Rebecca, coming up behind Caro and taking a supporting role after the tiger's restraining one. "The Viscount will stay in the carriage, but with our veils we may find a hidden place to observe."

Caro nodded, taking the veil from Rebecca and putting it back over her face. They skirted the trees surrounding the glade, the tiger leading the women to a place behind some bushes where they could watch unnoticed. They were now closer to Ravensbough's carriage than to their own.

Caro, once installed, cast her eyes over the top of the bushes and across the field that opened up before them. She saw two men in the centre, one in shirtsleeves, the other not having removed his black jacket, only conceding to unbutton it for ease of movement. She could see Felton was the one in the shirt, his chest heaving with the exertion of the footwork, sweat soaking the linen.

The meeting was energetic. Each man attacked whilst the other retreated, parrying the blows, before taking back the ground in the next few moments.

After a short time, it was easy to see that they were evenly matched, something rare at such a meeting.

"There is your brother," said Rebecca, tapping Caro's shoulder and making her jump. Caro only gave James a moment's consideration before returning her gaze to the duel.

"He does not look to have fought yet, and I see no wounds on the principal fighters," said Rebecca.

The tiger disagreed. "He's pinked my master's hand, he has."

At that moment the Marquis lunged again. Felton's injured fingers re-gripped his sword, but Ravensbough's fast-paced attack made him lose the balance of the blade in his hand. He caught it up just in time to save his side from being skewered.

"God forgive me for bringing this about," whispered Caro, causing the tiger to cast her a sideways glance she barely noticed. Her hand was fast upon Rebecca's who bore the pressure without a word of complaint.

Suddenly, the Marquis' coachman who was also watching the duel with interest stepped into their line of vision, unwittingly cutting off the hidden party's view. Caro was sent into a panic, the clash of metal her only knowledge of what was going on in the clearing.

"What's happening? We must see!" Caro hissed, her gaze flashing between Rebecca and the tiger. Before the latter could stop her, she shot past Rebecca and headed into the open by Felton's curricle.

"Miss!" hissed the tiger, running out after her. "Miss, you cannot be seen! My master said—"

"No one can see my face. Now let me stand or I shall beat you down myself!" The threat caused a sigh from the tiger but no other protestation as he had no wish to be further diverted from the duel.

The best he could do was to stand to the lady's right, hemming her in by the carriage and hoping nobody saw them. Rebecca joined, standing behind Caro and resuming her duty of holding the latter's hand.

"Your master will not be pleased," said the Viscount coming around the corner of the carriage, his voice making each of them jump. "But with a threat like that I am not surprised you surrendered. I too have come to gain a better view, though I would appreciate it if you could stand before me, Jedidiah, to shield my presence from the duellers."

"My lord." The tiger tugged his imaginary forelock again and moved before the Viscount so the aristocrat could look over his shoulder partially obscured.

"My master failed to explain the lady's temper," said the tiger, apparently feeling the need to justify himself.

"A temper that shall be put to use if you deter me," said Caro with force.

The Viscount smiled at this and would have offered a rejoinder if Felton had not let through a thrust from Ravensbough. The hit was to his side, far enough out not to damage his innards but painful enough to cripple him for a few moments.

It was then that the Marquis' plan was put into action. A look to his second brought that man onto the field at a dead run. The two men advanced on Felton, as he staggered back a few paces clutching at his side.

James let forth an exclamation and ran to join the melee. "Honour, men! Honour!" he cried as he ran, desperate to restore order. As he neared the men, he realised the calls were in vain. Their swords were raised and their plan was murder. He drew his own sword and prepared to meet them— although, without Felton, he had no hope of staving off two blades.

Suddenly, however, Felton straightened. Ignoring his bloody wound, he raised his sword.

This sudden revival took Ravensbough by surprise. The Marquis' advance was checked as Felton parried his sword and lunged forward. His blade entered his opponent's shoulder, and the Marquis screamed in pain.

James, at the same time, met Mr. Rivers, whose slashing was unpractised and ineffective. He repulsed each blow and drove the man back.

Ravensbough, goaded to anger, now charged ahead, shouting at Felton. Felton sidestepped Ravensbough and, as he flew past him, rammed his sword hilt into the Marquis' head, sending him sprawling on the ground. Blood soaked his black jacket.

Felton left Ravensbough on the ground to assist James as he dealt with Mr. Rivers. "Stand down!" shouted Felton. "I have my satisfaction!"

Mr. Rivers stopped mid-move and, after seeing his fallen friend, lowered his blade, swore, and stood down.

Felton immediately turned to the Marquis who was attempting to get up. He sprang forward with much effort and leveled his sword point at the Marquis' throat. His lithe frame overshadowed the sprawled figure of the Marquis, and his next words were spoken loud enough for all to hear, a proclamation to the world.

"I have taken your shoulder as satisfaction. You shall not

breathe another slanderous word about the woman who will be my wife. Angelica Worth has this morning made her escape to the continent where she will run from her creditors, though I will pay the outstanding debt she owes to you. But in return, Ravensbough, you shall relinquish any claim on or acquaintance with her."

From a distance, the ladies and the Viscount listened breathlessly to Felton's declaration. When Felton offered to pay her debts to the Marquis, Caro opened her mouth to protest. But a hand rested lightly upon her shoulder and stopped her from contradicting the hero's terms. It was the Viscount. He said nothing but continued to watch the proceedings.

"Come near her again," said Felton, "and I shall take more of your blood for my satisfaction."

Ravensbough, whose pride smarted as much as his shoulder, sneered at the proposal before spitting on Felton's feet.

"Did I fail to make myself clear?" Felton lunged forward, his boot landing on Ravensbough's shoulder, causing the man to cry out as blood spurted from the wound up around Felton's boot. "Come near her again, and I shall kill you! Do you understand?" The menace in Felton's voice and the murderous light in his eyes finally settled the situation in Ravensbough's mind. The Marquis looked suddenly fearful and sought respite from the pain in his shoulder by nodding his agreement to the terms.

"You are my witness," said Felton, pointing his sword at Rivers who visibly flinched. "Make sure, for your friend's sake, he keeps to this agreement."

The man nodded, and Felton was sure from the looks of disparagement he now shot at the fallen Marquis that he would be no more trouble. Once this tale spread around London, the Marquis would be kept in check and Caro would be saved.

Felton stood there, his sword in hand, until the Marquis and his second had slunk off to their carriage. He was still mistrustful of the aristocrat's guile, still afraid that he would try something dishonourable.

When their carriage finally began to move, the deed was done. Felton dropped his sword, his hand coming up to his side, feeling the wet blood that had soaked through his shirt. He staggered a little, grunting, only to be caught up by James who gave him his shoulder to lean on.

The sight of the Marquis coming towards them sent Caro and Rebecca into panic.

"Into my carriage—now," commanded the Viscount.

The tiger nodded, guided the women back to his lordship's carriage, and opened the door to usher the women and the Viscount inside before the Marquis could see them. Once inside, the Viscount shut the door.

"Oh, thank God! Thank God!" whispered Caro. "But how could he have promised to pay my debts? He cannot!" she spoke urgently to Rebecca who patted her hand and soothed her.

"All is well now, Caro. He has saved your honour."

"As your future husband, he most certainly can, though I do not understand to what debts he refers. Trust his judgment, my dear," said the Viscount, his voice kind.

"But he is not my future husband!"

"Dear child," said the Viscount, leaning forward and placing a hand upon the women's which were still joined, "you must go to him."

"I...I...." Caro stuttered, and then, as if it were her own idea she said, "I must go." She did not wait for assistance but opened the door and descended from the carriage in so much of a rush she almost collided with the tiger Jedidiah carrying bandages from the curricle to his master.

Rebecca stumbled across the field behind her toward the spot where Felton was being attended by her brother. Running ahead of them, Jedidiah brought the bandages and dabbed at the wound before pouring brandy from Felton's flask upon it. Caro saw Felton flinch at the burning liquid, but as his eyes re-opened they saw her coming across the field.

"Hurry up, Jedidiah."

"Hurry up," muttered the tiger, complaining as he dabbed the wound dry, and wrapped a bandage about Felton's torso. "Bleeding with a hole in him and he wants me to hurry up." The bandage was soon in place, however, and Jedidiah passed a rag to Felton for his hand just as Caro came upon them.

"A happy result!" said Felton, grinning from ear to ear, if looking a little pale, "though I wished you to stay out of sight."

"A happy result! You are bleeding and stabbed and, oh...." Caro began crying, great rolling tears falling down her cheeks.

James offered her a handkerchief rather awkwardly, but she refused, pulling out instead the one Felton had given her and dabbing at her eyes.

"Perhaps you could all give me a few moments with my betrothed? The wish of a wounded man?"

Caro was too busy blowing her nose to notice the others disappear, leaving her quite alone on the field with Felton who leant heavily on his sword.

"Oh, you are a fool!" she said finally, growing exasperated with the way he was grinning at her.

"A fool! Lady Etheridge was kind enough to call me a genius when I first put this plan to her. She would hardly call me a fool now, that I know for certain. I didn't die, did I?"

"Oh, how can you fun when you very nearly could have died? And all on account of me."

"And what if I had died?" asked Felton, something other than amusement in his voice, the question hinting at something deeper.

"Don't say such a thing! And now your father thinks us really engaged and says all sorts of silly things about you...." Caro faltered, her eyes which had been everywhere but looking into his own, suddenly glanced up. The deep green of his own eyes captured them, and where once she had seen only mischief, now she saw something much warmer, much deeper.

"What? What does he say?" coaxed Felton.

"Oh, nothing—now at least you can cry off," said Caro in a pathetic attempt to lighten the mood and change the conversation. "And how does your side and hand do? Are you in much pain?"

"Cry off?" Felton stepped forward gingerly, ignoring the later questions.

"Yes."

He took another step. "Oh, I don't believe I shall be doing that."

Caro's next questions were uttered so fearfully they were almost inaudible. "What? Why?"

"I am not in the habit of crying off from women I am in love with. When I said I would, I lied. Now we have both lied to one another. Fool me once, shame on you, fool me twice...." He let slip a grin and then a sly wink. "And I wish to kiss you again—you didn't think I did so for no reason before, did you?"

"Ridiculous! I am most ineligible," snapped Caro.

"So am I—quite a pair. Now I have fought for you, I wish to kiss you."

And he did, without the least hesitation. He wrapped an arm about her waist drawing her in, and his mouth found hers, his lips warm and persistent.

The movement of his mouth upon hers sent a pulse of

excitement running through her. The kiss that started so calmly became suddenly urgent, and before Felton was done he drew an illicit sigh from Caro who pulled back, out of breath.

"I have wanted to do that again for *far* too long. Tell me, do you love me?" asked Felton, his straightforward manner and the kiss he had just given her causing Caro to blush deeply. His eyes were intent upon her own.

"Oh, you infuriating man! You will not cry off?"

"Never!" said he, refusing to let her go.

She wavered for a moment. "Then yes," she replied, tapping his chest with fidgeting fingers but unable to return his gaze. He tipped her chin upwards, looking into her eyes with such loving warmth that another thrill passed through her.

"Have I surprised you?" she asked.

Felton's lips curled into an amused smile. She was putting off the inevitable, shyly keeping him from kissing her again, as she knew he intended, by word-sparring with him. But he knew this woman better than she knew herself.

"Surprised me by saying yes?" He released her a little so as to look at her more clearly, though his grip remained firm as, in all honesty, her attractive frame was doing much to keep him upright in his wounded state. "My dear, argumentative Caro, you did not fool me the first time." He looked at her reddened lips, tempting himself with the sight. "In fact, if anything, I have fooled you into trusting me, and into marrying me, a reprobate. I believe you have been in love with me for almost as long as I have been in love with you."

"I don't know what you mean."

"That phrase again." Felton laughed, but only for a moment. Before she could speak again his lips found hers, pressing, asking, yearning.

When he finally released her, Caro's breath was quick and light. "Well, shame on me then, Tobias," she said, smiling and kissing him again.

The End

REVIEW THIS BOOK

Thank you for reading *Fool Me Twice*.

If you enjoyed it, please share your review on Amazon, BookBub or Goodreads to help other readers find my book.

GLOSSARY

British Museum – the museum was established in 1753 largely based on Sir Hans Sloane's collections. It first opened to the public in 1759 in Montagu House. The museum is still in existence today.

Caraco – a woman's jacket, fitted at the waist, with three quarter / full sleeves and a skirt that dropped to thigh height. It was fashionable from the 1760s and usually made of patterned cotton or silk.

Chaise longue – a sofa designed for reclining with an arm only on one end.

Chemise /shift – a plain gown with or without sleeves and often made from linen. It was worn against the skin as the first layer of clothing beneath the stays, hip pads, petticoats, and dress.

Cravat – usually a strip of linen that was tied around a gentleman's neck, the equivalent of a tie for the 18th century gentleman.

Duel – a fight, usually between two men, to settle a quarrel or a point of honour. It was normally held at a prearranged time, involved swords or pistols, and the use of 'seconds'. The latter were men chosen by each combatant should the individual in question be unable to act.

Faro – a 17th century French gambling game using a deck, a banker and matching cards.

Gaming hell / hell – a secret establishment, often on the first floor of a building behind bolted doors, containing various games of chance for gentlemen to play.

Hazard – an English gambling game using dice popular in the 18th century.

Ices – a term for ice creams, often flavoured, in the 18th century.

John King – originally known as Jacob Rey, King was a well-known Jewish money lender in the later 18th century.

Mantua maker – a term for a dressmaker in the 18th century. Mantua, either derived from the place in Italy or from the French word for coat, was the name of a gown which originated in the last quarter of the 17th century. Originally a loose-fitting over-gown all in one piece of fabric (unlike the skirts and bodices of the previous decades), it was worn with petticoats and a stomacher.

Patch – patches, or mouches (French for flies), were false beauty spots usually made from black taffeta or velvet and cut into shapes like hearts or crescents. They were worn on the face, neck or chest to hide imperfections and highlight the whiteness of the skin. They became fashionable in the late 18th century, particularly as a way to hide scars caused by smallpox.

Piquet – a two player French card game originating in the 16th century.

Pot and Pineapple – a shop in Berkeley Square established by Italian pastry cook Domenico Negri for the selling of confectionary including ices. Negri took on James Gunter as a business partner in 1777. Eventually, Gunter became the sole proprietor and renamed the establishment Gunter's Tea Shop in 1799.

Robe à l'anglaise – a closed fronted gown. This type of garment fastened in the front over structured undergarments.

Robe à la française – an open-fronted gown. This type of gown did not meet in the front. It would be worn over a matching petticoat and stomacher.

Stays – a predecessor to the corset, stays were usually made of a heavy-weight material and had boning for structure. They were laced either front, back, or both and had adjustable straps to get the desired fit. They would be worn over a chemise.

Stomacher – a stomacher was a 'v' shaped piece of material worn at the front of the bodice to fill in the front of a robe à la française. It was generally boned or pad-stitched and the gown was either pinned either side or sewn closed when worn.

Wig – these were commonly worn by men throughout the 18th century for formal occasions. Women often wore artificial hair pieces to supplement their natural hair. These additions to the head were worn powdered to white or grey.

WANT TO BE IN THE KNOW?

Be the first to know about freebies, sales and when Philippa's next book releases by signing up to her newsletter.

Sign up below:

philippajanekeyworth.com/newsletter

FREE CHAPTER
A DANGEROUS DEAL

Ladies of Worth, book 2

Chapter 1

London, England 1775

Lady Rachel Denby faced the altar of the cold stone church trying her best to keep a straight face. The situation was hardly humorous. She kept telling herself that. But the dour, youthful curate, and the severe bridegroom beside her, were making the corners of her generous mouth twitch. The curate, obtained on short notice with her bridegroom's special licence, had just spent several minutes explaining the solemnity of the occasion. But still...

She took a deep breath, schooling her countenance, drawing her shoulders back and thrusting her chin up to better stare down her nose seriously at the fair-haired man clad in a white surplice before her. He had frowned at her twice when she had insisted on voicing her agreement to his statements. She could not help it. When Rachel came across individuals with an enhanced sense of their own status, taking them down a peg or two seemed the only right course of action. But apparently, the curate did not need confirmation from Rachel that God thought marriage was a holy covenant, or that it was to prevent fornication. It had quite put him off his recital of the marriage service.

She glimpsed Nellie out of the corner of her eye. Her loyal

maid had offered nothing but service faced with her mistress' sudden marriage. Then there was Viscount Arleigh's valet Jeffries stood beside the maid. That made up the entire party.

She risked a glance at her bridegroom. His gaze was fixed ahead, his lips tightly pinched, with no intention of staring lovingly into his bride's eyes. The thought almost sent Rachel off into peels of laughter. She clamped down on the rebellious smile. Her bridegroom had not appreciated her humorous asides to the curate and she did not think he would enjoy her laughter during his repetition of the vows.

His expression, as cold as the air in the church that morning, was not exactly the expression a bride would hope for on her wedding day. But Rachel was not a bride of the common sort. She had been through this before. When she was sixteen, a suitable match had been selected for her, she had participated in the mandatory period of courting, and she had married with all the neighbourhood in attendance. None of that rigmarole was needed here. It was understood. A simple business transaction between herself and Lord Arleigh. She needed Lord Arleigh just as he needed her. It was plain. It was simple. It was their deal.

"I require and charge you both…" The curate's crisp voice carried easily in the church. His grey eyes refused to catch Rachel's again. No more disruptions.

Good. She needed this alliance and the quicker they entered into it the better. Lord Arleigh had promised her security and independence. It was necessary, for she had been on the brink of throwing herself on her parents' mercy. Conditional mercy. That had always been the way. Do this, behave this way, marry that suitable gentleman. She would not be returning to the shelter of their roof. There was no need for such extremes—not now. She had no desire to be thrown into their power again, even now, when widowhood had overtaken her. Soon she would be a widow no more. Better than that, she would be indebted to no one, because her marriage to Arleigh was as much for his convenience as for her own.

Imagine if the curate knew the cynical nature of this wedding. Then again, this was how the ton operated. There was little room for love and affection where property and land were concerned. Those particular afflictions were a happy coincidence rather than a planned future and they happened to the few. Her first marriage had not been affected by such sentimentality. She had married where she had been bid, though—she noted with a quick upturn of her wide lips—she had not done so willingly. How she had screamed. The servants had mistaken the disturbances for someone dying and called the local doctor. But her father had always been relentless in his will, and though she had taken after him, there was only so much a woman could do, especially a young one. But she was no longer a young woman. Her position had changed and after this wedding, she would be mistress of her own fate. No master would be needed.

It had not been her intention to be widowed just yet. Not before she had provided an heir and secured her future at Godalming Hall. But nature was not always inclined to bend to the will of woman, no matter how desperate her desire. She pushed back the feelings that rose from some deep, dark place within her and focused.

She need only get through this marriage service and then she would be able to discard this stiff, uncomfortable gown that had already seen one wedding. She had not told the Viscount that. She doubted he would approve, but the speed of their wedding had necessitated the reuse of a gown. Of all the ones she owned, this one was, after all, the most appropriate. At least, she thought, as the curate droned interminably on, her dead husband's estate had backed onto a friend of Viscount Arleigh's. Otherwise she might never have met him and been given this opportunity for salvation. She had grabbed it with both hands, but then so had he. One must admit, Lord Arleigh's circumstances were less than normal. In fact, they were as peculiar, if not more so, than hers. It was the reason this deal had been struck.

After a respectable amount of time had passed, they would set up separate households and both their purposes would be served. Rachel would enjoy relative freedom, with a tidy sum for her independence. Lord Arleigh would have adhered to his father's oddly specific will, that his son marry by eight-and-twenty to receive his inheritance. To be perfectly honest, it was a very neat and tidy arrangement. Rachel was pleased with herself for thinking of such an excellent solution.

The curate was going on, rambling nervously so that Rachel lost interest. Fortunately she did not have to wait long for the important part.

"Wilt thou, Lord Julius James Andrew Arleigh, have this woman to thy wedded wife, to live together after God's ordinance in the holy estate of matrimony? Wilt thou love her, comfort her, honour, and keep her, in sickness and in health; and, forsaking all others, keep thee only unto her, so long as ye both shall live?"

"I will."

Fancy that. Without so much as a glance at her or a murmur of hesitation.

"And wilt thou, Lady Rachel Constance Denby, have this man to thy wedded husband, to live together after God's ordinance in the holy estate of matrimony? Wilt thou obey him, and serve him, love, honour, and keep him, in sickness and in health; and, forsaking all others, keep thee only unto him, so long as ye both shall live?"

"I will." That voice didn't sound like hers. All animation was lost in her pragmatic tone. "And if you could hurry a little, curate, my shivering limbs would be most obliged."

He jerked his head up and down, almost dropping his

bible, and her betrothed, for the first time, turned towards her briefly.

She saw his glance rise from somewhere below her neck to her eyes, catching them with an unfathomable look, and then turning away. He offered a curt nod to the minister which the frightened young man took as his cue.

It was hardly her fault that they were getting married at eight o'clock in the morning when the temperature was well below acceptable levels in this draughty old building. Even the Puritan Cromwell would have cursed the cold. Apparently her outburst worked, for the curate tripped along with the next bit of the service and before she knew it, he was passing her hand to that of her bridegroom. She felt the cold of the jewelled gold ring as it was threaded along her finger. It matched the temperature of his hands. She wasn't the only one feeling the cold. Or perhaps they were nerves on his part. It was his first wedding after all.

"With this ring I thee wed, with my body I thee worship, and with all my worldly goods I thee endow: In the name of the Father, and of the Son, and of the Holy Ghost. Amen."

With his worldly goods. That part was music to her ears. When the hastily bought ring was installed on its rightful finger, they obeyed the curate and knelt for his prayer of blessing. He held their hands together and spoke those fateful words,

"Those whom God hath joined together let no man put asunder."

Rachel's brows rose a fraction and for a brief moment she could not look the man of God in the eye.

He made the pronouncement soon after and spoke several more blessings. Then it was over. They rose and walked towards a back room in which the register was laid out. A few dips in the ink pot, slashes across the page in clear, bold lettering, and they were married.

Lord Arleigh thanked the curate and then offered his new wife a courteous arm.

"I had best fetch Nellie. She has barely had a moment to understand these rapid proceedings."

"I can assure you Jeffries will not leave her behind."

He didn't speak with a peeved tone, nor show a hint of frustration. He did not speak with any expression whatsoever.

Rachel did not budge.

"As you wish," he said when she did not respond. "I shall meet you at the doors, if convenient." He bowed her out.

Rachel strode from the room in the hopes that the quick movement might warm her chilled limbs.

"Well, I never," said Nellie the moment her mistress came upon her. She had dealt well with the shock of the sudden wedding, and Rachel was pleased to see a bright smile on her maid's face now. "Congratulations, my lady, Lady Arleigh. I only hope you do not catch a chill." Nellie's fine little hands grasped around at her large shawl pulling it tighter.

"So do I, Nellie. Come, we shall warm ourselves at his lordship's fires!"

Rachel hated to admit it, but for a brief moment her easy resolution had faltered when she had seen the ink dry on the register. Her talkative maid Nellie had been with her for years and she always had something to say which was calm and reassuring.

Feeling much more the thing, she took her gloves from Nellie's outstretched hands and marched with her maid in tow to the waiting man at the door. He dutifully took her on his arm for the few feet to the carriage and handed her up, while Nellie and Jeffries took the smaller vehicle behind.

"It is done then." He was turned away from her, his eyes on the rapidly retreating church outside the carriage window.

"Yes, and tolerably quickly—and you will be thankful to hear that will be the last time you need hold my hand." She refrained from adding, *and show me affection*, for even the thought of it caused her to start smiling. He could not have looked more coerced during the ceremony than if he'd had a loaded flintlock pressed against his spine.

Lord Arleigh did not respond. His lips purse even further.

"Just think what Rebecca will say," she mused aloud. And what of her parents? That particular musing could wait at least a day.

"You speak of your sister?" He asked in a tone that did not invite a response. He was being polite, Rachel thought, as though it were an ingrained behaviour he could not shake even in this unusual situation. She found his eyes briefly but he failed to hold her gaze.

"I imagine," said Arleigh in pragmatic tones, "she will believe, like the rest of London, that we have taken leave of our senses."

"Oh, she already knows that of me. You, I suppose, will be a shock." Rachel threw her gloves into a corner of the carriage and slumped back. "Oh come, 'tis naught but a joke," she replied to his frown. "You must know I have a sense of humour if we are to be married."

"We *are* married," he corrected without pause. "Three months," he said, looking back out the window. "That should be sufficient time to satisfy the requirements of my father's will."

"Well, then you shall only have to laugh at my jokes for that long. I am sure you shall do tolerably well." She pulled out her hat pin which had been ill-placed that morning and removed the whole from her head. She sent it the same way as her gloves and sighed in relief at the loss of pressure from her head.

"A pretty ring," she said, admiring the emerald gem on her wedding finger. "I feel a fraud wearing it — perhaps you had better order a replica in paste."

"Madam," said her new husband curtly. "Your flippancy is hardly appreciated."

"Very well," said Rachel, straightening in her seat and looking very much the injured party. "But I don't see why you should be in such a foul mood. I have just become financially secure and you shall receive your inheritance. It is our wedding day after all!"

She caught him grimacing at her crass mention of money.

"It is no done deal—sordid though it is. My family must be deceived or the sham will be found out and I shall receive nothing."

"Sordid! I am not sordid and nor is the deal I proposed to you. It is as ingenious as it is clean. As good as any business deal. You should at least acknowledge our initial success." When his expression didn't change, she added, "If you continue with that face of yours, the wind will change, and you will stay like that forever." She raised her hands in surrender at the look he flashed in her direction. "Very well. I shall desist in my flippancy, but not my relief."

"Of course—you are to be a rich and independent woman when this is over."

"You make me sound the very caricature of a fortune hunter," she said, matching the sharpness in his tone. He clearly regretted his decision already. This marriage was off to a triumphant start. At least they only had to bear with each other's company for three months.

"You knew my circumstances when you agreed to this, as I knew yours." She spoke those first words with amiability but not the next. "I would ask that you kindly stop making a cake of yourself."

He unfolded his arms at that.

"I shall uphold my end of the bargain," said Rachel, "and perform beautifully for your family, but a word of advice—it is your acting that needs polish. Perhaps one small smile on your wedding day?"

As they pulled up outside Lord Arleigh's London home in Grosvenor Square, there had never been a married couple more at odds with each other so shortly after their wedding. Rachel shot a meaningful smile at her new husband as she was handed down from the carriage. It was not long before Lord Arleigh displayed one too, but Rachel thought it more akin to a snarl.

Keep reading *A Dangerous Deal* by picking up your copy now:

philippajanekeyworth.com/ADD

philippajanekeyworth.com/ADD

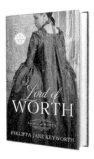

philippajanekeyworth.com/LOW

philippajanekeyworth.com/DOD

REGENCY ROMANCES

philippajanekeyworth.com/TWR

philippajanekeyworth.com/TUE

FANTASY

philippajanekeyworth.com/TE

ABOUT THE AUTHOR

Philippa Jane Keyworth, also known as P. J. Keyworth, writes historical romance and fantasy novels you'll want to escape into.

She loves strong heroines, challenging heroes and backdrops that read like you're watching a movie. She creates complex, believable characters you want to get to know and worlds that are as dramatic as they are beautiful.

Keyworth's historical romance novels include Regency and Georgian romances that trace the steps of indomitable heroes and heroines through historic British streets. From London's glittering ballrooms to its dark gaming hells, characters experience the hopes and joys of love while avoiding a coil or two! Travel with them through London, Bath, Cornwall and beyond and you'll find yourself falling in love.

Keyworth's fantasy series The Emrilion Trilogy follows strong love stories and epic adventure. Unveiling a world of nomadic warrior tribes and peaceful forest-dwelling folk, you can explore the hills, deserts and cities of Emrilion and the history that is woven through them. With so many different races in the same kingdom it's become a melting pot of drama and intrigue where the ultimate struggle between good and evil will bring it all to the brink of destruction.

facebook.com/philippajane.keyworth

twitter.com/PJKeyworth

instagram.com/pjkeyworth

amazon.com/author/philippakeyworth

bookbub.com/authors/philippa-jane-keyworth

goodreads.com/philippajanekeyworth

Printed in Great Britain
by Amazon